Praise for the works of C

The Other Side of Forestlands Lake

Elizabeth (*Gallows Humor*) delivers her signature blend of lesbian romance and murder in this suspenseful outing. Paranormal YA author Willa Dunn steps into her own ghost story when she returns to her childhood summer home at Forestlands Lake. She's hoping to work on her next book and reconnect with her half-sister, rebellious teenager Nicole, but her plans are derailed by a series of spectral visitations. When Nicole gets drunk and almost drowns in the lake, Willa's childhood sweetheart, Lee Chandler, saves her. Lee, now the director of a summer camp for LGBTQ youth, and her daughter, Maggie, join together with Willa and Nicole to investigate the haunting. Between ghostly possessions and cryptic conversations with mysterious neighbors, Willa and Lee rekindle the flame that was barely allowed to flicker back when they were both closeted teens. Though the story hits some speed bumps trying to juggle the tense mystery and the lighthearted romance, the charming characters will draw in readers, and the plot ultimately hangs together nicely. Fans of romantic suspense are sure to be pleased.
-Publishers Weekly

The author uses great descriptions and innocuous little details to give the community surrounding the lake a disturbing personality. This is a nice juxtaposition with the giddiness Willa and Lee feel over being reunited. I enjoyed losing myself in a paranormal story. I'm pretty set in my ways about sticking to the romance genre, but this was a nice change of pace. The book is well paced, and it's spooky enough to raise the hair on the back of your neck without making you need to sleep with the lights on.
-The Lesbian Review

It took only one book by Carolyn Elizabeth for me to decide that she was a must-read author. This is her third and it proves true again. I love Elizabeth's stories but even if I didn't, I'd read her books for the characters. She makes me fall in love with all of them.

There are many layers to this book, and so we don't get one mystery but two. Well-thought, complex and thrilling mysteries. Everything came as a surprise yet still made complete sense (in a paranormal way).

Carolyn Elizabeth is proving that she could write any genre and I'd want to read it. In this book, you get romance, paranormal and mystery all in one, with each element being as important and as well-crafted

-Les Rêveur

Gallows Humor

At this very moment, my coffee cup is raised in Carolyn Elizabeth's honor because she gave me the perfect blend of an angst-filled, budding romance with endless humor and an enthralling murder mystery that kept me up way past my bedtime. I still can't get over the fact that this story is her debut novel because Carolyn Elizabeth has knocked my fluffy bedroom socks off with her flawless writing and the witty and entertaining dialogue between the characters along with the vivid descriptions of the Jackson City Memorial Hospital and environs.

If you're looking for a story that will keep you on the edge of your seat and have you doubled over with laughter, then this is definitely the story for you!

-The Lesbian Review

I always enjoy reading good debuts. It gets me excited to find new authors. I would recommend this book to just about anyone. I think people will enjoy this read. I hope there is a book two because I will be reading it. Almost forgot, I also like the oddball title of the book.

-Lex Kent's Reviews, *goodreads*

Dirt Nap

Yes! This is how you write a sequel, you make it even better than the first. For those readers that were hoping for more of Thayer and Corey, including their relationship, you won't be disappointed. Their connection keeps growing, the chemistry is in your face and every romantic scene is just as good as the most exciting scenes in the book. All the story lines of this book really hit for me. From a little relationship angst to Corey's big problem with a trusted friend, there was always something going on that kept me flipping these pages.

-Lex Kent's Reviews, *goodreads*

This is a perfect sequel to *Gallows Humor* and met all of my high expectations. Sometimes sequels can be disappointing, but not this one. We have the same mystery, intrigue, and romance that we found in the first book. Corey, Thayer, and all the secondary characters are just as likable and easy to connect with. The romance is still as sweet, and it was fun seeing the two grow together through all the trials they had to endure. It was also fun meeting a few new characters and watching them develop. Ms. Elizabeth not only has the knowledge she needs in pathology and medicine for this story, she also shines in character development. This is what makes both of these books so great.

-Betty H., *NetGalley*

Great second book for Carolyn Elizabeth and a great second in the Curtis & Reynolds series. Just like her debut *Gallows Humor*, this one is also written in third person, from the point of view of both protagonists, Corey and Thayer. The plot is even more interesting, with a very well-done crime/thriller part, and continuation of a really good romance. The chemistry between the two well-defined and likable protagonists is excellent. Add to that a few other very well-written relationships, good pacing, nice ending...and you have a great read.

-Pin's Reviews, *goodreads*

I must admit that this is the second time that I was blown away with this author's captivating writing style. She has really outdone herself with this story because she gave me a riveting romantic thriller that has so many entertaining and laugh-out-loud moments embedded within it. This story kept me glued to my Kindle and hungry for more priceless wisecracks from Corey and Thayer. Even though Carolyn Elizabeth did a wonderful job of filling in some of the details and facts from her first book, I would strongly advise you to read *Gallows Humor* before you read this story so that you would get to know more about these lovely characters.

-*The Lesbian Review*

I reiterate from book one, the main characters of Dr. Thayer Reynolds and Corey Curtis are two of the most charismatic characters that I've had the pleasure of reading about in quite a while. Perfect leads in a book that begins in the foulest way, the discovery of a decomposed body. Although the remainder of the book unravels the answers to the mystery via good action and police work, the joy in the story comes from watching Thayer and Corey interact and grow as a couple and as individuals. They show tenderness and vulnerability in small intimate scenes that paint a picture of a couple falling hard and deep. I could easily read another ten of these Curtis & Reynolds books.

-Jules P., *NetGalley*

The Raven and the Banshee

Other Bella Books by Carolyn Elizabeth

The Other Side of Forestlands Lake

The Curtis and Reynolds Series
Gallows Humor
Dirt Nap
Zero Chill

The
Raven and the
Banshee

Carolyn Elizabeth

BELLA
B O O K S
2022

Bella Books, Inc.
P.O. Box 10543
Tallahassee, FL 32302

First Edition - 2022

Editor: Ann Roberts
Cover Designer: Kayla Mancuso

ISBN: 978-1-64247-240-0

PUBLISHER'S NOTE

Acknowledgments

A version of this story came into the world back in 2014 as an AU fanfiction for a fandom that will forever remain a secret. It's a story near and dear to my heart and one of my earliest efforts that helped build my confidence as a writer. It only made sense that one day I would develop it for publication. Today is that day.

Thank you to the Bella Books family for continuing to give me the opportunity to publish my stories and to Ann Roberts for continuing to help me make them the best possible books they can be. Many thanks to Tere for reading an early version and providing much needed feedback.

There are many more words where these come from, and I would be pleased to adapt more of the original for publication in the future. If all goes well we can continue our adventures with Captain Branna Kelly, Julia Farrow and the crew of the *Banshee*.

My wife tells me this one is her favorite. Time will tell what the rest of you think.

PROLOGUE

Charlestown, South Carolina 1705

Branna stumbled along behind her parents, Lochlann and Colleen Kelly. Her shoes were too small and pinched her feet as they made their way through the darkening, muggy evening, dodging the lamplighters on the downtown Charlestown, South Carolina, street. She breathed in the familiar heady scent of blooming crepe myrtles and freshly lit gas lamps on one side and the pungent seaport on the other.

Her belly fluttered with nerves, excitement, and unease while her left hand fidgeted with the heavy gold signet ring she always wore on her first finger. Her right hand pulled at the fabric of the ill-fitting, secondhand dress that once belonged to a young woman who filled it out much better than she could ever hope. It gaped in the bodice and had to be let out to accommodate her height, but still barely reached her ankles. It was once worn by the same young woman she was on her way to see, to profess her love for, and to say goodbye to—Julia Farrow.

Lost in thought, she didn't realize they had arrived and she bumped into the back of her tall, broad-shouldered father when he paused to turn up the walk to the Farrow estate.

"Aye, lass, pull yerself together." His eyes glinted with amusement despite the scolding. "That's no way fer a young lady to behave."

"Lady," Branna scoffed in a very unladylike manner, her accent nearly imperceptible after their many years in the colonies. "You must be speaking of your other daughter."

His eyes narrowed at his only child, looking her over from head to toe. Branna fought the urge to squirm beneath her father's intense scrutiny. She knew what she looked like and why she stood out so much from the other young women her age.

She was tall for a young woman of sixteen, towering over her peers, but still a head shorter than her father's outlandish six-foot-four frame. Despite inheriting her mother's lithe build, she was strong, broad shouldered and narrow hipped. She had long fingers on large hands, roughened from being raised in a life of hard work and sailing, which were a constant source of embarrassment when in high-class company.

Instead of a fair, rosy complexion and sun-kissed locks, she was gifted with straight black hair pulled back from sharp features darkened by the sun. Her eyes were so dark-brown they appeared black.

"There's only you, Branna, and I wouldn't have it any other way." Her father grasped her hands and raised them to kiss the knuckles of each, grinning with love and pride. "Now, let Mam fix yer dress."

"Yes, Da." She grinned back and turned around for her mother to adjust the pins she had added to help the dress better fit her shape, or as Branna thought, shapelessness. "Thank you, Mam."

Colleen spun her daughter and looked up at her. "You look beautiful, my darling daughter, and don't let anyone here tell you different, do you understand? You are every bit as worthy as them and quite a bit more so, if you ask me."

"Yes, Mam, I know." Branna lowered her eyes.

"It's not enough just to know, my sweet." Her mother tilted Branna's head up with a finger under her chin. "You must believe it, too. Hold your head up and be strong, be caring..." She trailed off, holding her gaze.

"Be true." She finished her mother's constant and favorite encouragement. "I do believe, Mam."

Her father feigned a sound of disgust at their sentiments and rolled his eyes, shining with emotion. "We've only a short time before a favorable tide so let's get on with it."

"You'll not forget to collect the satchel from Mr. Farrow this time?" Her mother pinched the back of his arm.

"Ow, woman, cease yer nagging." He jerked his arm away but couldn't hide the adoring twinkle in his eye. "It was only *one* time."

"One time that added a week to our voyage for having to return to port as we had no money and no contracts." She teased with no real anger.

"Aye, love." He smiled sheepishly. "I've not forgotten. Ye won't let me."

Branna laughed at her parents' good-natured bickering, her smile faltering as they neared their destination.

They walked the stone path lined with oaks and dogwoods to the Farrows' grand, three-story, brick double house. Branna, not knowing when she would lay eyes on it again, marveled at the sight of the columns across the piazza that overlooked the lush and impeccably manicured grounds and private gardens. She called to mind the many times throughout her young life she and Julia Farrow had run hand in hand and barefoot through the cool grass and lay together beneath the shade of the dogwoods in the muggy heat of the summer.

It was beneath one of those trees in the cooling air and dimming light that she experienced her first kiss—and the many that came after. The memory was so vivid she could feel the softness of Julia's lips against hers, the sweetness of her breath against her cheek, and the press of their still-developing bodies against each other.

Branna had never experienced anything so terrifying and tantalizing as that kiss and wanted nothing more than to feel that way forever. Now she had to say goodbye, for how long she didn't know.

Upon entering the house, her parents immediately split up in opposite directions to visit and make their goodbyes to their friends. Her father joined some of the other Farrow Company men and her mother went to their wives, including the heavily pregnant Amelia Farrow. "Despite being employees, Branna's parents were well regarded among the Farrow's elite business associates and her father was a highly sought-after ship's captain." Branna could not say the same and tensed as soon as she was left to fend for herself in the midst of the early summer party.

She glanced into the rooms to see distinguished, old white men in suits, twirling elaborate moustaches and sipping whiskey as they argued politics and trade while sophisticated women in summer frocks and hats fanned themselves while discussing whatever affluent women discussed.

Branna continued to the back of the house where she could hear lively music from a string quartet. She nervously fingered the battered, gold signet ring that bore the Kelly family crest. Her grandmother had passed it down to her before she was born. She stepped out onto the patio surrounded by groups of the young, unmarried elite in their best attire. They were all here to see and be seen, request dances, and lay the groundwork for possible courtships fueled by smart industry mergers, family legacy, and occasionally, genuine attraction and desire.

She recognized many of the faces, but since she had no social standing, she drew no attention, save for a smattering of derisive looks. She made one cursory glance across the crowd before her eyes settled on Julia Farrow and her heart jumped in her chest as it always did when their eyes locked. Julia, always insisting she believed they could sense each other even at a distance, was already staring at her with her trademark half-smile and sparkling eyes. Branna stilled, soaking in the sight of her—light blond hair piled atop her head, gray eyes and porcelain complexion. Though they were the same age, Branna thought she looked impossibly young with the splash of freckles across her nose from too many long days adventuring in the sun together.

Branna was reminded there was nothing childlike about Julia Farrow. Her gaze rested at Julia's full lips and strong chin with a hint of a cleft before continuing down her graceful neck and her shapely figure—full breasts and hips filling out her new dress, testing the seamstress's work. Branna's return smile crept across her face then fell into a scowl when she was jostled hard from behind.

"*Servants'* entrance is by the kitchen," sneered Cecilia Ainsworth as she walked by with her nose in the air.

She led the band of "snotty daughters," as Branna liked to call them, toward the dance floor—Daphne Blake, Agatha Eade, and the twins, Beryl and Violet Ivey. They were the young women of the wealthiest plantations, politicians, financiers, and merchants who judged and ridiculed anyone they deemed beneath them without restraint or censure.

Branna gritted her teeth, tamping down her anger as they each bumped her shoulder with varying degrees of force as they passed. She held Julia's gaze, seeing her playful smile turning to a frown of concern and sympathy, which further stoked Branna's ire. She was not to be pitied by anyone—especially Julia.

The last one who passed her, whose contact was a gentle hand on her arm, was Alice Farrow, Julia's older sister by a year. She offered Branna an apologetic look, but nevertheless followed along with the crowd. Alice was soon to be engaged to Cecilia's older brother, Arnold Ainsworth, thus establishing one of the most powerful family mergers in the South.

Branna met her gaze and forced a smile at the gesture. Alice had always been kind to her privately, but since she proudly wore the mantle of Farrow family status and expectations, she would never openly defy convention.

In contrast, Julia was a constant thorn in the side of her family, much to her mother's amusement and father's dismay. Branna loved her bold, outspoken ideas, fiery temper, and thirst for knowledge and adventure. If it weren't for her family's financial success and business prestige in the colonies, Julia would likely be as much a social pariah as Branna Kelly.

Branna exhaled a slow breath and could feel her shoulders sag as she watched the society girls tittering and casting her sidelong glances from across the patio. She made a half-turn to go back into the house and tell her father she was ready to leave when she felt a sharp tug on her arm. She was spun around to face the steely gray eyes of Julia Farrow.

"Not so fast."

Branna stumbled when Julia tugged her across the patio and right through the middle of the gossiping girls, scattering them, lest they be run over.

"Don't pay any attention to these venomous twats," Julia commented loudly as they passed through. Her language elicited a range of reactions—amused to aghast—from the other guests as was always Julia's intention.

Branna covered her laughter with her hand and flashed Alice a return look of apology. Alice just shrugged and rolled her eyes, quite accustomed to her little sister's outbursts.

"These bloody slippers are torture," Julia sighed, kicking off her shoes and flopping onto the grass beneath the shade of an old oak in a corner of the garden. They could still hear the music but were well hidden from the party.

Branna lowered herself carefully down next to her, mindful of mussing her dress. "My Da would skin me if he ever heard me using language like that."

"My father would have to notice me first," Julia said and reached for Branna's hand, lacing their fingers together.

Nerves got the better of Branna now that they were so close and all the words she had practiced fled her mind. "How is your mother?" she finally blurted.

"Exhausted. The midwife says her age will make this pregnancy and delivery dangerous, but my mother is strong, and despite her previous difficulties with childbearing, my father insisted on trying for the rightful heir to his fortune."

"Why not your sister? Or you?"

Julia laughed humorlessly and circled the back of Branna's hand with her thumb. "Girls don't inherit. And anyway, did you really want to spend our last night together speaking of my parents? How much time do you have?"

A shiver at Julia's touch froze her tongue for a moment. "An hour at best."

"Just enough time, I think." Julia's eyes shone with emotion.

She reached into the folds of her dress and deep into one of the pockets she secretly sewed into all her clothes to hide her treasures. "I have something for you. Close your eyes."

Branna eyed her suspiciously but complied. She never questioned when Julia Farrow asked something of her. She held out her hand and felt something irregularly shaped, cool, and hard pressed into her palm.

"You can look," Julia said softly.

Branna opened her eyes. In her hand was an intricately carved, black-jade raven in flight on a leather cord. "Oh." She sucked in a breath and turned it around in her hand, running her fingers over the smooth polished stone. "It's beautiful."

"I thought so, too." Julia waited until Branna looked up and met her gaze. "Like you." She took the necklace from Branna's hand and brushed her long hair off her shoulders. She held her gaze as she tied the cord around her neck so the pendant rested in the hollow of her throat. "Branna, beauty with hair as dark as a raven."

Branna's heart pounded in her chest with the warm breath of Julia's words against her lips. She leaned forward, a mere inch between them, her lips brushing against Julia's.

The world tilted when Julia leaned into the kiss, parting her lips to allow Branna in and sliding her hands around the back of her neck to pull her close while their lips explored tenderly and then more urgently. Branna couldn't help the soft moan of pleasure as she slid her hands up Julia's sides to rest against her breasts. "*Machree*," she whispered. The anglicized Gaelic term derived from *mo chroi*, meaning my heart, always made Julia shiver with pleasure. Not this time.

Julia inhaled sharply and pulled away, meeting Branna's startled gaze. Her expression, for but a moment, was unmistakably one of longing and regret before she laughed it off with a shrug. "I am so envious of you, Bran."

"Me?" Branna frowned, her heart pounding with uncertainty at Julia's abrupt change in mood. "Why? I have to leave."

"On an adventure," Julia gushed, her eyes alight with excitement. "What I wouldn't give for an experience like that."

Branna's heart stuttered at her beauty and vitality and the

idea that leapt into her head. She pinned Julia with a look of pure hope and desire. "Then come with us—with me. Your father wouldn't be sending mine on this route if he didn't trust that it was safe, and they're good friends..." She trailed off at Julia's musical laughter. "What's funny?"

"Can you imagine? You teaching me to sail and the two of us with our own ship, making a name for ourselves on the high seas?"

"Yes. I can imagine and I want nothing more."

Julia's smile faltered and her eyes darkened. "I'm afraid I'm destined for another course. You know that."

"I do." Branna stood, gesturing back toward the party. "To be married off to one of those dullards, drunkards, or braggarts for the price of a good business deal and a couple of male heirs."

Julia stood, too. "What would you have me do, Bran? You know who I am and what I am worth."

"I *do* know what you're worth, Julia. Maybe the only one who does." Branna closed the distance between them, reaching for Julia's hands. "Tell them your heart belongs to another. For god's sake, Julia, tell them what you want."

Julia held her desperate gaze for a moment. "I already told them."

"You did? When?" She frowned in confusion. "Then why—"

"I told my father when he was considering who he would send out on his newest ship, *Rebellion*, and who would be best to establish his interests in Port Royal that he should look no further than Captain Lochlann Kelly," Julia stated flatly.

"What?" Branna jerked back, dropping her hands. "Why? You must have known I would have to go, too. Why would you—"

"Because you don't belong here, Branna. You have more to do than work for my parents or your father. You should answer to no one. You are beautiful and smart and free and not beholden to family legacy. The rules are different where you're going and you can make a difference there. Heads should turn when you enter a room—with reverence not with disdain—and everyone should know your name."

"You don't get to decide that for me."

"It's decided."

"Julia, how could you—"

"You must go, Branna. There's nothing for you here."

"*You're* here." Branna twisted the battered gold ring from her finger and held it out. "I have something for you, too."

"Your family's crest," Julia breathed. She brushed her thumb over the design as it lay in Branna's hand. "Tell me again."

"The tower represents greatness and a place in society. The rings are fidelity and the rampant lions symbolize deathless courage, strength, and bravery."

Julia smiled wistfully at the ring for another moment before looking up. "It's so you, Bran. You must keep it."

"I want *you* to have it. I want you to have it as a promise that I love you and I'll be back and we can—"

"No. We can't, Branna. Don't be such a fool."

Branna felt the hot sting of tears behind her eyes and the pain in her heart grew. "What are you saying?"

"I'm saying I don't feel for you what you think. Our time together was just childish games. We're not children any longer and there's no room for you in my life. I will be married as per my family's wishes and I will entertain this ridiculous infatuation you have with me no longer." She snatched the ring from Branna's hand and threw it over her shoulder. Time stood still as they both heard it plunk down somewhere in the yard.

Branna gasped. She could feel her heart breaking. The pain was so acute she could scarcely take a breath. "I don't believe you. I know you're lying."

"You are beneath me." Julia stood close enough to touch but she was unreachable, her gray eyes cold and her expression one of contempt. "Just go, Branna. Don't look back."

"Branna, it's time to go, lass!"

Branna jumped at the sound of her father's booming voice and fled back through the yard, stumbling toward the street, barely able to see through her tears.

* * *

The summer storms had kept her inside for days and Julia stood motionless as the fat drops coursed down the outside of the window. She would weep with the sky if she had any tears left, but her heart was broken and her soul empty at the pain she had caused Branna. Her hand clutched the signet ring as if her life depended on it. It had taken her days of crawling through the yard to find it.

Remembering the pain in Branna's eyes and knowing she had caused it was more than Julia could stand, but it was all she could think about for the last several weeks. She had betrayed her best friend, the person who meant more to her than anything, and she didn't know if she would ever get the chance to make it right.

"Darling, please, come and join us for tea," her mother called from the doorway.

"No, thank you, Mama," Julia replied woodenly.

"I know what you had to do was awful but you did the right thing and Branna will be better for it, you'll see." Her mother's slippers were soft as she made her way across the floor.

"You should have seen her face, Mama." Julia's voice shook. "Better I pierced her chest with a blade than the cutting words I spoke."

Her mother sighed softly behind her. "I know what you feel for her, darling, I do."

"How could you, possibly?" Julia spun to face her.

"One day when you're older I'll tell you. I don't condemn you your love, but even if your father had allowed it, what kind of life could you have had together? Hiding and pretending? Would you have just married and kept her with your husband's house staff? As lady's maid, perhaps? I can't imagine Branna Kelly answering to anyone—even you. That's no way to live, Julia, or to love. Not for you or her."

"So, I'll just marry for money and name? That will be more fulfilling?"

Amelia Farrow smiled sadly at her daughter. "I know it's not the life you imagined for yourself and I know you are so much more than our family name. I believe that, in time, you will find your place and you must believe it, too."

Julia swallowed hard around her grief. "My place is with Branna."

"Miss Amelia?"

Julia's mother turned to address the housekeeper. "Yes, June, what is it?"

"There was a man with a message about the *Rebellion*." She shifted uneasily from foot to foot. "He's left just now but Mr. Arthur asked for you to join him in his study."

"I'll be right there, June, thank you."

"There could be word on how Branna's doing," Julia said excitedly as she raced off. "I know it's soon but maybe she got my letter in Port Royal and sent a reply. I don't care what father says anymore. I told her everything and explained what he made me do. She already knew I was lying. She'll forgive me, I know she will."

Julia stopped in the doorway of her father's office and paled when she saw him hunched over a small, battered wooden chest. There were small items and papers scattered across his usually impeccable desk. His face was blotchy and his eyes swollen as if he had been crying. She had never seen her father cry. "Father?"

He looked up, his face a mask of pain. "The *Rebellion* was lost."

Julia started in surprised confusion. "Lost? That's impossible. Captain Kelly is an exceptional sailor and—"

"Lost at sea. Destroyed. Taken by pirates and set afire." He gestured to the random trinkets and charred pages. "This is all that was recovered. There were no survivors."

The room spun and Julia never felt the floor as it rushed to meet her.

CHAPTER ONE

The Caribbean Sea 1720

The ship rocked gently in the calm seas as the captain of the *Banshee*, Branna Kelly, known throughout the Caribbean Sea as the Raven for the pendant she wore, stood hunched over her broad wooden navigation table. She studied the charts, absently running a finger across the thin, white scar slashing down her cheek from the corner of her left eye to her ear.

They would have caught the *Serpent's Mistress* by now if they hadn't lost the wind. She ground her teeth and swore under her breath. She couldn't lose him now. If the *Serpent's Mistress* held course they could be on her by morning of the next day, and she'd be running her blade through Captain Cyrus Jagger's heart by noon.

She threw her compass and pencil onto the table with a clatter and turned from the charts, which weren't providing any new useful information. She already knew where they were and where they were going. She shoved open the shuttered aft doors, opening her quarters to the afternoon light and the warm breeze.

She scowled at the beauty of it—the smell of the salty air and gentle lap of the three-foot swells along the hull as her ship rolled along through the crystalline waters of the Caribbean Sea. She sometimes wished the weather would darken to match her mood. So lost was she in her own thoughts she didn't acknowledge the knock at her door.

She turned when the door flew open, ready to vent her rage at the crewman impertinent enough to enter without permission, but she held her tongue when Augustus Hawke stepped into her cabin.

Branna eyed her first mate. He was tall and rangy with shoulder-length, sandy hair tied at the nape of his neck, weathered skin and sharp features befitting the name Hawke. He had perpetually hooded eyes that gave him an air of carelessness which often lead to being underestimated, offering him the element of surprise when things got confrontational. He was always allowed in her cabin and the reason was never far from her thoughts.

She owed him everything after he saved her life fifteen years ago when the ship on which he was quartermaster discovered her, half-dead from the elements, clinging to a scrap of floating wreckage with one hand and a sword clutched in the white-knuckled grip of the other. Her tattered clothes held to her by the snug strap of the locked, oiled, canvas satchel her mother had belted across her body before she died. She was the only survivor of her parents' raided merchant ship, all slaughtered at the hands of Cyrus Jagger.

Gus, ten years her senior, had been the first to reach her, secreting the satchel away when he realized its contents: fifty thousand pounds in South Carolina bank notes intended for negotiations between Farrow Company and new trading partners. He had taken responsibility for her after she had been orphaned, and she thought, at first, his motivation was only the contents of the satchel.

Many men would have simply robbed a young woman alone and injured as she was. Branna had been wary of his intentions for a long time. It was a year into their unusual companionship that Branna learned Gus once had a beloved younger sister. She was murdered by the hand of a man Gus despised, a man their parents had betrothed her to while Gus was at sea. Understanding loss, grief, and guilt as she did, she allowed Gus to work out his by aiding her—a benefit to them both.

He found a wealthy trader heading north to further his fortune in the colonies, one who was willing to purchase the South Carolina notes in Spanish gold at sixty percent of their face value. Gus protected Branna and taught her to fight so that she could protect herself. He mentored her for ten years in exchange for the financial security she could offer.

With no aspiration himself to captain a ship, she offered him a place as her first mate, her right hand, her friend and closest confidant and he accepted. Her ship, completed and christened five years ago, was a grand one and he took no small measure of pride in his contribution to that. The crew was highly trained, moderately educated, and with a few exceptions, loyal and honorable. Those who were not were turned out as soon as they were discovered. It was nearly impossible to hire a crew that weren't some measure of thieves, swindlers, brawlers or mercenaries, but she took pains not to bring on the worst of the worst. They were all killers, but there were no murderers and no rapists—at least none that she knew of, and it would stay that way.

"Captain," Gus said, apparently having grown impatient with her distance.

"Hmm?"

"A ship has been sighted," he reported, shaking Branna out of her reverie. "Less than a league off."

Branna stiffened. "The *Serpent's Mistress?*"

"I don't think so. Looks like a merchant galleon. Not one I'm familiar with."

"Heading for port?" She tucked her rumpled shirt into her leather pants. She gathered her weapons, buckling the belt of throwing knives around her hips. She slipped the scabbard of her sword across her shoulders—a simple double-edged hunting sword with a brass D-guard and leather grip. Her father's sword.

The one her mother pressed into her hands during the attack and the one with which she had every intention of running through Cyrus Jagger. She intended to fight. She always intended to fight. Cyrus Jagger and the *Serpent's Mistress* had eluded her for years, never leaving the area, always leaving his mark and staying one step ahead of her, challenging and taunting her.

"Not heading anywhere at the moment." Gus held the door for her. "Either out of wind like we are or damaged. Hard to tell from this distance."

Branna stalked from her cabin with Gus right behind her.

Ship's bosun, Nat Hooper—the English name given him by his previous captain—was a bald, dark-skinned, giant of a man with a voice so heavily accented and deep at times he was unintelligible, gave them a nod as they emerged.

"Captain on deck," he rumbled from the quarterdeck when Branna and Gus climbed the few steps to join him. The crew kept about their business but their movements became sharper, their faces more focused at the announcement.

Nat handed over the spyglass and pointed off the port bow. "Just below the horizon. We're closing on her fast, even in this piss-for-wind. I think she might be adrift."

Branna held the instrument to her eye as she sighted out the ship. It did look adrift, sails luffing and lines in disarray. They should have seen the *Banshee* by now and they weren't under way and there was no movement on deck.

"Ready all port guns. I want them trained and ready to fire at my command. We'll come along her starboard side. I want twelve armed men ready to board."

"Aye, aye, Captain." Gus and Nat moved off to see to her orders.

She turned to the wheel and jerked her head at Jack Massey, the quartermaster and ship's surgeon, currently on duty at the helm. "I'll take us in." She took his place at the wheel and adjusted their course to make way toward the larger ship.

"Aye, aye, Captain." The wiry and bespectacled young man jumped nimbly to the main deck.

The *Banshee* cut smoothly and slowly through the water, closing in on her target. Branna only had to make minor adjustments to their course as the wind remained low with only the sails of the main mast up of the three-masted bark.

She glanced up, squinting into the high sun to watch the crew across the yardarms furling the main sails as they approached. Her crew was so well trained she rarely had to give an order. Between Gus, her first mate, who handled her and all manner of ship's operations, and Nat, the bosun in charge of equipment and crew, the *Banshee* had a reputation as a force to be reckoned with in the open waters. Her crew, while in port, stayed out of trouble and was welcome at all the ale houses, brothels, and trading posts in Nassau and Port Royal.

The *Banshee* made her first score on an unclaimed bounty of a small sunken trading ship. It took them weeks to salvage what they could from a rocky bottom around a vicious reef, a rescue the shipping company thought too costly to undertake compared to what they may be able to recover. Branna's haul was considerable, for the small crew she kept along with her light and fast ship. With enough coin to grow her armory, they moved fast and hard against the ships trading and pillaging illegally in the shipping lanes. She had occasionally heard herself likened to the Robin Hood of English folklore except she didn't steal from the rich but stole back from those who did.

The foolish captains who refused to cease their piracy in exchange for a pardon from the new Bahamian governor, who had successfully wrested control of the islands from pirate rule and restored British control, were swiftly and summarily dealt with by Captain Kelly and the *Banshee*. Captain Kelly served a purpose, and as such, the Crown turned a blind eye to her own exploits and left her alone as long as she didn't go against the Crown's interests in the area.

Appropriately papered merchant vessels had nothing to fear from the *Banshee* and her captain. The rest had come to steer clear of her. When provoked, Captain Kelly could be as ruthless as the most hardened of the men, more so at times if she felt she had to overcome the perception that captain of a ship was no place for a woman, or that because she was a woman she would be merciful.

The Articles of the *Banshee* were drafted carefully to ensure that everyone received their fair share of any bounty and all adhered to the rules of her ship and the sea. There was no room for leniency or special considerations lest she be considered soft and lose the respect of the men. She had earned her place and she was well respected and trusted—if not well liked. Though she knew she had the unwavering support of her most senior officers, Nat, Gus, and Jack, and most of the crew, she could never let down her guard as there was always someone thinking that they could do a better job. Despite the fact the ship was hers, there were those that thought they would look much better as captain of the *Banshee*. Mutiny was always only one mistake away.

The men threw the boarding hooks across the gunwales of the galleon, painted with the name *Firelight*, securing the ships together. Gus called for boarding and the men swarmed the deck of the larger ship, pistols drawn and swords at the ready. The only sounds were the shouts of her own men as they cleared the main deck. There was no one there—no one living, anyway.

The main deck was littered with bodies and the stench was powerful, though no one reacted. Blood, dark and long congealed, stained the deck and tattered sails.

Branna made her way down from the quarterdeck. She pulled herself onto the gunwale of the *Banshee* and stood, gripping a stay line, surveying her men and their sweep of the deck as they picked their way around the bodies. Her gaze flicked to Kitts, one of her young, new crewmen, who grimaced as he slid a severed arm out of his way with the toe of his boot. She caught Gus's eye and called to him. "Go below. Sweep the holds."

He motioned for Nat and Jack to follow and disappeared below. Branna waited impatiently for Gus to return and frowned as he staggered back out onto the main deck several minutes later and doubled over, gulping air and retching.

"What's this, now?" she asked with a quirk of her mouth as she hopped over to the deck of the *Firelight*. Gus wasn't easily rattled.

He wiped his face with the back of his hand and straightened. "You're not going to thank me, but you need to come down to the hold."

She pursed her mouth and studied him. He wouldn't ask if it weren't important. Gus was fiercely protective of her as was his job as first mate and her closest friend. "Show me."

She paused at the foot of the ladder to let her eyes adjust to the gloom. It was hot and the air motionless and fetid. She swallowed heavily as he led her through the crew quarters, where the bodies were many—some dead in their hammocks. They descended again and weaved through the galley and gun deck. The final ladder led them down into the bowels of the hold.

The air grew thicker and the stench so vile Branna could almost see a greenish cast in the gloom. There was no mistaking the smell of rotting flesh and human waste. Her eyes watered and bile rose in her throat. She choked it back and pressed on through the narrow corridor that opened up into the forward hold.

Three bodies, in various states of rot, littered the floor. As the ship rocked gently, human juices dribbled trails and stained the floorboards.

"You wanted me to see this?" Branna choked, a hand covering her mouth and nose.

Gus swallowed heavily and jerked his head. "Over here."

They picked their way to a corner of the hold. Branna peered into the gloom at what at first looked like a pile of rags. As she approached, the dark pile jerked farther back into the corner with an inhuman shriek and she heard the rattle of chains against the wood. "Jesus Christ! There's someone alive down here."

"We know. And she's got teeth." Nat said and showed her the crescent-shaped bite mark on his palm.

"It's all right," Branna said as she approached the woman, her voice raspy from the foul air. "I promise I'm not going to hurt you."

The pile moved again and Branna caught a flash of pale skin from under filthy, matted, blond hair. "What's your name?" Branna tried but was met with no response. "Where are you from?"

Jack joined them, an arm covering most of his face. "These crates are stamped with a company logo out of Charlestown, South Carolina. This is a Farrow Company ship."

Branna stiffened as the familiar name prickled along her spine. "Haven't heard that name in a long time." She knew Farrow Company was running ships through the area, but so far they had all been small with little cargo of interest. They had gotten in and out fast and not drawn any attention to themselves. This was the first large ship in nearly fifteen years and apparently it met the same gruesome fate as the *Rebellion* before.

She looked back to the woman whose face was hidden in shadows and lank hair but whose raspy, frightened breathing was audible. There was a manacle around her bare ankle, chained to a bolt in the floor. "We can't stay down here any longer. We need to get her and get out. Jack, find me something to strike these chains."

Branna moved closer to the woman. She didn't have time to be gentle or the inclination. "We're going to get you out so don't fight me. Do you understand?" She wondered to the woman's state of mind. She'd probably been abused, starved, and watched these people, part of her crew no doubt, die and rot in front of her. No one would be surprised if she'd gone completely mad.

"Yes..." she rasped.

Branna's eyebrows rose in surprise. "Good." Jack had returned with a heavy iron mallet and iron spike. "Hold out your leg and keep still."

The woman did as she was told and Branna wedged the spike in the hinge of the manacle and brought the mallet down hard on the head of the spike. The clang of metal on metal rang out through the hold and the woman groaned, bending her head to her chest, but didn't move.

Branna brought the mallet down half a dozen times before the iron around her ankle gave way and she could pry it from her leg. "Nat, Gus, help her to the deck."

Branna blinked and shielded her eyes from the harsh sun while they readjusted. She gulped at the fresher air and grimaced at the smell of death that followed her like a cloud. Her clothes would be burned and she would wash her hair and scrub her skin raw as soon as she was able.

Gus and Nat emerged from below supporting the woman. She was weak and the sun, which she may not have seen for some time, blinded her. She cried out, hiding her face from the light.

"Take her below. Jack, get her cleaned up and check her out. Food if she's able, water and clean clothes. Search her clothes and then burn them. I don't want an infestation."

"Me?" Jack looked between the women.

"You are the ship's surgeon, are you not? I trust you'll be the perfect gentlemen. Get Ollie to help you."

"Aye, aye, Captain."

"The rest of you," Branna barked to the men, "do a thorough search. Recover all weapons. I want all bodies shrouded and brought up on deck. I want the ship's logs and all charts to me as soon as they are recovered. If you can't find the log check beneath the captain's bunk for a false plank. If there are any food stores that are still good, transfer them over. They'll be no good to anyone else."

"Aye, aye, Captain!" they chorused.

"You going to scuttle her, Captain?" Gus asked.

"No." Branna let her gaze travel the ship slowly. "This ship is new and well cared for. Someone will be looking for her and her crew. Not to mention the woman, whoever she is. You and Nat make sure the ship is seaworthy and assign a six-person crew to limp her back to port and anchor a way off. Keep two men aboard to keep watch while we're in port. Any volunteer will be paid well, though don't mention that part until after they've volunteered. We'll not wait. Whoever that woman is, she needs to get to land."

CHAPTER TWO

Branna braided her damp hair. She spent far more time than she usually allotted herself to clean up and she could still smell the stink of human decay. It was in her nose where she suspected it would linger for some time.

A knock at the door had her rushing to button her shirt. "Come."

Gus pushed his way in. He too was freshly scrubbed and in clean clothes. His mop of hair was still damp and he shook it out of his eyes. "That was unexpected."

"Was it?" Branna dropped into the chair at her desk, pulling out her private bottle of rum and two battered copper cups. She poured for them both and motioned him into the chair across from her. "I can't say I'm surprised by anything Jagger does anymore."

"You think it was him?" he asked as he lowered himself into the other chair and set a leather-bound book on her desk.

"Who else?" She sipped her drink. "Maybe our guest can enlighten us."

Gus barked a humorless laugh. "If she's not completely out of her mind. How long do you think she was down there?"

"Too long. They obviously kept her alive and they hadn't abandoned ship so long ago that she died of thirst."

"So we were supposed to find her?"

"Perhaps."

"What now? Go after him? He's probably close by."

"No. We head to Nassau. We're in desperate need of a refit and restock and the crew needs a break." They'd been at sea for weeks and Branna, feeling that they were close, was reluctant to abandon the chase now, but she needed the crew well rested and in good spirits for when they took on the *Serpent's Mistress*.

They had battled before over the years. The *Banshee* was better armed, but the *Serpent's Mistress* faster and their previous skirmishes always ended with Jagger getting in a few good hits and then running with Branna unable to follow.

He nodded his approval. "We're down a few hands since we tossed those three arseholes off the ship in Port Royal last month. We could hire on. And the damned cracked bowsprit is acting up again. We need to get it fixed properly or lose the whole spar into the sea and half the foredeck with it."

"I've charted our location." Branna glanced to her navigation table. "We'll come back and start here. There are only a few uninhabited islands a day's sail from here. He's probably hiding out seeing what we do. If he wanted us to find her, then he wants us to find him, too." She leaned forward and grabbed the book, flipping it open. "There will be a cargo manifest and crew roster in here."

Branna thumbed through the first couple of pages of the *Firelight's* log. She scanned down the list of crew and froze, her cup halfway to her lips. The air was sucked from the room and she felt the color drain from her face.

"Jesus, Branna," Gus said.

She heard him as if from leagues away as her head swam in shocked terror. She never thought she could again feel fear like she did fifteen years ago. The day she cowered beneath her mother's dying body, clutching her father's sword, while she listened to the screams of her crewmen as they were slaughtered around her.

"What is it?" Gus spun the book toward him, searching the page. "Holy Christ, she's Julia bloody Farrow. She must be worth a fortune. We could use that. Did you know her?"

"Where is she?" Branna stood on shaky legs.

"In the purser's cabin. Jack wanted to have some privacy away from the crew."

Branna nearly slammed into Ollie, the baby-faced ship's boy, on his way out of the cabin. He had stinking clothes tucked under one arm and a large knife gripped in the other.

"Beg your pardon, Captain," he blurted and looked down, clumsily sheathing the knife.

"What are you about, Ollie?" Branna asked.

"Getting rid of her clothes. And I, um, had to cut off her hair. There was no cleaning the blood and filth." He dug in his pocket and held something out to her. "Found this hidden in a pocket of her skirt."

Branna sucked in a breath at the familiar sight of her family's ring. The one Julia had thrown away the night she threw away their love. She took it from Ollie and jammed it into her pocket without looking at it further. "On your way."

"Aye, aye, Captain." He shimmied by them and disappeared.

Branna stood in the doorway, watching Jack move about the small cabin applying the thick salve to the raw skin around the ankle that had been shackled. Branna's heart thudded painfully in her chest as her gaze travelled along Julia's body eventually resting on her face. At one time it had been a face Branna knew better than her own, but now she barely recognized it.

"How is she?" Branna asked, working hard to steady her voice and clamp down on the emotions and memories threatening to roar back into her heart.

Jack washed his hands in a basin and wiped them on a cloth. "In and out. She's been through hell, I'd say. That she's alive at all is a bloody miracle."

"Tell me."

"She was pretty delirious from thirst, starved, and beaten, though not recently. No bones are broken as far as I can tell, though her leg is pretty bruised from the chains." He paused and swallowed hard, his face reddening. "I don't know if she was, um, I can't tell if they hurt her in that way..."

"I get it."

It would be hard to believe that a woman had been held on that ship and hadn't been raped, but maybe they afforded her some small mercy.

She looked at Julia, now covered only in a thin sheet and a clean, oversize shirt. Beneath the old bruises her skin was smooth and pale. Her once long, blond hair was hacked short, sticking out in ragged spikes and still matted with grime and dried blood despite Ollie's attempts to clean it. Her features, so familiar and yet so foreign, were thinner than Branna remembered. She had lost the softness of childhood and grown into a woman. "Can you wake her?"

"Are you sure? She's been through a lot."

"You've got a bad habit of questioning me today, Jack. Is there something we need to discuss?"

"No, Captain." He sighed and produced a small bottle of smelling salts and held it under Julia's nose.

She jerked and coughed, her eyes fluttering open and a hand coming up to push Jack away.

"Easy," Branna said and stepped to the side of the bunk. "You're safe."

Julia blinked up at her, her gaze unfocused, working her tongue around in her mouth. "Water..."

Branna took the cup Jack offered and held it to her lips, helping lift her head so she could swallow. "Just a bit," she said and moved the cup though she clearly wanted more. "You'll only be able to handle a little at a time."

Julia's head dropped back to the bunk, exhausted at even the small motion. "Thank you."

"Julia?" Branna whispered. "Do you know who I am?"

Her eyes widened at the sound of her name and she struggled to focus on Branna's face. She stared at her a long time, her eyes darting over her face and over her body, eventually coming to rest on the raven pendant at her throat. "Bran...Branna?"

Branna released the breath she had been holding. "That's right."

Jack blurted, "You know this woman, Captain?"

Branna ignored him. "Julia, can you tell me what happened?"

Julia stared at her, blinking bleary, confused eyes before they drifted closed and she sighed deeply. Branna swore and snatched the smelling salts out of Jack's hand. She waved the bottle under Julia's nose until she coughed and her eyes dragged open again.

"Captain, you shouldn't," Jack protested.

"Quiet. Julia, stay with me. I need to know what happened to you."

Julia swallowed several times, her gray eyes dull. "You died fifteen years ago," she whispered. Her pale, trembling hand reached to brush the tips of her fingers across the pendant. "And part of me died, too. That's what happened."

Branna scowled, shaking off her words. None of that mattered now. "Why were you left alive?"

"What?"

"I need to know if you were taken by Captain Jagger?"

Julia gasped, a small keening sound coming from deep in her throat. She closed her eyes tightly and turned away. "My crew."

Branna's chest tightened. "I'm sorry. They're all gone."

"Captain Jagger." She turned back to Branna and her eyes were dark with grief. "He told me I was a gift for someone."

Blood roared in Branna's ears and she heard Jack suck in a breath next to her. "A gift?"

"An anniversary gift. I don't know what he meant. He said I was to remain unspoiled...the men...they tried to but he wouldn't let them touch me."

Branna's jaw clenched and unclenched in anger. It was a message. A message for her on the fifteen-year anniversary of her parents' death. Jagger had taken another merchant vessel, killed the crew, and left Julia for Branna to find. She felt sick to her stomach.

Julia's breathing slowed again and she began to drift out of consciousness. "No." Branna reached for the smelling salts again. "I need to know."

Jack's hand closed firmly around her arm, stopping her from reviving her again. Branna jerked in surprise, her eyes going wide at his brazenness.

Jack cleared his throat and let go of her arm. "With respect, Captain. You put this woman in my care. She's sick and injured and has suffered more than any one person should." He stared pointedly at her. They all knew her past. "You need to let her rest. When she's stronger, I'll let you know."

"Fair enough, Jack. You know where to find me." She looked at Julia again. She knew all too well what it was like to suffer as Julia had—and would still.

Branna turned to Gus. "We should talk."

"Aye," Gus replied tightly.

CHAPTER THREE

Branna stood at the aft doors staring out at the ocean while Gus refilled their cups. They were underway again, heading back to their home port of Nassau. The *Firelight* grew smaller as the distance between them increased.

"Nothing to say?" She picked up her drink and dropped into the chair behind her desk.

"Plenty. But I'll listen first."

Branna was quiet a long time, her thoughts far away. "I never lied to you."

"You said you had no one back in Charlestown."

"I didn't *have* her."

"But she's the one? Jesus, Julia Farrow?"

"The one what?" she said coolly. She had overheard enough hushed conversations to know her friends suspected a betrayal of the heart in her past. Her preference for the love of other women was well known but never spoken of openly. Though her relations were frequent enough, there was rarely any real tenderness involved.

His lips thinned as he apparently thought better about whatever he had intended to say. "Why didn't you contact her? Let her know you were alive? Her family owns half of Charlestown. They would have helped you."

"What for? I had you."

Gus barked a laugh. "What happened between you and her?"

"Does it matter?"

"She's on the bloody ship, Branna, so yes, it matters. Does Jagger know who she is? Who she is to you?"

"If he knew who she was I don't think he would have given her up. But I bet he'll find out quick. And she's nothing to me. Not anymore." She slid open the only drawer in her desk and produced a stained and yellowing envelope. She tossed it across the table toward him. "If you want to know what happened, it's probably all in there. It caught up with me about three years after the attack. Found its way to Genevieve's."

Gus turned it around in his hand, squinting at the flourishing ink script across the front with Branna's name as well as the name of her father and his ship, the *Rebellion*. "It's unopened."

"I haven't read it."

* * *

Three days later the ship pitched and rolled all afternoon and Branna stood at the helm. The wind was high as they sailed toward Nassau. She had heard from Jack that Julia had been able to take food for the last day and was regaining her strength. Branna had to stop herself several times from going to see her again. She had waited this long. She could wait a little longer, and whatever she had to say wouldn't change their immediate plans. She knew enough. Jagger was waiting for her and she would be there to meet him.

Branna tightened her grip on the wheel, imagining her hands around his throat squeezing the life out of him. Her lip curled into a snarl as her thoughts never strayed too far from her sworn path of vengeance.

"I bet I know what you're thinking about," Gus said as he came up behind her. "Or, should I say, *who?*"

She jumped, startled at the interruption. "We're almost home."

"There's something else for you to focus your attention on," he said with a nod toward the main deck.

She followed his gaze and watched Julia climb out from the main hatch with a slight limp from her still-healing ankle. She wore a shirt and pants several sizes too large, belted tightly at her waist. Her ridiculous attire did nothing to detract from her beauty as she stood looking out at the sea. She swayed comfortably with the motion of the ship. Her short, blond hair was clean and blowing gently.

Branna's belly tightened and her breath caught. She was jolted by her unexpected, visceral physical reaction at the sight of her. She could feel Gus's eyes on her. "Take the wheel. I have more questions for Miss Farrow."

Branna gazed at her from behind for another moment before moving close enough to be heard over the whipping wind. "You've grown strong sea legs," she said and cringed inwardly at the absurdity of the comment.

Julia spun and stared at her intently, her breath visibly quickening as she moved toward Branna, a hand outstretched. "I was afraid it might have been a dream. You *are* alive."

Branna stepped out of reach. "Yes."

Julia stilled, her arms wrapping around her middle as if to ward off a chill. "Are you the only one?"

"Yes."

"Why didn't you come home?"

"To what? This is my home now." Branna's gaze swept out at the ocean and over the deck of the ship—her ship, her crew. She looked at Julia from the side. God, she was beautiful and seeing her again breathed life into the fire Branna thought was long extinguished. As the embers of emotion smoldered so did the pain. "I'll see that you get back to Charlestown safely, of course."

Julia swallowed heavily, her eyes never leaving Branna's face, as if she still couldn't believe she was here. "Of course."

"I'm sorry for what happened to you," Branna said. She was terrible at this. Empathy, compassion, warmth, tenderness and kindness were not words usually associated with Captain Kelly—the Raven—the person she had become. More often than not she heard herself described as cold, ruthless, savage and heartless. While she didn't agree with that assessment either, she let it stand as it suited her reputation and got her what she needed.

Julia tucked an errant lock of hair behind her ear and stared openly at her. "But you still want to know what happened to me. What I know of this Captain Jagger and what his plans are?"

Branna squirmed under her familiar stare. There was no threat here yet somehow she felt she needed to protect herself. Julia could always see right through her, expose her secrets and lay her bare for the whole world to see. Branna would rather Julia Farrow hold a knife to her throat then turn those knowing eyes on her again, and she took an involuntary step back. "That's right."

"I should have known. The anniversary is yours isn't it? The fifteenth anniversary of the loss of the *Rebellion* and all her crew—except you, apparently. *You* are who I was meant to be found by? To be left..." She laughed bitterly. "...*unspoiled* for?"

Branna pressed her lips into a hard line but didn't answer. She was sorry for what Julia had endured but she didn't owe her any explanations.

"Ah, I see. You're not going to tell me anything, are you?"

"It's none of your concern," Branna answered tightly.

"None of my concern? I spent, I don't even know how long, beaten and chained in the hold of my own ship while the vilest men tormented me by leaving my crew to die and rot around me and I could do nothing to help them. I could only push them away as far...as far as the shackle on my leg would allow."

"Julia, I'm—"

"My cargo destroyed, my friends slaughtered, everything lost! All so I could be left as a prize for *you*. The dead woman who, for the last fifteen bloody years, I thought I would never get over the pain of losing. And here you bloody well stand. And it's none of my concern?"

Panic welled in her chest. She felt the eyes of the crew on them. She couldn't let Julia get the best of her. Not in front of the men. She had to work fast and diffuse this or risk losing respect in the eyes of her crew which could be the beginning of losing everything. "Julia, I understand how you feel. You know I do."

"I don't know anything about you, Captain Kelly." Julia's eyes flashed with rage and for a moment Branna wondered if she would try to strike her.

Before she had time to think about the ramifications of what she was doing, Branna went to a place inside herself she never dared go. She closed her eyes and called up the memory of the terrified young woman she was fifteen years ago, the one who watched in horror and agony as her parents were brutalized and butchered in front of her. She looked at Julia and let the pain, rage and fear wash over her and darken her eyes to black. Naked grief and fury poured from her very soul before she slammed up her walls and shut it away again. "I *know* how you feel," she repeated.

Julia sucked in a sharp breath and visibly trembled, her eyes bright with tears. Branna kept her voice calm and held out her hand as if to a wild animal. "Please, Julia, let's go to my quarters and speak privately."

Julia's chest heaved with her ragged breathing and her eyes darted around as if searching for an escape.

"It's okay," Branna murmured, recognizing the unpredictably wild mood swings she herself suffered after her ship was lost— fear, anger, guilt, grief and shame warring for space within her. "It's okay. You're safe with me."

Julia stared at her for a long time until her breathing slowed and she came to the realization that, at the moment, she had few other choices. She nodded and allowed Branna to lead her from the deck, speaking so quietly Branna nearly missed it. "I don't believe I am safe with you."

Julia stepped through the door to the captain's cabin and stopped. It was spacious but not ornate or frivolous. The large navigation table took up most of the space. It was covered with charts, some rolled and some lay open, instruments strewn across the top. Behind the navigation table there were double shuttered doors open to the ocean astern.

The walls were recessed with shelves filled with books, more charts, tools and curios. To the left of the table sat a battered desk, the captain's chair behind and two chairs in front from which she would surely hold council with her most senior officers. Along the port bulkhead was the bunk, neatly made and large enough for two. Julia couldn't help wondering if anyone had ever shared that bed. She doubted it. Not here. Not in Branna's obvious sanctuary.

Branna moved across the room and made to close the aft doors.

"Please, leave them open," Julia said. "The fresh air…I can't stand to feel confined." She tried to explain, but her burst of anger had left her feeling weak, disoriented, and filled with so much grief she thought it might consume her.

"I understand."

Julia stood, wringing her hands, unsure what to do until Branna motioned her into a chair at her desk. She sat and let her head drop into her hands. She heard the cork pop from a bottle and liquid being poured into cups.

"Drink this," Branna said softly and held out a cup of amber liquid.

The biting, sweet, tang of rum filled her nose and her trembling hands brushed Branna's fingers as she grasped the cup. There was a flashing tingle across her skin as they came into contact with each other. Julia saw her eyes widen briefly before she pulled away. Branna felt it, too.

Julia sat back and clutched the cup with both hands. "Let's just get this over with. What is it you want to know?"

"Tell me what happened from the beginning."

Julia licked her lips and drained her cup, coughing at the heat of it. "Farrow Company has been shipping to Port Royal for several years now. Nothing big but we've had a presence here for a while, solidifying our contacts and trade agreements."

"I'm aware."

Julia stared at her blankly. "We commissioned three new vessels—galleons—and it was a good time to make our presence felt, or so we thought." Branna, blessedly, remained quiet and Julia stared for a long time into her empty cup without speaking, a confusing knot of emotions warring within her.

Branna rose from behind her desk with the bottle, holding it out and offering her more. She held up her cup, careful not to touch her again.

"Where were you boarded?" Branna finally asked.

"We were only two days out of Port Royal." Julia swirled the rum in her cup and gazed past Branna's shoulder, out the doors to the clear water, making every effort to recount the horrors without reliving them. "They came upon us at dawn. Our watch was light and I don't know what happened; it was so fast. They were nearby, I guess, hiding in the keys we had passed overnight."

Branna nodded for her to go on.

"We were boarded, rounded up on deck. There was some fighting, screaming, I don't even know who. There was a lot of blood." She trailed off and tried to distance herself from the pain and fear. "The men took me below and I didn't see a lot of what happened."

"It was the *Serpent's Mistress?*"

"I don't know. I was struggling, fighting them, but there were so many of them. They hit me over and over. I blacked out and when I woke, I was where you found me."

"It's okay," Branna said. "Tell me about Captain Jagger. Does he know who you are?"

"I don't know. He never called me by name, and I'm all but certain none of my crew would have offered my identity, but if he found the logs…"

"He didn't. I have them."

She shrugged, knowing he would find out if it mattered. "He came to me only once. He was shorter than the others but muscular, dark hair, dark eyes. He spoke well, like he was educated. He told me I wouldn't be hurt." She gave a small laugh. "*Any more*, I suppose he meant. And that I was, like I said, a gift for someone to mark an occasion, an anniversary, and that once I was found, he expected he would be thanked appropriately."

Branna's expression hardened and darkness filled her eyes. "Where?"

"Where it all began." She had given all the information she had. She could do no more to help, if in fact help was what she had done. "I'd like to go back and lie down now," she said softly. She imagined she looked as bad as she felt—pale, weak and exhausted. She was worn out physically and emotionally.

Branna snapped out of her trance and eyed her with what almost looked like concern. "We'll be in Nassau by morning. I'll see you somewhere safe and help you make arrangements to get home."

"Thank you, Branna." She cleared her throat. "It's so strange to say your name again after all this time. I appreciate your efforts and I owe you my life. I'm sorry for the way I spoke to you earlier on deck. I should never have been so disrespectful."

Branna frowned at the apology. "I'm afraid it is I who should be apologizing to you, Julia. You've been caught up in a battle that's not yours and I regret that very much."

"My clothes, what happened to them?"

"They were disposed of."

Julia winced at one more blow to her already shattered heart. With Branna standing right in front of her she wasn't certain why the ring still mattered, but it did. It still served as a reminder of what they once shared between them. A love that seemed just as impossibly out of reach with the Branna Kelly standing before her, than if she had remained dead. "I understand."

Branna moved from behind her desk and held open the door to her cabin. "Ollie!"

He must not have been far away as the boy appeared within seconds.

"Please, escort Miss Farrow back to the purser's cabin and see that she has everything she needs."

"Aye, aye, Captain," he warbled, his voice just beginning to change.

Julia followed him without another glance at Branna Kelly.

CHAPTER FOUR

"Drop anchor," Nat called as the sails were furled when the *Banshee* bobbed in the water several hundred meters from port. They would moor outside the port and take the boat to land. "Lower the dory," he commanded and the crew tended the lines that would lower the boat to the water. Nat pushed the rolled rope ladder over the gunwale.

Branna dropped to the main deck next to him. "Is the watch schedule finished?" she asked though she knew the answer. Nat was thorough and an excellent bosun. He took his duties seriously and kept the crew running smoothly.

"Aye, Captain. Six-man watch teams as long as we're in port. We'll bring a barge out to unload the cargo as soon as everyone is ashore that's going. Gus and I will see to its sale or trade."

"Excellent." She nodded and turned to Gus. "And the repairs?"

"I'll have to head down to the repair yard and get some estimates. It's a big job and may take a few days."

"That's fine. We'll be staying at least a week. I have some things to take care of in town. We need to restock the stores and get the word out about the *Firelight* and find someone to see to her proper disposition and get our crewmen back."

Gus nodded. "I'll see to it."

"Nat, what are your thoughts on crew replacements?"

"I may have some leads. I'll have to ask around."

Branna looked past his shoulder as Julia emerged from belowdecks, escorted per Branna's request, by Jack. She looked better than she had yesterday but still with lines of exhaustion and tension around her eyes.

She was squinting and shielding her eyes from the blinding sun, but the small smile at her mouth was unmistakable when her gaze came to rest on Branna. Branna, as was her custom when in town, was dressed to intimidate in loose-fitting cotton shirt open at the neck, tucked into tight black leather pants. Heavy black leather boots reached to just below her knees. Buckled around her waist was a wide black leather belt gleaming with the hilts of eight throwing knives, four across each hip.

She carried her father's sword, the one she would run through Cyrus Jagger. It was not at her waist but slung in a scabbard across her back like a quiver of arrows so the hilt rose up behind her right shoulder and the blade angled across her back ending at her left hip. The strap of the scabbard crossed her chest snugly and her hair was in its usual braid ending between her shoulders.

"Good morning," Julia said politely as she approached them. Her eyes flicked over Branna. "Are you expecting trouble?"

"Always." She turned her attention to her men, knowing they hadn't yet been formally introduced. "Julia Farrow, these are my most senior officers, Gus Hawke, first mate, and Nat Hooper, bosun. Of course, you already know the quartermaster, Jack Massey."

Julia placed a hand over her heart and looked at them each in turn. "Thank you for everything you've done for me. I don't know how I can ever repay you."

Gus actually blushed. "No need, Miss Farrow. We're just happy we were able to help."

Branna asked, "Ready to go ashore?"

"Yes."

Jack assisted Julia into the boat and Branna said to Nat and Gus, "See to the pay of the crew and to your duties then come ashore and meet me for supper at Genevieve's tonight. You'll both be off duty until tomorrow night so plan accordingly."

"Aye, aye, Captain," they both replied enthusiastically.

Branna levered herself over the side and climbed nimbly down the ladder after Julia.

Nassau swarmed with people and Julia was assaulted with sights, smells and noise. It was not unlike Port Royal, but because of what had happened since, she felt vulnerable and anxious. She was saved from complete madness by the wide berth people gave Captain Branna Kelly when they saw her striding down the laneway.

The crowd thinned as they came to the entrance of their destination. They walked under a wooden arch, carved with the words Travers Trading Post, overhanging with palm trees and shaded from the sun. The arch opened into the large stone courtyard of a U-shaped, two-story building dotted with more palms and tables scattered throughout.

Julia looked around at the open space and the men and women who occupied it. The men were obviously all some flavor of sailor, merchant, or tradesman by their dress. The women were dressed shockingly provocatively in loose flowing skirts, hiked above their knees and tightly laced bustiers leaving little to the imagination. Their faces and hair were made up as if ready for a theatrical performance, which, she supposed, was not far from the truth.

Above her on three sides, the courtyard was rimmed by a balcony leading to rooms, some closed, some not. There were more couples and other single men and women drifting around and in and out of the private spaces.

"Well, well, well, if it isn't the lusty Raven," a throaty-voiced woman called as she approached them. Unlike the other women she was more modestly clothed in sturdy boots, long brown skirt and leather underbust corset laced over a white blouse. She was tall and thin with deeply tanned skin and straight, brown hair. She was probably at least a decade older than Julia. All sharp features and angles but put together in such a way as to make her striking. She walked toward them with a confident grace and was very obviously in charge.

"Been a while, Gen," Branna said.

"Too long or not long enough?" the woman teased before turning her curious gaze on Julia. "Who do we have here?"

"Genevieve Travers, meet Miss Julia Farrow, though I'd thank you not to repeat that, for now. We picked Miss Farrow up a few days ago. She needs some help."

Genevieve's eyes flicked to Branna with a question, but apparently she knew better than to ask it at present. If she recognized Julia's name, she gave no indication. "Of course. If you don't mind my saying, honey, you look done in."

Julia forced a smile. She was fading fast from tension and overstimulation. "It's a pleasure to meet you, Miss Travers."

"Genevieve, please. Better yet, my friends call me Gen. Welcome to Travers Trading Post."

"Gen runs the trading and shipping company. We do a great deal of business together. As you can see"—she gestured around the courtyard to the men and women transacting their personal business—"there are other services offered, as well."

Julia smiled thinly. "I see."

"Julia needs a room for a while." Branna looked pointedly at Genevieve. "A private one."

Gen cocked an eyebrow at her. "Follow me."

Genevieve pushed open the doors to a spacious room with double doors at the far side that opened to a private balcony view of the harbor with undeveloped land between. There was a large clean bed draped with mosquito netting, and a table and chairs with an ewer of fresh water and a bowl of fresh fruit atop. Along one wall was a divan and two other wicker chairs.

Julia looked around the room and sighed. She longed for that bed and some privacy to get some rest and collect herself. She needed some time to figure out what she was going to do.

"Make yourself comfortable, honey," Genevieve said. "The captain and I have some things we need to discuss."

Julia blushed wondering about the real nature of their relationship. "I have no way to pay you right now but I can assure you—"

"Don't worry about that." Genevieve waved a hand.

"You'll be safe here," Branna said. "I'll check on you tomorrow."

Julia nodded, not trusting herself to speak. She was all of the sudden overcome with emotion at being left alone. She swallowed hard and steeled herself. "Thank you."

Branna and Genevieve stepped out onto the interior walkway and closed the door behind them, leaving her alone. She heard them move off a few steps and the unintelligible murmur of low voices as they stopped nearby. The door was blessedly silent when she cracked it softly to listen.

"Julia Farrow? Branna, please, tell me I heard you wrong."

"We found her chained in the hold of her own ship half mad and nearly dead the only survivor. You'll find the Farrow Company galleon *Firelight* in the harbor in a few days. I need you to get word back to Charlestown for someone to claim her."

"Jesus. Jagger? What a bloody mess."

"You have no idea. She was a message to me. We're going to finish this once and for all. He wants to meet on the anniversary where he took down my parents' ship."

"That's in a fortnight, Branna."

"No one knows the date better than I. There's much to do between now and then."

Julia heard the jingle of coins and strained to hear more as it sounded like money was changing hands.

"Keep Julia here and don't let her leave. It's not safe for her, especially when word gets out that she's here. Look out for her. She's under my protection so get her whatever she needs. She'll need passage back to Charlestown as soon as something comes up. Safe passage."

"I'll see to it, personally. How long are you staying?"

"We have to refit and restock. At least a week."

"Hmm. Merriam will be pleased."

"You can let her know Jack will be ashore tonight. She can have him all to herself for a bit. Don't worry, Gen, Gus will be here too. I've given them both the night off."

"A whole night? Golly, Captain Kelly, that's very generous of you."

"That's why I'm so well liked."

Gen snorted. "What about you? You've been a long time out there. What do you need?"

Julia heard nothing further and moved from the door to the bed. She flung the netting aside and dropped onto the clean linen. It was luxurious. She replayed what she had heard. Branna was going after Captain Jagger. She tried to hold on to her ragged thoughts but felt herself drifting away. The last thing she thought, ridiculously, before sleep claimed her was how alluring this unfamiliar Branna was to her.

CHAPTER FIVE

Julia awoke with a start, her chest heaving and her face damp with tears. She had been dreaming of the attack on the ship and the sounds of her crew's screams still rang in her ears. She had no idea what time it was but the sun was low in the sky when she looked out across the harbor.

She crossed the room and poured fresh water from the ewer into the matching porcelain bowl. She washed her face, neck and chest and had three buttons unfastened on her shirt when there was a soft knock on the door.

She hastily raked her hands through her short hair trying to tame the irregular tufts when someone pushed the door open slowly.

"May I come in?" an unfamiliar female voice called out.

"Yes."

Julia turned to see a young, petite blond woman, twenty years at most, with wild hair and artfully displayed cleavage in an ornate dress that looked far too snug to be comfortable. Julia smiled curiously at her and ignored the pang of disappointment that it wasn't the enigmatic Captain Branna Kelly. If she dared, she could examine that emotion another time.

"Hello," the woman said. She held a pile of clothes in one hand and a plate of food in the other. "Gen sent me up with supper. Poor thing, ya must be starved."

"Thank you, yes." Julia took the plate and set it on the table.

The woman dropped the stack of garments onto the bed. "I'm Merriam Beeson." She introduced herself with a hand over her chest. "Call me Merri."

"Julia Farrow." Julia winced inwardly, wondering if providing her name indiscriminately was a mistake.

Merriam seemed not to notice and made herself at home. She dropped onto the bed with a sigh, kicking off what looked to be a pair of very uncomfortable high-heeled boots and massaging her feet. "Ya don't mind do ya, Julia? I been going like mad all day?"

"I don't mind." Since Merriam Beeson felt comfortable Julia didn't think she would mind if she ate in front of her and started in on her food. "Do you work here?"

"It's temporary. 'Course, I been saying that the last five years." She laughed. "Gen's good to me. I get to meet some interestin' people, ya know? And some right arseholes. But they all got coin, so it has its perks."

Julia nodded, though she really had no idea. "Merriam? I heard your name mentioned before. Are you a friend of Jack Massey?"

Her eyes sparked with life, and Julia thought, lust. "I am, indeed. Do ya know 'im?"

Julia wasn't sure how much to say. "We've met, yes. I came in on the *Banshee* this morning."

"I heard Captain Jagger left someone alive. That you?"

Julia blinked, her face falling. "I, uh, yes, that's me."

Merri gasped, her hands covering her mouth. "I'm so sorry. My mama, if I knew who she was, would be ashamed. Are ya okay? I mean, it musta been awful. Is there anything ya need?"

Julia couldn't help but be charmed by the young woman and quickly forgot her discomfort. "I'm okay, thank you. Captain Kelly and her crew have been very kind."

Merri snorted. "*Kind* and Captain Kelly are not words ya often hear put together."

"You know her?"

"Everyone knows the Raven. Or knows *of* her. She cuts a wide swath in case ya haven't noticed."

"Oh, I've noticed." She considered for a moment. She wanted this woman's opinion of Branna but didn't want to be rude or come across as too nosy. "How would you describe her? In a word."

"Indomitable."

Julia's eyes widened. "That's high praise."

"Is it? Damn. That's Jack's word for her. I ain't even sure what it means. I thought maybe it meant cold-blooded bitch."

Julia stared at her in surprise before throwing her head back in laughter. Merriam laughed with her and Julia felt, if only for a moment, normal again. "Thank you, Merri," she breathed, wiping tears from her eyes.

"I almost forgot." She jumped up and began to unfold the clothes from the pile on the bed. "Gen asked me to gather some clothes that might fit ya. Something *appropriate*, she said. I said, Jesus Christ, Gen, ya run a fuckin' brothel. If ya wanted appropriate ya should raid a convent."

"You said that?"

"Sure did." Merri nodded, preoccupied with the clothes. "'Cept not as nice as that."

Julia laughed again and perused the clothes Merriam had procured for her. They were far less modest than she was accustomed to but looked as though they would fit well enough. "These are great, Merriam, thank you."

"Don't mention it." Merriam beamed and flopped back down on the bed.

Julia returned to her food and considered her plate for a moment as something occurred to her. "If you're bringing me my food, does that mean I'm not allowed to leave?"

Merriam squirmed under her gaze. "I'm sorry. Gen said yer to stay here. Didn't know why 'til ya told me. I 'spect it's under the orders of Captain Kelly."

"Will I be stopped if I try to leave?"

She quickly pulled on her boots and backed out of the room. "T'was really nice speakin' with ya, Julia. I'll see ya soon."

Julia nodded dumbly. She was a prisoner again and her temper flared, this time directed at one Branna Kelly, captain or not.

She wasn't so angry that she couldn't eat and finished her plate as the sun set. The noise from the courtyard had been steadily growing louder and as the night wore on, she couldn't hold back her curiosity any longer.

She stepped out the door to her room and peered over the railing. Torches lit up the courtyard, and the air was filled with the music of guitar and drums, ribald laughter and conversation and the smell of rum, smoke, and ocean.

Rooms were filling up fast as women led men, taunting and teasing, behind closed doors. She looked to her right and left down the walkway and saw, at each end, a large, armed, stone-faced man staring off at nothing. She suspected she knew why they were there and took a few steps toward the man nearest her. He turned to her, arms crossed, and shook his head.

Julia seethed, staring hard at him before turning back to her room. She was just about through the door when a woman's voice caught her attention for no particular reason.

"Come on, Captain, let me help you relax." The deep, lyrical voice floated up over the din.

Julia turned back to the rail and peered down into the courtyard. A buxom woman with blond hair, swinging hips and sultry eyes was leading Branna through the crowd by her hand. Julia's eyes narrowed and her blood heated.

She sucked in a breath and searched to find the words to describe what she was feeling. She had no claim to Branna. She saw to that herself fifteen years ago. Branna Kelly owed her nothing. They had barely spoken but for Julia to scold her and she to interrogate her in return. Why should she care whose bed Branna warmed? Why could she not look away?

Julia's gaze tracked them as they wended their way across the courtyard and she saw Branna stiffen, her hand going to the hilt of her sword as if sensing danger and her head whipped around the courtyard searching for the threat. Her focus darted up, finding Julia. Her grip on her sword relaxed, but she held her gaze for a long moment, her expression unreadable.

Julia shuddered as both fear and desire skittered its way across her skin. She dragged her gaze from Branna with a sharp breath and slipped back into her room.

CHAPTER SIX

Julia bolted upright in bed as iron bands of fear tightened mercilessly across her chest. She groaned with the pain of her loss and struggled to breathe. Throwing off the thin sheet, she staggered to the table, pouring herself a glass of water with a shaky hand.

There was a soft knock at the door and she jumped, her heart pounding still. It was hours before dawn.

"Julia? It's Gen. Are you all right?"

She wore nothing but the oversize shirt they gave her from the *Banshee* and her hair was a lopsided mess but it was Genevieve and she deserved an answer. "I'm fine, thank you," she said shakily as she opened the door.

"My room is right next door and I heard you cry out." Genevieve took in the room, the tangled bedclothes and Julia's face, flushed and damp with tears. "Bad dreams?"

"Yes." Julia took a shuddering breath and moved from the door to drop herself down into a chair at the table.

"I'll be right back," she said and disappeared. She returned a moment later with a bottle and two glasses and joined Julia at the table, pouring her a generous amount of rum. "Care to talk about it?"

Julia ran her finger around the rim of the glass, making it sing for a moment before tossing it back with a grimace. "I'd rather talk about something else."

"Something in particular?"

"Captain Kelly and Captain Jagger," she said and met Genevieve's eyes. "What happened between them?"

Genevieve sipped her drink and stared out at the inky night. "It's not a secret. It's well known that they've been after each other for years."

"Fifteen years."

"Well, that's when it all began, but the chase has been on for much less time than that. Fifteen years ago Jagger overran the merchant vessel Captain Kelly's parents sailed. Branna was only a young woman then. Jagger gave her that scar on her face and she watched as they slaughtered her parents and the crew. He left her alive, though. I guess the idea of it amused him."

"I know most of that." Julia's heart ached anew for the young girl she remembered. "What happened to her after?"

"Gus took her in, helped her, trained her, and protected her and her money until she could take care of herself. She lived here off and on when I was just getting my start. It's actually how Gus and I met. He got her work, taught her to fight, taught her to sail these waters like she'd been born to it. He handpicked her crew, whatever she needed. They're very close—like family."

Julia shook her head. "I'm grateful she had him—all of you—but I don't understand why she didn't just come home. Why she let us believe she was dead all these years."

"Don't you?"

Julia flushed and looked away. "She told you about me?"

"No. But I've always suspected it wasn't just the death of her parents that hardened her. Seeing you two together for even a moment and it's plain to see you share a painful history."

"What do you mean?"

"The air between you positively crackles with unfulfilled longing."

Julia forced a laugh. "No, you must be mistaken."

"I passed along a letter a long time ago. You have beautiful penmanship."

Julia jerked up in her chair. "She got my letter? So, then she knows. She knows what really happened. What my father made me do."

"She got it. Didn't seem at all interested in reading it. That was over ten years or so now and I've never asked and she's never said. Anyone who knows her well, and admittedly I can count that number on only a few fingers, knows there is a part of her that is untouchable. It's pretty clear you have something to do with that."

Julia sighed, sadness for the loss of Branna and the woman she knew overwhelming her, more so than losing her crew. She'd never felt so alone. "She's going after Captain Jagger isn't she?"

"Did she tell you that?"

"I overheard your conversation earlier."

"Captain Kelly has a lot of rage inside her that she doesn't feel will be quieted until Jagger is dead."

"By her hand."

"Yes."

She had figured all this out already. She wanted to know more. "And all that rage? Where does it go in the meantime?"

"Nowhere. It burns so hot in her sometimes I think she's on fire."

"Does she have someone? I mean, to talk to?"

"Are you offering?"

"It's not like we don't have anything in common and we knew each other well once and we were…" She trailed off uncertainly.

"True. I don't know what Branna Kelly was like with you before all this, but Captain Branna Kelly is a complicated woman, Julia. I'd be cautious if I were you. When people run that hot those around them tend to get burned."

"Are you warning me off?"

"I just want you to be aware what you're getting yourself into by involving yourself with her."

"And the others Captain Kelly is *involved* with? Do you warn them as well?"

"What others?"

* * *

Branna walked into the courtyard in the late afternoon, finally having completed her duties for the day. She had told Genevieve she would be checking on Julia and Gen was waiting for her with a sly grin.

"What's that look for?" Branna asked suspiciously.

"I've spent some time with your Miss Julia Farrow," she said coyly.

"She's not *my* anything. *Her* choice, if you must know."

"I doubt that very much."

Branna sighed. "And?"

"And if I'm not mistaken, and I rarely am, you've met your match, Captain Kelly."

"In what way?"

"Well, I daresay she couldn't best your sword but in every other way that matters."

Branna scoffed and waved her off, heading up the stairs. The door to the room was open and Branna raised her hand to knock on the wall. She froze, her fist poised in the air, when she caught sight of Julia standing in the doorway to the balcony at the far side of the room. Her back was to her, one arm raised above her gripping the molding as she rested her head against her arm and gazed out across the harbor.

The cross-breeze rippled through the room and the thin skirt hugging her hips fluttered, revealing a thigh high slit and the smooth, fair leg beneath. Branna took a slow breath, her lips parting slightly. Julia had grown into an astonishingly beautiful woman, with long legs, slender waist and full curves.

Julia, like always, must have sensed her presence in the room. "You're staring, Branna," she said without turning around.

Branna straightened and recovered herself. "The view is breathtaking."

Julia turned, mouth quirked in a half-smile.

"The view of the harbor."

"Of course."

"Are you finding you have everything you need?"

"Gen and Merri have been very attentive." She gestured to her hair which, while even shorter, now was neat and even.

"Looks good," Branna mumbled and found she was at a loss for what to say. The next thing she wanted to tell her was that she hadn't stayed with Selina last night but she would sound like a complete arse if she blurted that out. Why did she even care what Julia thought? And, what made her think Julia cared whose company she kept?

"Is your business here being taken care of to your satisfaction?"

Branna nodded, knowing she was fishing for information. "It is. There's always much to do when we're in port."

"You're going after him aren't you?"

"Who?"

"You know damn well who, Branna. Captain Jagger."

"What makes you ask me that?"

"I overheard you speaking with Gen yesterday after we arrived. I think—"

"*I* think, Julia, you should be very careful whose conversations you overhear. And anyway it's—"

"None of my concern?" Julia finished tartly. "You know what *is* my concern? This gilded cage you're keeping me in."

Branna felt herself losing control of the conversation again. "If there's something you need, Julia, just ask."

"What I need, Branna, is to get out of this room. I can't stand feeling that I'm a captive again. Surely, you can understand that?"

"I *do* understand, but it's not a good idea for you to go out."

"Can't you just come with me and do that thing that you do?"

"What thing is that?'

"You know, be the *Raven*. Swagger about with your pointy knives and your fearsome scowl that parts the masses like the Red Sea."

"You don't know me, Julia, and you insult me," she said tightly and turned to leave. "You're safe here."

"Wait. Don't go. Branna, I didn't mean to offend you. I'm just frustrated."

Branna stopped but didn't turn back around even when Julia stepped close enough that Branna felt the heat of Julia's body against her back.

She placed a hand on Branna's arm. "Please, Branna. What I meant was, I *do* feel safe with you."

Branna ignored the tingling warmth from Julia's fingers against her skin. "You were right the first time—you shouldn't."

Julia's hand dropped away. "You're a liar."

Branna's fists clenched instinctively at the challenge and she rounded on her. "Watch your tongue, Julia!"

"Don't!" Julia flinched and stumbled backward, her hands coming up as if to protect herself from a blow.

Branna sucked in a sharp breath. "I'm sorry...Julia, I would never..." she stammered and backed away from her, unable to meet her eyes. She backed out the door, leaving it open as she found it.

Branna stalked a few yards down the walkway and grasped the iron railing in a white-knuckled grip. "Bloody hell!" she hissed through gritted teeth.

She was truly furious now, not at being challenged but because Julia was right. She *was* lying. She wanted nothing more than to keep Julia safe for the rest of her life. Instead she had frightened an already traumatized woman into thinking she was going to strike her.

She'd handled that completely wrong. Julia was suffering. She had been through so much and had opened herself up to Branna, allowed herself to be vulnerable and ask for what she needed and Branna had stomped all over her for it. She never meant for that to happen. She took a steadying breath and glanced down to the courtyard. Genevieve met her gaze with a wide grin and mimed applause.

"Go to hell," she mouthed over the side.

Genevieve gestured to the door and raised her eyebrows. Her expression was unmistakable. Get back in there and make it right.

Branna stepped quietly back to the doorway. Julia sat with her head in her hands, shoulders trembling with quiet tears. Branna's heart lurched. The horrors Julia had faced and Branna hadn't seen her shed a tear until now. Maybe she *was* as heartless as people thought. She didn't want to be that person. Not with her.

She cleared her throat and Julia jumped to her feet, swiping at her eyes. "I'm sorry, Branna. I didn't mean—"

"Don't apologize to me. I should never have treated you like that. I was out of line."

Julia smiled hesitantly. "Do you think we can, maybe, start over?"

Branna crossed the room and met her gaze. "It's a beautiful afternoon, Julia. Would you care to take a walk around town with me?"

CHAPTER SEVEN

They stood at the entrance to the laneway that would lead to the main square and watched colorful throngs—villagers, merchants and sailors—stream past and go about their business. Within moments of their arrival the path cleared as people, previously shoulder to shoulder and jostling to move past one another, stepped to the side. Julia's mouth quirked into a near smile.

Branna's face heated. "Just say what you're thinking."

"I'm not saying a word," she said over her shoulder and stepped out onto the walk.

Branna caught up with her in three quick strides and kept a hand at the small of her back to keep her close and out of harm. At least, that's what she told herself. The gentle warmth of Julia's skin radiated to her hand, even through her blouse, crept up her arm and heated more distant parts of her body. She never wanted the feeling to go away.

She tried to move them quickly through the market but Julia slowed every few steps to admire the wares, smell the food, flowers and oils, or simply chat with the vendors. She eventually gave up and settled for keeping a wary eye out. It had been years since Cyrus Jagger had been allowed in Nassau but that didn't mean he couldn't have agents nearby. He had let Julia live intentionally, but she was also the only surviving witness to his latest brutality, and no doubt he would find out who she was—assuming he didn't already know. Branna wasn't going to let her guard down.

She scanned the crowds and couldn't help but notice the looks shooting their way. She was used to getting a fair amount of attention but this seemed different somehow. It took her another moment to realize the people weren't looking at her but at Julia.

She turned to see Julia leaning against the stall, oblivious to the eyes on her, drinking something from a wood flagon. One leg peeked daringly from her sheer white skirt and the blouse had slipped down over her shoulders, her breasts straining against the laces across her chest.

Her skin was smooth and fair in a way so different from many of the locals, and droplets of sweat beaded on her chest in the evening's heat. She was magnificent and it was no wonder others didn't fail to notice. Julia glanced up to see Branna staring at her and smiled, laughter dancing in her eyes.

"Have you ever tried one of these? It's wonderful." Julia held the drink out to her.

"No, I haven't."

"Try it," Julia encouraged and thrust it into her hands. "It's called mango and papaya. They're fruit."

Branna's mouth quirked. "I know what they are."

"Then how have you never had one?"

"I guess I never took the time." She took a sip and a sweet, tangy taste burst across her tongue. She licked her lips and tried some more.

"Good, right?"

"It's fine." She handed the flagon back to her.

"Oh, come on, Bran, do you enjoy nothing in this place you call home?"

"I enjoy many things in this town." She dug in her pocket and flipped a coin to the vendor, ushering Julia through the square.

"Like what?"

She considered for a moment. "The harbor is expertly run and they are extremely efficient at getting the ship refitted and restocked. Gen is always able to find buyers for my cargo and there's no shortage of new crew when I need to take on men.

Julia was quiet a long moment. "And when you take on women?"

"There's a service for that as well."

"So I've seen. That's not really what I was trying to say, though. It's so vibrant here. There's so much energy, so much life, so many stories and things to explore. I can't believe you don't know more about it."

"I know everything I need to know," she said, feeling inexperienced for the first time. She really knew nothing of these people and their daily lives—where they lived, how they arrived, their names, what they celebrated and why. Maybe, when this was over, she would change that.

"Captain Kelly," Nat boomed, striding toward them. People hurried out of his way lest they get run over by the big man. "Miss." He nodded toward Julia as he approached.

"I'll just be a moment," Branna said to Julia and turned her attention to her officer.

"I have some men interested in signing on to the crew. Would you care to meet with them?"

"I would." She considered her schedule for the next couple of days. "Tomorrow night. At the bar."

"I'll let them know." He strode back the way he had come.

Branna turned back around and Julia was gone. Her stomach dropped as she looked around wildly. All she saw were vendors, customers, and children playing in the square. "No," she growled.

Her fists clenched and her throat tightened. She was about to move back to the juice vendor when she heard a rich, melodic laugh nearby. She followed the sound and peered over the half wall of a booth to see Julia sitting on the ground covered with squirming orange and white kittens.

Julia looked up at her and beamed, laughing as one of the little creatures batted at her hand. "Aren't they sweet?"

"Adorable," she grumbled, her heart still pounding.

"Let me guess. You're a kitten hater, too?"

"I don't hate kittens," she insisted and moved around to the other side of the wall.

One kitten, the smallest, moved from Julia's lap and tottered over to Branna, winding herself around her legs and mewling up at her.

"You have an admirer," Julia said as she eased the others off her lap and stood, scooping up the tiny creature between Branna's feet. She held the little animal up to look at her and frowned. "What happened to her?" she asked the boy in the stall, indicating the scar where it appeared no fur could grow, slashing over one eye.

"She is the littlest," the boy replied. "The others tried to force her out but she fought back. She is small but she has a brave heart."

"A kindred spirit," Julia said, her eyes alight with humor as she dumped the little animal in Branna's arms before she could refuse.

"Wait," Branna blurted, fumbling with the creature.

Julia laughed as the kitten purred and nuzzled against her. Branna's eyes went wide in surprise. "I think she's yours."

Branna scowled and adjusted the wriggling animal in her hands. "Why the hell would I want a cat?"

Julia crossed her arms and arched a brow. "You know in many cultures cats are worshipped as deities. Have you never heard of Bastet? A fierce feline and protector of the innocent of Ancient Egypt. I think, perhaps, you'd like her."

Branna's scowl softened but she still remained skeptical.

"Fine." Julia took the kitten back from her. "But you can't tell me your ship doesn't have a rodent problem. I don't care how good a shape you keep it in. I've seen them. I know," she whispered the last conspiratorially.

Branna was hopelessly charmed. For a moment it was like nothing had changed between them and no time had passed. If Julia had suggested she adopt a manatee she would have happily found a way for it to be loaded onto the ship. She couldn't help herself and she laughed.

"Why, Captain Kelly, what a beautiful smile you have. Don't worry I won't let anyone know the Raven has a sense of humor."

Branna straightened and pressed her lips together, though laughter still fluttered in her belly. She was enjoying herself and she couldn't remember the last time she could say that. "How much for the little beast?" she asked the boy.

"For you, Captain, a gift. I cannot sell this one anyway because she is damaged."

Branna stared at him for a moment, the irony of his statement not lost on her. A wounded animal for a wounded woman. She dug out another couple of coins and dropped them into the boy's hand before turning to Julia. "We should be getting back, Julia."

Julia clutched the kitten to her, hiding her expression in its fur, and simply agreed with a nod.

CHAPTER EIGHT

Julia set the kitten down in her room and it immediately scampered off to bat at the drapes across the door billowing in the breeze. "Thank you, Bran." She placed her hand over her heart, feeling immeasurably better. "Going out. Seeing the town was just what I needed."

"You must be hungry. Can I have something sent up for you?"

"Will you stay? Have supper with me?"

She opened her mouth to speak but held silent for a long moment. "Yes."

Julia had thought for certain she was going to say no and beamed at her. "Excellent."

"I'll be back in a few minutes." Branna fled the room, but not before Julia caught the flush of heat creeping up her cheeks.

As soon as she was out the door, Julia poured fresh water in the bowl and pulled the laces at her blouse. She washed sweat and dust from her skin and ran her fingers through her short hair, messy from the breeze.

She heard footsteps on the balcony and rushed to pull herself back together. She paused, the laces of her blouse partially tied, and let them fall. She pushed up the short corset Merri had provided her, revealing the swell of her breasts.

Branna returned followed closely by a serving girl carrying a tray of food. The young woman set the tray on the table and hustled out of the room without a word. Branna held two glasses of pink juice in one hand and a bottle of rum in the other.

"I have something for you to try," she said with a gleam in her eye. She popped the cork on the rum and poured a generous amount of the amber liquid into the glasses. "This is how mango and papaya should be consumed."

Julia tasted it and nodded her approval with a smile. "Very nice."

"Do you mind if I wash up?"

"Please."

Branna lifted her sword and scabbard over her head, leaning it against the end of the bed. She stretched her shoulders and neck, and Julia imagined it did get heavy after a full day.

She rolled her sleeves up to reveal the powerful muscles in her forearms rolling under her skin, crisscrossed with old scars, as she washed her hands. She ran her wet hands over her face and neck and smoothed them over her hair to pull the unruly, escaped tendrils off her face.

When she was through, Julia gestured to the table by the window and they took chairs across from one another. The kitten immediately leapt into Branna's lap when she sat down. Julia smiled as she picked at the plate of fresh fish and fruit. "What are you going to name her?"

Branna offered a piece of fish to the kitten who gratefully accepted. "Morrigan."

"That's a beautiful name."

"I don't need beautiful. Morrigan is an Irish goddess of battle and war and protector to her territory and people. She's often depicted as a crow—appropriate, don't you think? I need a name to strike fear into the hearts of vermin everywhere."

Julia laughed, enjoying a glimpse of the Branna she remembered. "Ah, I see."

"I like the sound of it. It's menacing without being vulgar."

"Is that how you see yourself now—a warrior and protector?"

"I don't know, maybe."

"Why didn't you name your ship Morrigan?"

Darkness clouded her expression and Branna toyed with her glass for a long time before she spoke again. "Right before the *Rebellion* was attacked, I was asleep and I woke to a scream unlike anything I had ever heard, echoing in my ears—not man, nor beast. My mother comforted me, insisting it was just a dream but I knew what it was and I was right—the wailing woman heralding the death of loved ones. *Banshee* seemed the right thing to name her when I had her built."

Julia fought tears, her own sorrow mirrored on Branna's face. "I'm so sorry, Bran."

"It was a long time ago," she said and took a deep breath, meeting Julia's gaze. "It gets better."

"It doesn't seem like it's gotten better for you," she replied softly.

Branna sighed wearily and attempted a smile. "Tell me of your family."

Julia knew it was only a matter of time before Branna would ask what had happened in the last fifteen years. "My mother, she was only months away from having the child when you left."

"I remember." Branna's smile was genuine. "Did your father get his son?"

"Another little girl."

"Healthy?"

"Yes, by the grace of god. My mother, though, did not survive the birth."

Branna sat up in her chair. "No."

Julia raised her glass in salute. "You're right, it gets better."

"Your father?" Branna asked hesitantly.

Julia smiled grimly and looked away. "My father's descent into madness began the moment he heard of the *Rebellion's* destruction. It was his failure and his cross to bear. He hardly ate or drank unless you count whiskey and he only slept when he passed out. He would have lost Farrow Company but for me propping him up, literally and figuratively. Then my mother died and he didn't even have the son he was counting on into whom he could pour what was left of his soul. He couldn't even look at the babe. He died in his sleep a year after my mother."

"Oh, Julia, I didn't know."

"How could you? You were dead. I was left to raise my sister and take over Farrow Company. My father, after all his perceived failings and disappointments felt he could make one thing right, and even against the fierce objections of his associates and solicitor, he changed his will. I never let him forget how he wronged me and what I was owed, so he left me everything."

"Owed you for what?"

Julia arched a brow and finished her drink, choosing to ignore the question. "I intended to run Farrow Company from the ground and not from an ivory tower. I would never ask the crews to do something I couldn't or wouldn't do myself. I learned to sail and I kept my own books and negotiated my own contracts. I learned everything I could from anyone who would teach me."

"That's admirable and good leadership."

"I thought so." Julia turned the glass around in her hands. "Some leader I turned out to be...getting my entire crew slaughtered."

Branna's gaze was piercing. "That's not your fault, Julia."

She held Branna's gaze for a moment then moved on. "Alice got married right on schedule and had four children. Three boys and a girl, all healthy and bright, apples of their parents' eyes."

"Not you?"

"Not me, what?"

"Married? Children?"

"That was never what I wanted."

Branna was quiet a long time. "And your little sister? She'd be nearly fifteen."

Julia beamed, her heart swelling at the mention of her. "She's with Alice being schooled with her family while I left on our new galleon's inaugural shipping run. She's so clever and thoughtful and beautiful. She's going to change the world."

"What's her name?"

"Well, admittedly, I got some grief for it. Alice insisted it wasn't appropriate for a girl and Arnie—that's her husband—was apoplectic, but I named her Kelly." Julia smiled at the shocked and curious look on Branna's face. "Don't let it go to your head. You're dead, remember?"

"I should go," Branna said abruptly and stood, the kitten dropping to the floor with a mewl of protest.

"I'm sorry. I didn't mean to make you feel—"

"It's okay, Julia. You don't have to keep apologizing to me. It's late and I need to get back to the ship."

Julia bit her lip to keep from protesting again. She wanted her to stay so badly and tamped down her disappointment as Branna slung her scabbard across her back. "Thank you, Branna, for a lovely evening."

"The pleasure was mine, Julia." Branna said, her voice husky as she turned to leave. "I'll see you again soon."

"Wait." She scooped up the kitten, holding her out. "Don't forget Morrigan."

CHAPTER NINE

Captain Kelly stood on the deck overseeing repairs to the bowsprit all morning. It was taking longer than anticipated and part of her was feeling anxious to be back under way. The other part, god help her, longed to be with Julia. She wanted to smell the salt air on her skin and watch as the ocean breeze ruffled through her hair. She wanted to feel the warm hum under her hands that happened whenever she touched her. She wanted to hear her laugh. She wanted to hear her gasp in pleasure under her touch.

"Captain Kelly!" Nat nearly shouted in her ear indicating he'd been trying to get her attention for some time.

She spun, snapping out of a delicious daydream, her cheeks reddening as if her thoughts were appearing in the air above her head. "What?"

Nat fidgeted uncomfortably.

"Out with it, Mr. Hooper," she barked at him, her tension and confusion making her unnecessarily harsh.

"The meeting with the crew hopefuls is tonight. I have four men lined up but I need to know if you want to replace the purser. I don't know if any of them are qualified so I'll need more time to look around if you do."

Branna considered his question. She'd had the position filled for a year. As far as anyone had been aware, he was clever with the accounts and the crew was paid on time. Too clever, as it turned out and it came to light, literally by accident, that he had been cooking the books. He had been going with the lowest bidders, recording funds spent for repairs that weren't made, and keeping a tidy sum for himself.

His fraud against the ship was discovered when the stay line of the foremast, which was supposed to have been repaired, snapped and dropped Jack from thirty meters into the sea. He suffered broken ribs and a head injury and was laid up for weeks.

Branna had happily keelhauled the purser before marooning him, bleeding and naked, on a deserted island. His saving grace was that it was in the path of a shipping lane and a frequent stop for repairs and respite. She wasn't a total monster. She had heard he'd been picked up within a week and survived. They had never replaced him and she, Nat and Gus kept the records and managed well enough.

"No. We're fine and we only need two crew. I don't want to worry about training too many right now."

"Aye, aye, Captain. So, I'll see you later for the interviews?"

"Yes."

* * *

The sun was low as Julia walked back out to the walkway and looked down on the courtyard. As usual, the space was filling fast and raucous laughter, music, and suggestive conversation filled the air.

She saw Genevieve working her way through the crowd, greeting people and seeing that their needs were met. Everyone that desired it had food, drink and company for the night. Gen must have sensed her gaze and looked up at her, offering her a smile and an apologetic shake of her head. Julia sighed and returned to her room, shutting the door to dampen the noise of the festivities.

She heard the soft knock a few minutes later. She skipped across the room and flung it open, her face falling dramatically at the sight of Genevieve.

"I'm sorry," Genevieve said. "I know you were hoping for someone else."

"What?" Julia forced her face into a more pleasant expression. "No, I just thought...I'm sorry, Gen. I didn't mean to be rude. I am pleased to see you."

"I'm sure. The good news is I'm not staying." She pulled something from behind her back and held out a narrow wooden case about a foot long. "I thought you may appreciate borrowing this while you're here. Maybe it will help you feel more in touch with the world."

Julia frowned and took the case from her. In it was a brass spyglass. "What's this for?"

"You might like to get a better look at the comings and goings in the harbor. See what people are up to. That kind of thing."

A small smile played across her lips. "Thank you."

"I better get back to work."

Julia wasted no time. There was little light left. She removed the instrument and extended it to its full length. It took her a moment to get her bearings and find the *Banshee*. She could see her clearly now, rocking in the gentle waves of the protected harbor and her breath caught at the beauty of Branna's ship. For the first time she could see the figurehead. It was an intricately carved, ghostly woman in a flowing gown. Her white hair fanned out behind her from the unseen wind, black eyes and ethereally beautiful features frozen in a mournful scream.

She moved the sight away from the haunting image so she could see the skeleton crew moving around the deck and she strained to see if she recognized anyone. She didn't.

She traced a slow path along the water looking for a dory bringing people to shore but saw none and continued scanning toward the shore and along the dock. She sucked in a breath, her heart quickening at the sight of Branna striding along the dock toward Travers. She looked determined and Julia wondered what she was about. She was coming close and Julia hoped she would come to her door when her business, whatever it was, had finished.

Captain Kelly entered the bar off the main courtyard. It was quieter and usually reserved for more intimate meetings and business transactions. She had cleaned up and dressed to intimidate in all black, her weapons gleaming in the torchlight. When meeting prospective crew for the first time, it was best they see her at her most severe lest they come on board thinking her an easy mark.

Nat was at a table with the four men and he rose when he saw her. Two of the other men followed his lead, standing as the captain strode purposefully to their table. The other two men seemed not even to notice her. One was paying attention only to draining his mug while the other was equally attentive to picking something out of his ear with a long, grubby fingernail.

Branna stared hard at them. The one with his face buried in his pint of ale she knew. Virgil Bunt had applied to her crew several times in the past and she had denied him every time. The other man she'd only seen around, but she'd seen enough. They were slovenly and disrespectful, unshaven and unkempt and looked like they would rather be anywhere else. She sighed and gave Nat a sharp shake of her head.

Nat smacked Virgil Bunt in the back of his head to get his attention, causing him to splutter on his drink. "You're both dismissed."

The two men straightened at this and stared at him in confusion before noticing Captain Kelly standing before them. They both started to protest at once and Branna cringed inwardly when she got an up-close look at the dozen teeth between them. She shook her head again at Nat.

"The interview is over," he rumbled. "Be off!"

They sneered and swore at her and Bunt grabbed his crotch obscenely. "You'll get yours, Kelly!" he snarled before lumbering off.

She ignored him and pulled up a chair at the table, gesturing for the other men to sit.

"Captain Kelly, these gentlemen, Cuddy Hurst and Bartholomew Griggs are interested in a position on the *Banshee*."

Branna nodded at the men and sipped the drink a serving girl had slid in front of her without being asked. She eyed the men. Hurst was the standard seafaring type. He was large and hard-looking with beady, furtive eyes and rough, calloused hands. Griggs, on the other hand, was clean shaven, good looking and dressed in fitted pants, crisp white shirt and waistcoat befitting a man of high station. He had sharp, intelligent eyes and a relaxed air about him.

Branna decided to start with Hurst. "Mr. Hurst, how is it you come to be looking for work?"

"I was on the *Sea Sprite* for seven years," he said, his voice rough and unpleasant. "I don't suppose I need to explain further."

She nodded. He didn't. The *Sea Sprite*, a good ship with a solid reputation, sank in a storm two days out from Tortuga a few weeks ago. There weren't many survivors. "That was a loss. Is there anyone left here who can recommend you?"

He was silent for a long time, his jaw clenched. "No, Cap'n."

She turned to the other man, eyeing him hard. "Mr. Griggs, is it? You don't look like a sailor."

"What does a sailor look like, Captain?"

She narrowed her eyes. "Someone who looks like they know what the hell they are doing."

His smile faltered. "I assure you, Captain Kelly, I am experienced at sea. My uncles were merchants. Just smaller vessels, mostly. None that you would have heard of, I'm afraid. I was raised at sea and learned to walk on deck. I left the life for a time in favor of a formal education and tried my hand at the other end of the import/export business running the accounts…"

Branna's eyes flicked to Nat. A purser after all, perhaps? She held his gaze for a moment before a soft laugh drew her attention. She turned, expecting to see Julia and was disappointed when an unfamiliar serving girl appeared to be the source.

The interruption caused Branna to totally lose her focus and she found she was unable to drag her attention back to her task at hand. She vaguely heard Mr. Griggs droning on about his life at sea as her eyes drifted toward the second floor where she knew Julia would be. Was she sleeping? Gazing out into the harbor? Thinking of her?

"Captain?" Nat called to her.

Her attention snapped back to the table and she noticed it was just the two of them. The other two men were standing over by the bar. "What?"

"I asked them to excuse us so we could speak privately. Are you interested in taking them on?"

She didn't want to spend too much time thinking about this. She was shorthanded and she already ran with a lean crew. She didn't want to go into battle weak. At the same time, she didn't want to go into battle with crew unfamiliar with each other. Two men were as many as she was willing to take on and she didn't have the time to be picky. These two would have to do. "Yes, fine."

"I can finish up the paperwork and go over the Articles with them if there's somewhere you'd rather…" He cleared his throat. "If you have other business to attend to."

This got her attention. She was distracted. Thoughts of Julia Farrow were creeping up on her when she least expected and now it was affecting her work. She gave her head a sharp shake. She couldn't afford any distractions right now and it angered her. "No. I'll handle it."

Branna rose after hours of sitting reviewing the Articles, discussing the pay schedule, discipline, duties and answering their incessant questions. She was tired and disturbed at how easily she had been rattled. Before Julia Farrow came back into her life she had one purpose—to find and kill Cyrus Jagger and destroy the *Serpent's Mistress*. Now, in a matter of a few days, she'd had daydreams, wet dreams, and a cat. She was disgusted with herself and her fists clenched as her eyes drifted back toward the courtyard.

She growled under her breath and stalked out of the bar without another glance, determined to let nothing stand in her way.

CHAPTER TEN

Julia awoke from a long night of tossing and turning from worry, grief, and uncertainty. She lay in bed for a long while as the sun rose higher. The thought of spending another day alone in this room frustrated her beyond words.

She had been selfish and irresponsible. The pain of the tragedy that befell her ship and her crew was acute and she couldn't hide from it here. She had responsibilities to her family and to manage her company's affairs. She had to gather her wits and get back to Charlestown and let them know what had happened. The ship would have been due to return soon and they were going to be missed. Families would be waiting for their loved ones to return.

She'd nearly died and had been given a second chance. It was time to start taking charge of her life. She walked to the window and gazed out at the harbor. The *Banshee* was a familiar sight and she felt the early stirrings of longing for Branna's company. She pushed the thoughts away and stopped herself from taking out the spyglass again.

She threw open the door to the walkway and stalked to her left, approaching her guard with purpose and determination. He turned to her with a look of surprise as she said, "Please, inform Miss Travers I would like to speak with her at her earliest possible convenience."

By early afternoon, Julia was deep in thought, pencil in hand, hunched over a scrap of cloth offered to her for writing, running through what she felt she needed to take care of upon her return. She looked up at a knock. "Come in."

Merriam stood in the doorway and Julia smiled. She had such a fiery presence that it was hard not to be energized by it. "Merri. This is a surprise."

"Thought I might find ya here."

If it had been anyone else, Julia would surely have bristled at their insensitivity to her situation. "You just caught me. What brings you here?"

"Gen sent me to escort ya to dinner with us downstairs if yer feelin' up to it."

Julia stood and stretched the kinks from her back and neck. "I can think of nothing I would enjoy more."

"Oh, I bet ya can. But, in the absence of any dark, disagreeable ship's captains, we'll have to do."

Julia laughed. There didn't appear to be any love lost between her and Branna Kelly, but she suspected it had more to do with the fact that Branna was the other woman who stood between Merri seeing more of Jack. Julia was so delighted for the change of scenery she didn't even dwell on the mention of Branna.

Genevieve was directing a serving girl to set up a table for them when they descended the stairs and the three of them sat as the young girl poured drinks and distributed platters of fish, fruit and bread.

"I have good news," Genevieve said with a smile.

"Oh?" Julia's brows rose in interest.

"There's a ship leaving in a few days for Boston. They are reputable and have agreed to provide you passage to Charlestown. You could be home in a couple of weeks."

Her eyes widened in surprise. She didn't think it would happen so soon and was, for all her planning, nervous now about returning home. Up until a few days ago she thought Farrow Company was her life. Now, Branna was alive and she felt she had another choice. A second chance.

Genevieve studied her. "I thought you would be pleased."

"I'm sorry. I am. Thank you, so much for everything you've done. I guess I'm just feeling a little overwhelmed."

"I'd be concerned if you weren't. You've been through a lot and you're facing an uncertain future."

"Yes," Julia mused, grateful for her understanding.

"Ya could always stay," Merriam suggested around a mouthful of fruit.

Julia looked at her curiously.

"A woman a yer talents would have no trouble findin' work 'round here."

Julia gasped at the suggestion she work at a brothel and Genevieve glared at Merriam.

Merri looked between them. "What? Oh, I didn't mean it like that. Meant this is a shipping port and ya know the trade."

Julia relaxed and gave a small laugh. "This is truly a remarkable place and there are many things I find captivating about it…" She lost herself in thoughts of one captivating thing in particular. "But I have responsibilities to my family's business and I need to return and see to them—and my sisters."

The three women ate and drank well into the evening and Julia was grateful for their company, sharp minds, and good humor. Her mind rarely drifted to dark, disagreeable captains.

Branna closed her door on Nat and Gus. She had kept them with her, strategizing, far longer than was necessary. She was afraid of what would happen once she was left alone with her own thoughts.

She kicked off her boots and settled onto her bed with a leather-bound copy of *Robinson Crusoe*. Anything to take her mind elsewhere. She intended to read until she fell asleep. Morrigan appeared out of nowhere and hurled herself at Branna with a cry before curling up on her chest, purring loudly.

She slammed the book closed sometime later, unable to recall anything she had read and not feeling the least bit tired. She sat up at the edge of her bed, dislodging the kitten, before striding to her desk and yanking the drawer open. She picked up the ring, clutching it for a moment before jamming it into her pocket.

Next to the ring was the letter and she lifted it gently, running her fingers over Julia's faded handwriting. She slit the seal with a throwing knife and pulled the papers free for the first time, unfolding them carefully.

She scanned the three pages, filled with Julia's perfect script. Her throat closed painfully when she read the words she had wished for years had been true. Julia *had* been lying that day in the garden. Her father, the bastard, had given Julia an ultimatum—cease their unnatural relationship and cut herself off from Branna or he would dismiss her family from his employ without a reference. Despite her family's solid reputation if they had been blacklisted by the Farrows, it would have devastated her father and ruined them. Julia knew that and did the only thing she could to protect them—bend to her father's command.

Branna dropped into her chair, the pages falling from her hand to litter her cabin floor. She could have gone home. Julia loved her and would have been the healing she needed to recover from the loss of her family. She would have been there to help Julia through the loss of hers. They could have been together, worked together, raised her baby sister.

Branna stepped into her boots and slung her sword across her back.

"Captain?" Nat said when he saw her throw the rope ladder over the gunwale down to the dory. "Is everything okay?"

"Aye. I'm going ashore."

"I'll take you."

"Not necessary. I'll row myself."

"Aye, Captain."

It was late by the time Branna reached shore. The dock was quiet with few people about. Even the courtyard of Travers Trading Post was nearly deserted. She looked around and her eyes fell to Genevieve behind the bar.

Gen looked up when Branna entered, pausing cleaning the last of the glasses. She offered a smile and a nod in the direction of the stairs, not that Branna needed her permission.

Branna paced back and forth outside Julia's door for several minutes. A couple of times she stopped, raising her hand to knock, before letting her arm fall and resuming her wearing of the wood floor. This was a mistake.

She stopped outside the door again, resting her head against the wood, her heart pounding. Was it so wrong to want something good in her life? She was about to raise her hand to knock again when she heard a terrified cry from inside.

Her head jerked up and she shouldered open the door, her right hand reaching for the hilt of her sword. She looked wildly around the moonlit room. There was no danger that she could see and she released her blade.

Julia cried out again. Branna pulled aside the bed netting and saw her—tangled sheets plastered to her sweat-slicked body—caught in the throes of remembered terror and pain.

"Julia." She sat at the edge of the bed and gripped her flailing hands. Julia pushed weakly at her arms and chest, crying in her sleep, unable to wake from her nightmare. "Julia, you're safe."

"No!" Julia's eyes flew open with a strangled gasp and she struggled against Branna's grip.

"It's all right, *machree*," Branna soothed. The term of endearment that hadn't passed her lips in years coming so naturally. She released her hands. "It's not real."

"It is real, Bran. It happened," she choked out, wrapping her arms around Branna and sobbing into her neck.

Branna hesitated for only a moment before enveloping her, running a hand down the bare skin of her back in comfort. "I know. I'm so sorry. Tell me what I can do."

They embraced for a long time before Branna noticed a subtle change in Julia's breathing. The feel of hot tears on her neck changed to the feel of warm lips as Julia began to kiss along her throat and jaw.

"Julia," Branna gasped in surprise and pulled away.

"Please, Bran," Julia whispered and met her eyes. "I *was* lying. You know I was. You've always known."

Branna brushed a lock of hair from Julia's face and smiled sadly. "It doesn't matter anymore."

"It matters to me. I thought you were dead and the last words I said to you…" She hiccupped a breath. "I was so cruel. I'm so sorry I hurt you. I didn't mean it. I thought I was protecting you," she said as she pulled at Branna's shirt.

"I understand now." Branna grasped her hands to stop their roaming, her blood heating under the sizzle of her touch. "But, Julia, you don't want this. Not me. Not anymore."

Julia sobbed a breath. "I need to feel something good. I need to feel you."

Branna sucked in a breath when she realized Julia was naked beneath the sheet and it had fallen away to her waist, revealing her full breasts, nipples peaked in the cooling night air.

Julia kissed her neck again and ran her tongue along the hollow of her throat. "Please, touch me, Branna. I've longed for you all these years but you were only a ghost haunting my most treasured dreams. I never thought I'd have this chance."

Branna groaned at the sound of her name spoken with such passion. Julia's confessed desires, the sight of her body, and the feel of Julia's hands and mouth on her sent her reeling. All Branna's sensibilities and her very sanity fled. She crushed her mouth to Julia's with a similar passion and need born of shared grief, overwhelming longing, and loneliness.

"Take this off," Julia demanded breathlessly, as she pulled at the strap of her scabbard across her chest.

Branna lifted it over her head, letting her sword clatter to the floor. She moved over Julia, pushing her back to the bed, their lips meeting again in a clash of tongue and teeth. Julia's fingers fumbled with the buttons on Branna's shirt, eventually giving up on the last few and ripping it open. Julia's hands snaked across her taut belly and the strong muscles of her back as she worked her way down to encourage her out of her pants.

Branna groaned at the touch, her insides boiling with need. Her nerve endings crackled and spots danced in front of her eyes as her hands stroked Julia's breasts, belly, and sides, feeling the soft heat of her desire. Julia's back arched, her lips parting in a ragged exhale, as Branna kneaded her breasts and teased her nipples.

Branna's hands never stopped moving over every swell and curve. Her mouth never left Julia's skin, tasting every part of her, her ears ringing with every desperate moan and sigh she coaxed from her.

Branna was wild with a nearly painful need and Julia responded to her with abandon, sending her heart racing and her breath coming fast and quick. Heat coiled in her belly and fanned through her core when Julia threw her head back, exposing her neck and chest to her touch. When Branna's hand slipped down between Julia's legs, Julia opened for her, pulling her close and clawing at her back.

Branna entered her slowly and held still, holding Julia's bright-eyed gaze, waiting for her to either move with her or push her away. Julia gasped and bit her lower lip, thrusting her hips against Branna's hand when her walls contracted powerfully around her fingers. Branna didn't need further encouragement and wrapped her left arm around Julia's lower back to hold her close.

They rolled, naked and sweating—their scents mingling with the ocean air—and struggled with each other for dominance, demanding and claiming everything the other had to offer long into the early hours. Branna, usually so controlled in her passions, gave up everything. Julia was as generous in return and held nothing back as their hunger for each other consumed them time and time again.

CHAPTER ELEVEN

Branna woke with a start, the sun streaming in through the open balcony door to the harbor, and all her fears returned. This was wrong. She couldn't do right by Julia Farrow. She had a family and a life far away from here. Branna could never be what she needed. Maybe Arthur Farrow was right to do what he did. Being with Julia was extremely selfish and would only end in heartache for them both—or worse, endanger Julia. There were more than a few people who would pay their weight in gold to see the Raven swing from her own yardarm and happily use Julia to make it happen. She could never risk Julia like that.

She sat up slowly, removing Julia's hand from across her chest, careful not to wake her. She lay sleeping deeply still, her face turned toward the sun—relaxed and satisfied. Branna squeezed her eyes shut and clenched her hands tightly to keep from running them down her back, her heart aching to touch her one more time.

She slipped out of bed, dragged on her pants, and looked for her shirt. She was only able to button it partway but she didn't care. She needed to go before Julia woke and Branna lost herself again in the fantasy that she could have something more. That's all it was, a fantasy.

Grabbing her boots and sword, she slipped quietly out of the room. A shadow loomed over her as she bent to wrestle her feet into her boots. She straightened to see Gus standing there with a tray of food, presumably heading back to Genevieve's room.

"Good morning, Branna," he said straight-faced.

"We're leaving."

"What?"

Her eyes flicked to the tray and she took pity on him. "Make your goodbyes, round up the men on shore and meet me at the dock." She slung her sword across her back. "I'll let Jack know."

Branna hastily braided her hair as she took the stairs two at a time. She looked right and left, trying to remember where Merriam's room was. There, on the other side of the courtyard, she stalked over to it.

Merriam answered her sharp knock a little breathlessly and with a beaming smile that turned abruptly to a sneer. "Oh. It's you."

"Is he here?"

Merriam opened the door wide. Jack was lounging in the bed covered only with a thin sheet across his lap. He gripped the sheet to cover himself more and sat up, a look of horror on his face. "Captain! What—"

"We're getting underway with this evening's tide."

"I don't understand," he said. "The repairs aren't complete."

"The repairs will have to do," she said, aware it was unlike her to cut corners on the ship's maintenance. Especially after Jack's accident. She just needed to get out of here before she changed her mind. "Get yourself together and meet me at the dock."

"Aye, aye, Captain."

Merriam slammed the door with a grumbled noise that sounded like "bitch" when Branna had barely crossed the threshold. She headed for the archway that would lead her to the harbor and had almost made it when Genevieve came hurrying after her, tucking her blouse into her skirt as she weaved between the tables.

"What the hell is going on?" she asked when she caught up to her.

"Nothing. Change of plans and we're heading out today."

"So, you're sneaking out like a thief in the night?"

"It's day. And what makes you think I'm sneaking?"

"Tell me I'm wrong."

Branna's jaw clenched, her eyes flicking to Julia's door. "I can't be what she needs."

"Shouldn't you let Julia decide that? How do you know what she needs?"

She didn't want to have this conversation and she was wasting precious time. "She's been through a lot. She's not thinking clearly."

"One might argue it's you who's not thinking clearly. I've spent some time with Julia and I think she's one of the most levelheaded women I've ever met," Genevieve stated plainly.

"Clearly not."

"Bloody hell, Branna. Is it so hard for you to believe that someone could really care about you?" She stepped closer and waved her hand over her, gesturing to her sword. "That she could see through all this to the real you? You were close once, why not again?"

"This is the real me. That other girl died with her family on the *Rebellion*."

Genevieve eyed her and stepped back again. "Right. You're ruthless, immovable, and uncaring."

"Careful, Gen."

"What are you going to do about it, Branna? Leave?"

Branna stared at her hard for a moment before she turned away.

"What do you want me to tell her?"

"She's a smart woman. She'll figure it out."

"Why, Branna? Why can't you let her into your heart?"

"What heart?"

Julia woke slowly and smiled at the sun glinting off the water as she stared out the door to the harbor. She stretched languidly, her body deliciously relaxed and sore in all the right places. She reached her arm out to the side of the bed and sat up at its emptiness.

The sheets and pillow were cool to the touch and her stomach dropped. She knew Branna had not just gone to get something for breakfast. Julia scrambled out of bed and wrapped the sheet tightly around her before flinging the door open and stepping out onto the walkway.

Genevieve was moving from table to table emptying ash buckets and collecting empty glasses. She looked up and saw Julia standing at the rail, barely covered. She couldn't hold Julia's gaze and turned away, going back to her work with a shake of her head.

The look on Genevieve's face told Julia everything she needed to know. Branna had run as far and as fast as she could, without a word of explanation. She dragged herself back into her room and closed the door.

The pain in her heart was acute. As fulfilled and as hopeful as she felt last night, she now felt that much hurt and disappointment. "Goddamn you, Branna Kelly!"

She crossed the room and threw open the wooden case, dumping the spyglass on the table with a clatter. She stepped onto the balcony and jammed it to her eye. It didn't take her long to spy the dory bobbing up and down alongside the ship. The men were waiting their turn to ascend, and as Julia moved her view up she saw Branna, standing tall on the gunwale, gripping the shroud, staring straight at her.

Julia jerked the spyglass away. She couldn't possibly see her—could she? She put it back to her eye and studied Branna. Her expression looked thunderous, and even from here, Julia could see her vibrating with tension and what? Sadness? Regret? She knew that feeling all too well.

Julia felt a tightening in her belly, a longing to smooth the worry from Branna's face and hold her again, followed immediately by the rage of being abandoned without so much as a goodbye. Branna had her so twisted up she could barely breathe and her frustration boiled over. Before she knew what she was doing, she slammed the spyglass onto the iron railing, denting the brass and shattering the lenses.

She threw the ruined instrument onto the table and went back inside, closing the doors to the harbor. She didn't want to see the *Banshee* leave.

She sat slumped at the table, fiddling with the pieces of the shattered spyglass when a knock came at the door. She didn't move or bother to look up. She already knew who it wasn't. "Come in," she said listlessly. Her anger and hurt had flared out, leaving her nothing but empty.

Genevieve joined her at the table and picked up a piece of broken glass. "Did that help?"

"I'm sorry. I'll have it replaced."

"No need. It was Branna's."

Julia breathed a small laugh before her face fell again. "I don't understand."

"And you shouldn't try." Genevieve placed a hand on her arm. "Captain Kelly is—"

"Complicated?"

"Maybe that wasn't the right word. Maybe determined?"

"To what? Die alone?"

"She's had her life planned very carefully for a long time."

"Fifteen years. I know."

"And you've come into her life and blown her off course and I think it scares her. She doesn't know anything else. She's not made room in her heart for anything but rage and vengeance since she was a child and it frightens her. You frighten her."

"Me? The indomitable Captain Kelly frightened of me?"

"Of how you make her feel. Of what could be possible if she let someone in. Yes, more than frightens her. Terrifies her."

"It doesn't matter now, does it?"

"Who knows? They have to wait for the evening tide. Maybe she'll come to her senses."

Julia felt the seed of an impossible idea take root in the back of her mind at Genevieve's words. Maybe not an *impossible* idea, but most certainly a *terrible* one.

"Is there anything I can get you?" Genevieve asked.

"Yes, actually," Julia said, determination of her own flaring in her chest. "Could you send Merri to see me as soon as possible?"

Julia pulled down the large floppy cap and turned to face Merriam. "How do I look?" she asked and pasted a scowl to her face.

"Ridiculous," she answered with a laugh. "I don't understand why ya wanted me to bring ya men's clothes. Or, should I say, boys' clothes 'cause in order to find somethin' that'd fit I had to go to the kitchen lads."

"Because I can't sit in here all day, not after what happened with Branna." She settled the rope strap of the waterskin across her chest, making sure it didn't accentuate her breasts too much. She felt badly about playing on Merri's sympathies and betraying her trust but she couldn't let things end this way. She wouldn't be abandoned again. And it wasn't as if she too didn't have a vested interest in seeing the *Serpent's Mistress* to the bottom of the sea. "I must get out of here. At least for a little while, and with this disguise and your help I can get past the guards. I'll be safe dressed as a man. No one will recognize me or harass me. You'll help me won't you?"

Merriam chewed her lip, her brow creased with worry. "Give me five minutes to clear the guards out. Then ya must hurry. And make sure yer back before anyone misses ya or Gen'll skin me alive."

Julia could only nod, unwilling to make a promise out loud she knew she wasn't going to keep. She pulled Merriam into a quick embrace. "Thank you."

Merriam ducked out and Julia scrawled a quick note, leaving it on the table beneath the crooked spyglass and then stood by the door. She worked to slow her pounding heart and relax her breathing as she counted out five minutes.

She cracked the door and peered both left and right. The guards were nowhere to be seen. She moved quickly down the stairs and through the archway, taking pains to walk hunched, head down and hands jammed in her pockets.

As she had hoped, the dock was its usual frenzy of activity made even more chaotic by the *Banshee's* early departure. Men and boys scrambled to load the crates of supplies on the barge that would make the last trip out to the ship before it left. With the shouting and confusion, it was shockingly easy to grab a crate and heft it up the ramp to the flat, overladen boat. She squeezed herself between two stacks of crates and waited for the barge to make its laborious way out to the *Banshee.*

At the other end the barge floated some ways off the starboard side of the *Banshee* and a ramp was raised so the hands could carry the crates aboard instead of working to haul them all by hand using ropes. Julia chose the largest, lightest one she could find and carried it in front of her to better hide her body. Her cap was low over her eyes which served to keep her unrecognizable, but nearly sent her toppling off the ramp when her inability to see caused her to misstep.

She recovered to jeers from the laborers and crew alike and moved to wrestle the crate down the ladders and into the hold with the others without another incident. Again she squeezed herself between the crates and settled as comfortably as possible.

She tried to relax and stretch her cramped muscles in the confined space. The ship had gotten underway an hour ago but she needed to remain hidden until they were far enough from port that Branna wouldn't turn around and take her back to Nassau. That is, if she didn't just throw her overboard first.

She sucked quietly on the waterskin. She was glad she had thought to ask for it, as it was brutally hot this far below. She thought for sure Merriam would be suspicious, but in the end she praised Julia for her cleverness in completing her look with the detail.

Between the heat and the gentle rocking and creaking of the wooden crates, Julia managed to doze. She didn't know how long she'd been asleep before she heard someone moving around in the hold. She held her breath listening for the sounds of them having discovered her and heard nothing. She exhaled slowly in relief just as a giant meaty hand came down on her shoulder and dragged her out of her hiding place.

"Well, well, well," a rough voice said, as he shifted his grip to the back of her neck. "Ain't the cap'n gonna be surprised to see you."

CHAPTER TWELVE

Branna danced back and parried another thrust from Gus's sword, turning to meet Nat's blade in a clash of iron. She grinned wickedly as sweat poured down her face. She could hear the labored breathing of the two men as she battled them both while the rest of the crew watched, cheering and placing bets. She had already taken out Jack who laid panting and clutching his middle where he had taken a solid kick from her boot.

The wind was light and they were far from their destination. She was taking them to a stretch of deserted islands a day's sail from where they were to meet the *Serpent's Mistress*. They had several days of sailing and she wanted to get in all the training she could. She needed herself and the crew sharp for the battle that was yet to come.

Gus rushed her and again she knocked his strike past her and swung an elbow to his gut. He doubled over with a grunt and she laid her sword across the back of his neck. "You're dead."

She turned her attention to Nat when a string of shouts interrupted their game.

"Cap'n!" a gravelly voice shouted to her.

"Can't you see I'm busy, Mr. Moyle?" she barked, not turning around. She circled Nat, waiting for her opening.

"I've caught you a stowaway," Moyle growled.

Branna straightened and she felt the deck vibrate beneath her as a body landed behind her at her feet.

"I can't think of a better way to end the day than..." Her words died on her lips when her eyes landed on the person struggling to push themselves up at her feet. "Julia," she whispered.

"I'm sorry," she mouthed, her eyes wide and terrified.

Branna looked around wildly, her heart thudding in her chest. This couldn't be happening. She couldn't be here. Her gaze fell to Gus who looked stricken. He knew what this meant. He met her gaze and his lips thinned in determination, one hand by his side gestured her to calm.

Branna took a deep breath and stalled by handing her sword off to Nat. "Miss Farrow, I would have thought you'd seen enough of this ship to last a lifetime."

There was a nervous chuckle from the crew while Julia pushed herself to her knees, but blessedly remained silent.

She continued, hardening her voice to keep it from trembling. "We work hard on this ship, Miss Farrow, and we don't take kindly to those who think to steal from us. And make no mistake. Being here without my permission is stealing."

"Captain, I'm—"

"Hold your tongue! I save your life and this is how you repay me?" Branna roared, causing Julia to flinch. Her throat tightened at seeing Julia afraid of her. She could do nothing about it now. She had to treat Julia as she would any other stowaway or risk losing the respect of her crew. If they thought her weak, they would never follow her into battle. They would not trust her and she would not be able to trust them.

Branna's head swam. She couldn't do this. She stalled more as she paced the deck in front of a trembling Julia and an anxious crew.

The new man Bartholomew Griggs spoke up. "Captain, if I may. I have, as you know, reviewed the Articles quite recently with regard to the punishment for stowaways and perhaps, considering the circumstances"—he gestured to Julia—"we can come up with an alternative."

There were shouts from the crew some in agreement and some not.

"I got an alternative," Cuddy Hurst, the other new hire, shouted. "Instead of three days tied to the mast, how 'bout three days in the hold with the crew?"

There was a ripple of laughter, lewd gestures, and shouts of agreement from some of the men.

Branna's stomach lurched and bile rose in her throat at the thought. She had to regain control of the situation. "I think not. If we change the Articles for Miss Farrow, however lovely she may be, we will need to change them for all."

A grumble of displeasure grew louder from her crew.

She glared around the circle of men and grabbed the ugliest one she could find by his collar, jerking him forward. Her mouth twisted into a mocking sneer. "And what happens when the next stowaway looks like Mr. Gribble? Are you going to spend three days in the hold buggering him?"

The grumbling stopped and the men roared with laughter.

"Captain, please, I have a suggestion," Bartholomew Griggs persisted.

Branna kept her face expressionless and hoped she didn't look as terrified as she felt. "Aye, Mr. Griggs, I'm listening."

"Conscription."

Branna stilled and could tell from the chatter among the crew not all of them knew the word. "Explain, Mr. Griggs." Her eyes flicked to Julia who still knelt on the deck, hands clasped tightly in front of her and eyes downcast.

"I apologize and mean no disrespect if I am overstepping my place, but I am aware, as are we all, that we are shortly to cross paths with Captain Jagger and the *Serpent's Mistress*. Crossing paths means crossing swords."

A low rumble began among the crew.

"Aye." Branna nodded. "It's true."

"We are not so many that we couldn't use another capable hand." He gestured to Julia who had raised her head and was watching him with wide-eyed intensity. "She may not be able to fight but she could perform any number of other critical tasks that would free up another fighting man and decrease casualties on our side."

The rumbling of the crew became louder and sounded supportive of what Griggs was suggesting. None of them wanted to be on that casualty list.

Branna felt her insides begin to uncoil and saw her opportunity to spare Julia a slow painful ordeal likely to end in her death from thirst. She pretended to consider as she met Julia's fearful gaze and tried to send her strength. "What say you, Mr. Hooper?"

"Aye, Captain. I can work her until her fingers bleed—mending lines, sealing decks, and oiling blocks. She can swab the heads, too."

His agreement elicited a cheer from some of the crew. Branna nodded and shot Nat a desperate look of thanks for naming some of the most hated chores aboard. She could do this.

"What of her punishment?" Hurst sneered, his eyes never leaving Julia, who hunched further over as if to hide herself from his leer.

Branna bristled as his glittering eyes raked over Julia. He wanted to hurt her and Branna regretted taking him on, but she could not ignore the demand from her crew. Julia would not escape unscathed, but her life would be spared and she would recover. Branna met and held her eyes. She wouldn't let her go through this alone. "Twenty lashes," she stated with finality.

The rumbling of the men quieted and Branna raised her voice and turned to the crew. "Are we in agreement?"

"Aye, Captain," the men chorused.

"I'll get the whip." Branna turned again to face Julia, whose eyes were bright with unshed tears, and her breathing labored. Branna's jaw clenched and unclenched savagely around words she couldn't say, her heart shattering. An anguished, inhuman growl came from deep within her chest before she snatched her sword back from Nat and stalked away.

Branna crashed through the door to her cabin using the hilt of her sword, hoping the crew was well out of earshot.

Her gaze darted around the room, her chest heaving like there wasn't enough air in the world. Howling in rage she rushed into the room, hacking and slashing her blade across any available surface.

Wood splintered, charts shredded, and instruments were bent and scattered across the floor under her relentless barrage. Books were cleaved in two and glass shattered as she whirled around the room on a crazed path of destruction.

"Captain!" Gus yelled over the din of wreckage and mindless screaming.

Branna was tiring and she swung her sword mightily, embedding it into the bulkhead before dropping to her knees and sobbing for air. "Dear god, no."

"Jesus, Branna," Gus said as he dropped to the ground next to her, a hand on her back. "Calm yourself. It's going to be okay."

Branna wrapped her arms around her middle, her stomach roiling, and retched onto the floor of her cabin.

"You did the right thing," he stated.

"How can you say that?" she ground out and wiped her mouth with the back of her hand. "I'm about to have an innocent woman whipped like a criminal because she dared to care about me."

"And you her?"

"Yes." Branna pushed herself to her feet and shook off his hand, staggering toward the door. "Yes, goddamn it. And me her."

Gus gripped her arm to slow her and blocked her way. "What do you think you're doing?"

"I'm calling this off and getting her off my ship." She tried to push past him.

"To where? You can't stop this, Branna." Gus gripped her by the shoulders and pinned her with his gaze.

"The hell I can't. Get out of the way, Gus."

"Branna, listen, she wouldn't want you to do that."

"What the fuck do you know about what she wants?"

"Because you just told me. Listen to me. She cares about you and she wouldn't let you do anything to put yourself in danger for her."

"At best she'll be scarred for life and I've seen twenty lashes kill, Gus."

"It won't. I won't let it."

Branna felt helpless tears spring behind her eyes at the thought of Julia being whipped. "How?"

"Do you trust me, Branna?"

"Aye." She took a shuddering breath. "With my life."

"Then trust me with hers. Follow my lead and don't back down," he said and looked around the disaster that was her quarters. He bent to pick up the cat-o'-nine-tails from beneath her desk. He turned his back to her for a long moment before turning and handing it to her. "Take this. You need to get back out there."

Branna stared in horror at the vicious, long-handled whip. "You want *me* to do it? I can't."

Gus placed a hand on her shoulder and waited for her to meet his gaze. "It has to be you. Don't waver. Julia needs you to be the Raven, right now. So do I."

Her hand shook as she closed her fingers around the leather grip.

CHAPTER THIRTEEN

Branna emerged from her quarters with cool determination as she stalked across the deck with Gus following. Inwardly, her guts churned and her legs felt leaden as she hauled Julia to her feet with a hard grip on her arm. She kept her expression carefully blank when Julia gasped in surprise and pain.

She pulled Julia toward the main mast, whispering under her breath, "It will be okay."

"Don't worry about me," Julia whispered back and Branna's throat tightened at Julia's attempt to ease her mind.

"Mr. Hooper, bind her." Branna gestured to the iron ring set high above her head. A low murmur of displeasure rippled through the crew at her command. It gave Branna some comfort that when confronted with the reality of it, most of her crew did not want to see a woman get the lash.

Nat swallowed hard several times but stepped forward to tie Julia's hands together with a length of rope and pull them above her head, leaving her stretched onto her toes and secured tightly to the mast.

Branna could hear nothing but Julia's ragged breathing as she struggled to steady her footing while Branna stepped up behind her and slit her shirt up the middle of her back, leaving the collar attached to try and protect her from being seen by the men. She touched the bare skin of her back with her fingertips as she spread the fabric wide, feeling the familiar heat when they touched but which offered her no comfort this time.

"Count out twenty lashes, Mr. Hooper," Branna commanded with a steady voice despite her racing heart and twisting gut as she measured out the distance. Her gaze flicked to Gus whose hooded eyes held hers intensely. He gave her an almost imperceptible nod.

She closed her eyes briefly, offering up a silent prayer and cocked her arm back. She let fly with the whip, hearing it whistle through the air. Her arm was nearly jerked from its socket and she staggered when Gus's hand gripped her wrist, stopping her swing.

"No!" he bellowed over the rumble of surprise from the crew.

Branna gaped at him in shock, before snapping back to the moment and trusting in Gus's plan—whatever it was. She wrenched her arm from his grip and roared her displeasure, taking a step back before driving her boot into his middle, dropping him to one knee with a grunt.

"You defy me, Mr. Hawke?" she growled standing over him. "Do you wish to be separated from my service?" She backhanded him, rocking his head back.

"She'll be of no use to us if she's dead," he mumbled and spat a wad of blood onto the deck.

She glanced up, giving Gus a chance to catch his breath, to take the measure of her crew. They conversed amongst themselves and shifted uncomfortably at the scene unfolding before them. Gus was beloved among them, but he had openly defied orders. From their expressions of confusion, she knew they were conflicted about what should happen next.

"Her transgression against me and this ship cannot go unanswered. How shall that be satisfied—and my anger appeased?" She struck him in the head with the butt of the whip, sending him all the way to the deck.

"I'll take her punishment. As it is written in the ship's Articles." He levered himself slowly to his feet and straightened in front of her.

Her lips parted in surprise. There was an allowance in the Articles for a surrogate to volunteer to suffer in place of the transgressor. It had never been done before. From the increasing rumblings of the crew they were equally as surprised. Her gaze darted to Julia who struggled in her bindings, trying to ease her obvious discomfort.

"So be it," she snarled. "Let's not stand on ceremony." She let fly with the cat, catching Gus off guard and lashing him in his side. He spun, instinctively trying to protect himself, but made no effort to move away. She hit him again. There was a loud crack as the thick leather strands connected with his back, rending his shirt. He grunted but stood his ground.

The third strike caught him across his now exposed skin in a brutal lash that sent him to the deck and left the head of the whip dangling from the snapped handle by a single strand of tattered leather. Branna frowned at the ruined whip, clearly seeing where it had been cut—by Gus.

Her lip quirked into a smile she turned quickly into a sneer. She screamed in fury and hurled the cat over the gunwale into the sea where no one else could see what he'd done.

She pulled a knife from her belt and there was an audible gasp from her crew. Stalking to Julia, she sliced through the rope tying her to the mast and she sagged into Branna's arms with a groan.

Branna gripped her by her still-bound hands and helped steady her. She glared at Gus and then the crew. "Miss Farrow will see out the remainder of the agreed-upon punishment in my quarters. Does anyone have issue with that?"

The men gaped at her. Some shook their heads and others murmured their agreement.

"I didn't think so. The offender's punishment will be fulfilled. She will then become a part of this crew with all the rights and responsibilities therein. She will be treated with the respect granted every other member of this crew." She looked pointedly at Hurst who met her stare with an icy one of his own. "Are we in accord?"

"Aye, Captain," the crew shouted in unison.

"Mr. Hawke," she said coolly.

"Aye." Gus was upright again, standing stiffly.

"Clean yourself up and see me in my quarters. If the explanation for your defiance doesn't immediately earn you my blade through your gut, you may be able to retain your position as my second."

"Aye, aye, Captain."

"We've been idle long enough," Branna barked. "Back to work."

The crew was more than happy to have something else to do and scattered to all corners of the ship.

Branna kicked the door to her cabin closed with her heel. Julia was trembling, a fine sheen of sweat coating her skin, her hair plastered to her brow. She sat her on the bed and held her hands, cutting through the ropes.

Julia gasped in relief. She flexed her fingers and rolled her hands. "Thank you."

Branna knelt on the floor at her feet. "Are you all right?"

She swallowed heavily several times. "Yes. Branna, I'm so sorr—"

"Not now. We're not out of this yet." She looked around her ruined cabin from her earlier rampage. There was an unbroken glass bottle on the floor. She kicked it with a furious cry, shattering it against the bulkhead. One of the chairs already had a broken leg. She picked up the chair, smashing the rest of it onto the floor with a bellow of rage.

Julia gasped. "What are you doing?"

"Beating you senseless." Branna stalked around her quarters, stomping and kicking any loose items.

"There's not a mark on me," Julia said and stood.

"I haven't figured that out yet."

"I caused this with my foolishness, Branna. Do what you must." She raised her chin.

Branna eyed her and laughed humorlessly. "I think there's been enough foolishness for one day, don't you? As crazed as you make me, Julia, I'd never strike you—you should know that." She went back to making as much noise as possible for anyone curious enough to listen in on Julia's punishment.

"I do know that. If you won't do what needs to be done, I will."

"Hush, Julia, and let me think." Branna kicked a tin cup across the room with a growl.

"Your aft doors are stout," Julia said.

"Aye. I didn't damage them."

"I might."

"What?" Branna looked up just as Julia jerked hard on the door, opening it fast and slamming the edge into the side of her face, splitting her brow.

Blood dripped down her face as she eyed the door with a wince. "That'll do."

"What in god's name are you doing?" Branna gasped and started for her. Julia smiled grimly and whipped the door open, cracking it into her face twice more before Branna reached her and pulled her away.

Julia staggered into her and they both went down hard onto the floor with a shout of pain, Branna wrapping her up in her arms to protect her as best she could. She scrabbled out from under her and up to her knees. Julia's lip and brow were split and bleeding freely. Blood trickled from her nose and her cheek swelled behind a dusky bruise. "Julia, bloody hell. Are you mad?"

Julia's tongue roamed the inside of her mouth, inspecting the damage. "How do I look?" she mumbled, spitting out blood.

Branna frowned. "Like I just beat you senseless."

"See?" She smiled and groaned softly. "I feel sick."

"Christ, woman," Branna sighed.

"Captain Kelly," Gus called through the door. "Permission to ent—"

"Granted! Get in here and close the door."

"Jesus, Branna. What did you do?" Gus slammed the door and rushed over.

Branna glanced at him. His eye was swollen and lip bloody, but otherwise he looked uninjured. "It wasn't me."

Julia's head wobbled on her shoulders. "I did it. She's far too kind."

Gus snorted and scooped Julia into his arms, settling her into Branna's bed, propped up on pillows. "The lashes on my back say otherwise."

Julia gasped, tears springing to her eyes. "I didn't mean—"

"Never mind. It worked out as I intended. What can I do?"

Branna sat at the edge of the bed and grimaced at Julia's battered face. "Find a clean shirt somewhere in this mess. And pour the rum if you can find the cups." Branna carefully removed Julia's already torn shirt and slipped the fresh one of hers Gus handed her over her head, pulling it down to cover her.

"Thank you."

"Here." Gus handed them each rum in dented cups and raised his. "To not dying today."

Branna scowled and drank hers down. "The day isn't over."

Julia sipped hers carefully. "Don't be so dramatic, Bran. The day ended with me in your bed, so all is well."

Branna tensed and stood. "What did you say?"

Gus stepped between them, handing Julia a damp cloth for her face. "This should help."

Julia smiled her thanks and held the cloth to her face gingerly, her gaze never leaving Branna's. "How many other women have you had in this bed?"

Fear and rage over what had nearly happened—what could still happen—washed over Branna nearly choking her and spilling over. "Do you think this is funny?"

Julia's smile faltered. "No, Branna, I don't think this is funny at all."

"Do you have any idea what could have happened to you?"

"Branna, I—"

"Do you know what those men wanted to do to you? These men on my crew, they're not the worst, but some of them aspire to be. They would have hurt you, Julia. In ways that never heal."

"I'm sorry," she whispered as the first tear slipped down her face.

"You're sorry? Are you fucking mad? Why would you do this? Do you have any fucking idea of the position you put me in?"

"Branna," Gus said. "She understands. Lower your voice."

"I don't think she does—but she bloody well will."

Julia began to tremble, her breathing coming in short gasps as she raised a shaky hand to cover her face. "Please, stop swearing at me."

Branna stalked back and forth through her quarters. "Did you think about me at all when you decided to do this?"

"Probably as much as you thought of me when you crept from my room without a word."

"Is that what this is? Revenge? Are you getting back at me for leaving you?"

"No, that's not—"

"Is this a fucking game to you, Julia?"

"Branna, please. This isn't what I wanted."

"What did you want? What did you think was going to happen? We were going to sail off into the sunset together?"

"I couldn't lose you again."

"Branna, enough. You've made your point," Gus said.

"Lose me? You threw me away! Did you think I was going to give up everything I've worked for my whole life for you after the hateful things you said to me that night? Or, did you just want to be ship's whore?"

Julia sobbed. "Branna...stop..."

Branna jerked back, her mouth opening soundlessly. Julia was shattered. Branna realized her words were more savage and cruel than any physical pain she could cause. Julia shuddered as wracking sobs consumed her.

Branna didn't know what to do. The only one hurting Julia in ways that may never heal was her. Maybe it was better this way. Maybe it was better that Julia hate her. Then why did Branna want to drop to her knees, pull her into her arms and beg her forgiveness?

Branna swallowed thickly, unable to look at her any longer. "You may stay in my cabin until you're feeling better. There will be someone outside at all times to attend to whatever you need."

"Captain Kelly," Julia choked out.

Branna turned and met her gaze, the anguish she felt mirrored in Julia's heartbroken expression.

"If you care so little…" Julia took a shuddering breath, her gray eyes steely. "Why didn't you just let them have me?"

Branna looked away so Julia couldn't see the sorrow, shame, and longing warring within her. In the end, Branna didn't answer but just stepped quietly out the door.

Gus followed her out and she rounded on him. "Do you have something to say?"

He looked at her hard. They had known each other a long time. She knew he would do anything for her—he had just proved that again today. Except right now all she saw was disgust and disappointment in his eyes.

"I love you, Branna, but right now, I'm ashamed of you."

"She shouldn't be here."

"It's too late for that. She is here. And you better figure out how to handle it. Before you sink us all."

Branna sucked in a sharp breath, her eyes burning and her chest tight as she watched him disappear back into her cabin.

Julia heard the door open and tensed, levering herself up on her arms, not ready for another confrontation with Branna, but it was Gus who came back into the room.

"Whoa, Julia, what do you think you're doing?" he said as he pressed her gently back to the bed.

"Mr. Hawke, I'm so sorry. Are you hurt? I couldn't see what happened."

"It's just Gus and I'm fine. But you really did a number on yourself. You need to take it easy."

"I can't stay here." She dropped back to the bed. She wasn't certain she was capable of going anywhere. Her head throbbed and she felt too wrung out.

He pulled up a chair. "You'll be more comfortable here."

"No. I won't."

"I'll tell you what. Stay tonight, and tomorrow when you're feeling a little stronger, we'll find some quarters for you. I have an idea but I first need to run it by Jack."

"Not the captain?"

"Jack is the quartermaster. I think between the two of us we can find appropriate quarters for our newest crew member without the captain's help."

"I'm fairly certain she'd just as soon set me adrift—or afire."

Gus scowled. "I'm sorry. She should never have said—"

"Don't apologize for her. She's a grown woman. She knows what she's doing."

"Ah, see, that's where you're wrong."

"How do you mean?"

"In many ways she's still the terrified girl who's seen horrors that you can't even imagine."

"I can, actually," Julia said sadly.

"Of course, you know. The difference is she was still a child and she couldn't deal with what happened. She couldn't handle it and never has. The only thing she could do was wall herself off and protect herself from it ever happening again. She's hardened herself against ever caring about anyone again lest she might feel the pain of losing them."

"I know I played a big part of her experience with loss," Julia admitted.

"It's all she knows. And then you appear out of nowhere and without even trying you started tearing down those walls. She started to feel again and when you turned up here, she had to put you through that…honor the Articles and… She just, I don't know, I've never seen her like that before. She was out of her mind with fear."

"It's okay. You don't have to tell me."

"No. You need to hear this. What she said to you. It was wrong but you need to understand she was terrified for you, and what's worse she was the cause of it. She felt so helpless, like that young girl all over again. All she knew to do was to get those walls back up in place as fast as she could and make them stronger than before to keep you out."

"I understand." Julia couldn't stop the tears as they began to fall again. She was hurt and exhausted, but she felt a little better for having Gus's perspective.

"I've taken up enough of your time. We need to be clear on something, though, and then we won't speak of it again."

Julia nodded. She knew what was coming and she met his gaze.

"I am very sorry for what has happened to you, but you are far from blameless in all of this. Your recklessness put a lot of people in danger, Branna more so than anyone." He looked at her hard. "She did what she had to do to save your life—and hers. And so did I."

Julia nodded, tears falling softly. "How do I make this right?"

"You are right with me."

"And with Branna?"

"That, I can't tell you. Get some rest, Julia. Tomorrow, I'll get you settled somewhere you'll feel safe. And be prepared to be put to work as soon as you're able. Everyone pulls their weight around here."

Julia smiled at him. She was grateful for his counsel. She settled back against the bed, overwhelmed physically and emotionally. She had made a mistake and she had paid for it, and it seemed Branna was going to see she continued to pay for it by keeping her away in order to protect herself.

CHAPTER FOURTEEN

Branna stayed away well into the next morning, sleeping on the quarterdeck as she sometimes did and busying herself on deck and with other tasks she had been putting off. She needed to get to her charts now and couldn't wait. She wanted to check on Julia, too.

She had left things so badly between them and her heart ached for it. She needed to apologize but she wasn't sure she knew how. Part of her, though, thought it would be better to leave things as they were. Julia would be safer if she stayed away.

The door to her cabin was ajar and there was movement inside. She raised her hand to knock and then frowned. It was her cabin and she had every right to enter at will. She pushed the door open to see Ollie on the floor, sweeping up broken glass and picking up the mess she left. Her cabin was otherwise empty. "What are you doing?"

Ollie jumped to his feet, startled. "Captain. Mr. Hawke asked me to clean up. I thought now was a good time."

"Where is Miss Farrow?"

"Oh. You just missed them. Mr. Hawke asked me to prepare the empty purser's cabin for her. He's escorting her there now." "Carry on," she said and hurried to the deck.

They weren't hard to find as they moved slowly across the deck. Julia looked unsteady and Gus had his arm around her waist to help her to the main hatch. Despite their harsh words last night she was still captain of this ship and Julia Farrow, against all good sense, was now a member of her crew and she had a responsibility to the safety and well-being of all her people.

She hurried to catch up with them as they hovered around the steps leading to the officers' quarters. "May I help?" she asked as Gus reached a hand up from below to help Julia.

"No, thank you, Captain," Julia said coolly. She reached for Gus's hand and started down. "You've done more than enough."

Branna stood, mouth agape at her abrupt dismissal. She got exactly what she asked for and Julia, it seemed, wanted nothing to do with her. Then why did it hurt so much to see the coldness in her eyes?

* * *

Branna tried to push all thoughts of their newest crew member out of her mind as they continued their journey. By the next day Julia was on deck and on the schedule for light duty. She spent the morning rebraiding lines and mending sails—jobs she could do without exerting herself physically. Unsurprisingly, she needed little instruction and oversight. Julia had always been the most determined and capable person Branna knew.

Though Branna had no need to interact with her, her very nearness prickled along every nerve ending and rattled her focus. Branna needed an outlet for her helpless frustration and she dressed for battle—all in black with her sword across her back. She braided her hair tightly to keep it off her face, and laced her boots.

It was another hot and still afternoon as she climbed to the quarterdeck. Nat offered her the wheel and she declined with a shake of her head. "You keep it. You'll be safer."

His eyes widened. "Aye, aye, Captain."

She stood out at the edge of the deck. There were at least a dozen men on duty. That may be enough to slake her thirst for violence. She checked that Julia was safely out of the way. She was in the shade on the forecastle with Ollie, who met her eyes. Branna gave him a look and jerk of her head. He grabbed Julia's hand and pulled her as far to the edge of the deck as they could go without going overboard.

Branna inhaled deeply and drew her sword. The metal sang as it was released from its scabbard. She called to the deck, "All hands, arm yourselves!"

All the men on deck stopped what they were doing and looked to her, shielding their eyes from the sun. They glanced at one another for a beat before dropping whatever they were doing and scrambling for anything that could be used as a weapon against her—ropes and blocks, knives, gaff hooks or broom handles. She rarely included this much of the crew in her battle games but she could think of no better outlet for her fear and worry.

She gave them to the count of three before she leapt from the quarterdeck and unleashed her attack.

Her mind went still and instinct and training took over. Her ears filled with the clash of blades, excited shouts and taunting, and thundering feet as Branna took on half the crew. Her violence was carefully controlled as she slashed her way through the crew, spinning, kicking, and sending them to the deck with cries of surprise and pain.

She laughed gleefully while she somersaulted off the capstan, landing behind Gus and driving the hilt of her sword into the small of his back. He dropped to his knees with a groan and was out of play. There were only three men still on their feet, the rest having crawled or limped away to nurse their wounds. They circled her in the middle of the deck. Her eyes darted between them, anticipating which one was going to make the first move.

The three of them rushed her at the same time from different directions and while she held off the two in the front the third man got his strong arms around her, pinning her sword to her side and lifting her off her feet with a shout of triumph. The other two came at her and she kicked out at one, catching him square in the crotch and sending him to the ground with a wheeze.

She snapped her head back into to the face of the man holding her. He grunted, as blood spurted from his nose. He released her, clutching his face. She dropped to a crouch and swept her leg out, taking out the feet of the last man, sending him crashing to the deck on his back. It was Hurst and she smirked in victory as she leapt to her feet and held the tip of her blade to his throat. "You're dead."

Branna sheathed her sword and glanced around while her crew was picking themselves and each other off the deck. She was momentarily satisfied but she knew it wouldn't last. It was barely midday and she could already feel her tension and anger building again. "You're going to have to do better than that if we hope to have any chance against the *Serpent's Mistress*."

Some of the men glowered at her. She was being unnecessarily hard on them. They were a solid crew, good fighters and smart. It would not serve her well to push them too hard. "Thank you. I'm tired," she added, wiping sweat and a trickle of blood from her brow with her arm.

The same glowering men looked at her with surprise. She rarely ever admitted a weakness and they puffed up at having been the source of it.

Branna turned to the foredeck and met Julia's gaze. Julia was watching her but quickly looked away.

The wind had picked up again and they made up for lost time as they sailed toward the desolate shoals where she wanted to practice some maneuvers and simulate battles before they met with the *Serpent's Mistress* in several days' time.

* * *

Branna called her officers to her cabin to review their progress and go over the charts again. Ollie had done an admirable job of repairing her charts and navigation equipment and they were able to get through their meeting with her dividers only falling apart twice.

Branna straightened and stretched a kink out of her back. "Anything else?" she asked to close down their meeting.

Nat, and Jack shook their heads and looked away and Gus cleared his throat. "All the crew are fit and ready for full duty."

Branna eyed him. "I should hope so. We've been at sea for nearly a week."

Gus shuffled his feet. "What I mean to say, Captain—"

"Oh." She finally caught on. Julia was well and she was relieved to hear it. "By all means put her on a watch starting tomorrow. She claims experience. Let's see what she can do."

Branna was up on deck with the morning watch. The sun was bright and hot and the swells high, a result of the high winds overnight. They were at full sail and moving well. The ship lifted and dropped gut-churningly into the sea over and over again.

She stood next to Gus at the helm and frowned down at the deck. The crew was circled around the main mast, laughing and shoving each other in good humor. "What's with them?"

Gus cleared his throat. "The lines are fouled at the main top gallant sail. Someone has to go up to clear them."

Branna looked to the top of the thirty-meter mast and squinted into the sun. "So send someone up."

"She's on her way."

Branna whipped her head back to the deck to see Julia swinging onto the gunwale and and beginning her climb up the shroud. She wore pants, sturdy boots and a bulky shirt, belted tightly with a dagger at her hip. "Send someone else."

"A couple of the men were up already. The lines are too crowded and they were too big to get in there."

"Bollocks!" she shot back and pulled out the spyglass, training it at the top of the mast. The clew and bunt lines were a knotted mess, winding and snarling around each other, the sail, and the stay lines. "There's no way that happened because of the weather."

"Come on, Captain, you know how it is. The men are always tough on the new crew. She needs to earn her place if she's going to be safe here. You can't protect her from that."

She did know but she didn't like it. Julia was already at the fighting top of the mainsail and heading up again. She was fast and sure-footed, climbing when the ship dropped down into a trough and gripping tight to the shrouds when they crested a swell.

"She shouldn't be up there." Branna continued to argue. "She's—"

"A woman?" Gus finished for her and cocked an eyebrow at her.

Branna flushed. Is that what she was going to say? She had to battle against the prejudice her entire life. She knew how hard it was to earn the respect of seasoned male sailors. "I was going to say...not ready."

"She looks ready enough to me." Julia was at the top and skillfully picking her way through the matted lines, bracing herself against the stay lines and yardarm for balance. "If you interfere, Branna, you'll not be doing her any favors."

Branna swore under her breath. He was right. She had to give Julia a chance or she would never find her place here. The men, of course, had chosen the most difficult challenge for her. She, herself, had faced this particular test when she was nineteen. It had taken her all day and nearly sent her into the sea a couple of times.

She trained the spyglass back up to the top. Julia had one leg wound through the ropes to secure herself, her knees bent to take her weight with the rolling of the ship. She leaned back against the mast as she used both hands to work at the knots, the blade in her teeth. She looked determined, focused, and capable.

As much as Branna wanted to keep an eye on her she couldn't stand there all day. Julia was on her own now. The men had already drifted away, laughing and making bets on whether or not she would succeed. Branna gritted her teeth to keep herself from knocking *their* teeth out.

The sun rose high and many of the men were taking shelter in the shade of the sails on deck, passing around the water bucket. It was hot and Julia was totally exposed. Branna was worried about her so soon after her injuries, however self-inflicted. She pulled out the spyglass again and checked on her. She had one side of the sail free and it flapped wildly in the wind. She had moved around to the other side of the yardarm, found her footing and began working the next mess of snarled lines.

Branna dragged her attention back to her duties and focused on the compass in front of her, holding course for their destination. They should be there in another couple of days.

Her attention was drawn to the men when a cheer went up from the deck. They were grinning and clapping, exchanging coins as they looked to the top of the mast. She followed their gaze as Julia freed the last line and the sail snapped out, filling with the wind. She had done it. Hours faster than Branna had managed and Branna felt her heart swell with admiration. Julia was impressive to be sure, and unexpectedly, Branna's blood heated with desire.

Julia descended carefully. She had been up there for five hours and looked exhausted. When she jumped down to the deck, she staggered a little. Her shirt was plastered to her back and her bruised face dripping with sweat.

The men clapped her roughly on the shoulders in congratulations. Griggs, the previous newest recruit, held out the water bucket and ladle. She drank greedily before moving to a shaded area of the deck and dropping to her knees.

All the men had moved on but for Hurst, who continued to watch her with narrowed eyes. Branna trained her gaze on him, her gut twisting as he licked his lips while staring at Julia. He was trouble and she would be watching him very closely. He must have felt the heat of her stare and turned, his eyes flicking to her for a moment before he moved off to get back to his duties.

Branna looked to Julia again. She returned Branna's gaze, her expression unreadable. Branna held her stare for another moment but was the first to look away this time.

* * *

The crew worked tirelessly across the last few leagues out to the shoals, repairing sails and lines, cleaning and oiling rifles and cannons and running rigging and tacking drills until they were near to dropping. Julia held her own with the men. What she lacked in sheer strength, she more than made up for in speed, knowledge, and instinct. Whenever she was on deck, Branna couldn't help but watch her. She moved with confidence and grace and seemed to be enjoying herself.

Branna noted Julia spent much of her off hours with Bartholomew Griggs. She shouldn't have been surprised. They were of equal status on the crew and he was educated, good-looking, and well-spoken, in addition to coming from a similar merchant family background. She often saw them talking animatedly together, sometimes seriously and sometimes jokingly. About what, Branna had no idea.

She wondered if Julia talked about her family and about what happened. She wondered if she was taking comfort from him. She wanted to provide that comfort. Julia should have been talking to her, laughing, sharing her stories, her dreams and her pain. Branna had ruined it, possibly beyond repair and her heart ached for the loss of what could have been.

Branna moved belowdecks coming up from the hold. She needed to check the stores, assess their supplies, and estimate how much more they would use before they went underway to meet the *Serpent's Mistress*. She wanted to readjust her speeds for the change in weight—leaving nothing to chance.

Working her way down the passage through the officers' quarters, she slowed as a door slid open in front of her and Julia emerged, hands behind her neck, tying a scarf around her head.

Julia looked at her in surprise. They really hadn't seen much of each other at all and certainly not alone, though it seemed they were both aware of the other at all times. Their continued connection was both unsettling and comforting.

"Captain," Julia greeted with a nod and moved to edge past her in the corridor.

Branna's throat tightened at the sight of her, the nearness of her as she made to move by. She looked so strong and whole. Her bruises had faded. Her skin had darkened a shade in the sun and her hair had lightened. She smelled of salt, sweat, and sea air. Branna wanted so badly to pull her into her arms and taste her skin, feel their bodies pressed together and tell her how sorry she was for everything she had put her through.

She wanted to tell Julia she gave her hope for something better, that maybe when this was over there could be a chance for them. Branna wanted desperately to know if Julia thought there was a chance for them.

Julia squeezed past her and Branna reached out, a hand on her arm to stop her. "Wait, Julia."

Julia pulled from her grasp. "I'm expected on deck."

"Please, *machree*," she said, her heart pounding and her mouth going dry.

Julia froze at the name and turned, Branna's own sadness and longing reflected in Julia's eyes as she met Branna's gaze. "I'm sorry, Captain. I don't think you should call me that anymore."

Branna swallowed hard, her guts twisting at Julia's words, and watched her move down the passage.

CHAPTER FIFTEEN

The *Banshee* lay still in the water, anchor down, though the wind was high. She had all the sails furled and Branna wanted to run a full rig from nothing to see how fast they could get underway. She looked out at her crew, waiting anxiously for her command.

"All hands, weigh anchor! Full sail!" Branna commanded from the quarterdeck and watched with pride as the crew sprang into action. The booted feet of half a dozen men pushed against the deck in rhythm like the drums of war as the capstan was turned, bringing up the anchor.

The crew swarmed up the shrouds, picking their way across the yardarms to let loose the reef lines and drop the sails while the deck crew tended the lines from below. The ship moved through the sea in a matter of minutes and was soon knifing through the open water.

Branna grinned at Gus who manned the helm.

"That was fast," he said.

She nodded, pleased. They were ready. In three days' time they would sail for the islands and meet the *Serpent's Mistress*.

She clenched her jaw and her fists as she thought of the coming battle. She would give the crew a couple of days off before. They had worked hard and deserved it.

She was torn from her thoughts by a commotion at the bow. Gus frowned, but didn't seem to know what was going on. Branna jumped from the quarterdeck and made her way along the deck.

The crew was circled around the bowsprit. The jib-sail line had snapped and the sail dragged in the water. The ship crested the swells and dropped, sending spray across them all. The sail needed to be brought in which meant someone needed to go out on the bowsprit and get it. So why were they just standing around?

She frowned at Nat who looked on a little helplessly. "The lines are frayed." He cleared his throat. "The repairs were cut short."

That was her fault and everyone knew it.

"Even Jack weighs twelve stone. It won't hold," Nat said with a grimace. "Maybe Ollie?"

Branna wanted to order someone out there but she knew she couldn't expect them to take that risk when she was the reason it was dangerous. She began to unbuckle her knives as she stepped up to the bow and eyed the snapped line.

Nat stood in her way. "Captain, you can't. We need you here. If something were to happen…"

It was not her place and they couldn't afford to have her get injured or worse.

Julia stepped forward. "I'll go."

It was the right thing to do but Branna wanted to keep her safe. She glanced at Nat who nodded. She needed to let her go. "Not without a line." Branna grabbed a coiled rope and stepped toward Julia who was leaning out across the bow to survey the damage. "Turn toward me."

Julia turned and raised her arms and Branna wrapped the rope around her waist, looping it several times. "You don't have to do this."

"You think I can't?"

"That's not what I said." She brought the free end around and knotted it at Julia's waist.

"There's no one else."

"There's me."

"You're the captain. It's not your responsibility."

"I'm the captain who left port before the repairs were complete." Branna tugged the line to make sure it was secure. She had no one to blame but herself.

"Yes, well, I'm sure you had your reasons."

Julia wasn't going to make this easy for her. Nor should she. "Julia—"

"We're going to lose the sail!" one of the men shouted.

Julia pulled away from Branna and turned to the task at hand. She climbed up onto the bow and stepped out onto the inner bobstay, working her way slowly to the end of the bowsprit.

Branna stepped back and to the side, playing the line out for her but keeping tension on it. She wasn't going to let go for anything. Julia made it out to the end in a matter of minutes and hugged the beam tightly when the ship plunged down into another trough, nearly submerging her.

Branna gritted her teeth, her entire body tensing. Julia shook water from her face and leaned further out, gathering in the sail. It was wet and heavy, the weight of it dragging at her. Julia pulled her knife, cutting the remaining line holding the sail and started to make her way back to the ship, pushing the crumpled sail along the spar.

The men leaned out and grabbed the end of the sail, gathering the soaked canvas and hauling it aboard. Branna exhaled loudly, relaxing her grip on the rope, and Julia grinned triumphantly. A split second later the stay line on which she stood snapped with a loud crack and Julia dropped into the sea off the bow.

The rope streaked through Branna's hands, burning the skin from her palms before she could slow it, jerking it tight as the ship passed over where Julia entered the water. The men came around behind her and grabbed the line to take some of the weight and guide the line to the port side.

It all happened in less than a minute but it seemed to have taken much longer. Julia retched up water as Branna and the men hauled her up and over the side, easing her down to the deck, shaken and disoriented.

"Breathe, Julia," Branna commanded and laid a hand on her back.

Julia coughed and gasped, tugging at the rope which had tightened viciously up around her chest. "Get this...off..."

Branna pulled a knife and sawed at the thick rope until it gave. Running her hands down her back and sides caused Julia to jerk away with a hiss of pain. "Take her to my cabin." She no longer cared what anyone thought.

Nat picked Julia up and moved hurriedly across the deck, Branna following. As they passed under the quarterdeck Branna looked up to Gus. "Take us back to the cove and anchor for the night and send Jack to my cabin."

Julia gritted her teeth against the pain in her ribs as Nat laid her on the bed.

"Try to relax," Branna soothed and brushed wet hair off her face.

"Told you I could do it," she grunted, squeezing her eyes shut with a groan.

"I never doubted you."

Jack burst into the room. "What happened?"

"She went over off the bow and the safety line may have busted her ribs," Nat said.

"Let me see." He motioned for Branna to move out of the way and took her place at the edge of the bed. "May I?" He gestured to her shirt and Julia shifted, allowing him to raise it to just beneath her breasts so he could look at her chest. He winced at the sight. Her skin was raw and purpling in a thick line around her torso from the tightened rope.

Jack gently pressed against her ribs with his fingers and walked his hands slowly up and down her body. Julia grimaced at the pressure but stayed still. "Not broken but badly bruised. You're lucky."

Branna moved to her desk and pulled the cork on the bottle of rum, pouring a generous amount into a cup. She crouched next to Julia's head. "Drink this."

Julia nodded and pushed herself up, taking the cup with a shaky hand. She downed the contents in several large gulps before dropping back to the bed.

"Light duty for you again, I'm afraid." Jack offered her an encouraging smile.

"I'll be all right." Julia's eyes closed to slits with pain and the beginning effects of the rum.

"Don't argue. Just rest," Branna ordered.

She awoke sometime later. Branna was in a chair next to the bed, head bowed and hands clasped in front of her face. Julia frowned when she saw the bandages around both her palms. "Your hands," she murmured.

Branna looked up with a small smile. "Welcome back."

"What happened to your hands?"

"What?" Branna looked at the bandages, as if seeing them for the first time. "It's nothing. Rope burn."

"From saving me?"

"From endangering you—again."

Julia sighed and stared up at the ceiling. "So, here we are—again."

Branna fidgeted, looking anywhere but at Julia and taking a long time to say what was on her mind. "There's never been another woman in this bed—until now."

CHAPTER SIXTEEN

Branna left Julia asleep in her bed and returned to the deck in the afternoon. The anchor had been dropped just off a pristine sandy beach. The land dropped off precipitously and the ship could anchor a mere thirty meters offshore. They were protected from the wind and the water lapped gently at the hull.

"All hands." She waited until she had the crew's undivided attention. "You all know why we came out here and where we're going," she said as she looked down at their eager faces. Most of the men on her crew had an unpleasant history with the *Serpent's Mistress*, her crew, or Captain Jagger himself. It was one of the biggest reasons she never had trouble replacing them. They all wanted a piece of revenge. That and the *Serpent's Mistress* was rumored to be laden with riches.

"We sail for the *Serpent's Mistress* in two days. We're ready and…" She was unprepared for the swell of emotion she felt as she addressed them. She swallowed hard. "I'm proud to call myself your captain."

Her words were met with utter silence. She had never praised them like that as a group and the looks on their faces ranged from stunned to total disbelief. "We'll anchor here until we're ready to set sail. You all have permission to leave the ship."

A riotous cheer went up and Branna's mouth quirked into a half-smile. "We still need to reduce some weight. To that end, I'll be lifting the rum and ale rations for tonight only. I expect you all to do your part in lightening our load."

If possible the cheer was louder than before. "Lower the boat!"

The men scrambled to her command, and some not currently on duty simply leapt over the side and started the short swim to the beach.

Branna returned to her cabin to find Julia sitting up, propped against the bulkhead. Morrigan was curled comfortably in her lap and she stroked her soft fur. Branna sat down in the chair next to the bed. "How do you feel?"

"Really sore, but I'm okay."

"You know, I'm glad you weren't more seriously hurt but there is an upside to this."

"Oh?"

"I've been racking my brain trying to figure out how to keep you out of the fight and now I don't have to."

"What are you saying?"

"Isn't it obvious?" Branna gestured to her. "You're staying here, in my cabin where you'll be as safe as possible."

"You can't do that."

"Julia, don't be ridiculous. You can barely move. And anyway, however skilled a sailor you may be now, you're not a fighter and most certainly not a killer."

"You were wrong before when you said this battle wasn't mine. It is. Every bit as much as it is yours and your crew. Of which I am now a member might I remind you."

"Julia—"

"You can't deny me this. You don't have the right."

"Christ, how did we get here again?" Branna shot out of her chair, tipping it backward, raking her fingers through her hair as she paced her quarters. "All right. Get up."

"What?"

"I said on your feet, crewman."

Julia's eyes flashed with anger and she dropped Morrigan unceremoniously to the deck. She swung her legs out of the bed and stood, sucking in a sharp breath at the movement.

It was the only way to make Julia see reason. She wavered slightly before finding her footing. Branna slid a knife from her belt and pressed it into Julia's hand before stepping back a few paces. "Attack me," she said stonily.

Julia looked at her uncertainly, gripping the knife in her hand.

"Did you hear me? I said, attack me."

She still hesitated and Branna stepped closer to her. "How about now? Think you can handle it?"

Julia's lip curled at her mockery and she lunged, staggering a step before she dropped to her knees, the knife slipping from her hand. She clutched her bruised ribs. "Damn you, Branna."

Branna stood over her, fighting the hot sting of tears behind her eyes. "Don't you get it, Julia? I can't have you out there. I can't have you in danger again because of me."

"Branna…"

She dropped to her knees to face her, breathing heavily as she searched her eyes. "I can't do this if I'm thinking about you. And don't you know"—she cupped her hand against Julia's cheek—"all I do is think about you?"

Julia sighed and tipped her head so their foreheads pressed together, their lips so close they were sharing the same air. "I'm sorry," she whispered as she laced her fingers around the back of Branna's neck.

"Why do you keep apologizing to me? I forgive you everything—always."

"It's either that or tell you to go to hell."

Branna laughed. "Come on. Back to bed."

She nodded in agreement and let Branna settle her back on the bed. Branna sat at the edge of the bed and looked at Julia for what felt like the first time, and she began to hope again.

"What?"

"Nothing." Branna shook her head, not ready to share her thoughts lest Julia think her foolish. "I've given the crew leave for the next two days. There's chaos on the beach and I should make an appearance. Will you be all right here for a while?"

"I'll be fine."

She scooped up Morrigan who was hiding under the bed and deposited her in Julia's lap. "I won't be late."

"Are you coming back here tonight?"

"Is that okay?"

"Yes."

Branna called the boat and Jack came out and picked her up. There was a bonfire on the beach and a separate fire spit-roasted an enormous leatherback sea turtle. The men were well into the first crate of rum and barrel of ale, and a shout rose up when the captain hit the beach and joined the party.

Gus pressed a cup of rum into her hand and stood over her until she finished it before filling it up again. Someone had managed to produce a sad leather ball and a brutal game—without any apparent rules—of kill the ball carrier had broken out on the beach in the waning light.

She was surprised to see there was music too, and her jaw dropped as Ollie, the ship's boy, tore up the fiddle like a young man possessed. She hadn't planned to stay long. She wanted to get back to the ship and get back to Julia, but before she knew it she had been challenged to a knife-throwing contest by some of the men.

She tried to decline but they stayed after her, mocking and jeering until she knew the only way to shut them up was to put them in their place. When next she checked, hours had passed and her head was swimming from wood smoke and rum.

Branna extricated herself from the conversation she had been paying little attention to. She searched the beach for Jack and found him by the fire eating a large slab of turtle meat off a stick.

"Jack," she called.

He jumped and spun around, a chunk of meat hanging out of his mouth. "Captain, did you want some?"

She grimaced. "No, thank you. I need to get back to the ship."

"Why? Everyone is here."

"Not everyone."

Julia was dozing, Branna's copy of *Robinson Crusoe* open across her chest and Morrigan snuggled around her neck. She heard the cabin door open quietly and the open doors to the stern let in a gentle breeze. She cracked her eyes when Branna lifted the book and the kitten from her.

"You're back," she said sleepily and frowned, propping herself up on her elbows and wrinkling her nose. "What is that god-awful smell?"

"Rum, smoke, and roasted sea turtle. I'm sorry to wake you. I'm just going to wash up. Go back to sleep."

Julia dropped back onto the bed but didn't close her eyes. Branna stood by the light of the open aft doors and stripped off her shirt, the muscles of her back and arms rippling as she moved. She poured fresh water into the basin and scrubbed at the grime a life at sea left behind.

Julia licked her lips when Branna unbraided her hair, dampening it to clear out some of the smoke, and brushed it out. She pulled on a clean shirt, buttoning it partway before kicking out of her boots and pants.

Julia felt heat building in her belly. She was beautiful and Julia longed to touch her.

Branna turned, clearly feeling the heat of her stare. "Are you all right?"

"No," Julia breathed. "Not until you touch me."

"Julia, you don't know what you're getting into."

"I don't care." She held out her hand. "Please, come here."

Branna approached the bed and laced her fingers with Julia's. "Are you sure this is what you want?"

Julia had thought to be cautious this time, but seeing Branna now, hearing her confessions of earlier…she couldn't hold back anymore. She wanted it too much. "I've never been more sure of anything."

Julia scooted over and Branna eased next to her, mindful of her ribs. She lay down along her length, her head propped up on her hand, and brushed a finger down Julia's face. Branna studied her and frowned.

"What's wrong?"

"I'm so sorry. For how I treated you. The things I said and for everything that's happened."

"Thank you," she whispered. She knew how hard that was for Branna to say and she wanted to respect her efforts at sharing her feelings but she didn't want to talk anymore. Desire swirled in her belly and quickened her heartbeat. She traced her finger slowly down Branna's throat, stopping for a moment at the raven pendant before continuing between her breasts as far as her shirt would allow. "Why do you still wear this after all these years?"

"Why do you think?" Branna closed the distance between them, her hand around the back of Julia's neck, pulling her close. Their lips met, shyly at first and then more urgently when Julia's tongue slipped past her lips, deepening their kiss as she teased her mouth.

Branna groaned softly and she moved her hand across Julia's shoulder and down beneath her shirt to cup her breast, eliciting a delicious groan from Julia in return.

Branna pulled away. "I don't want to hurt you anymore."

Julia unbuttoned Branna's shirt and slid her hand down to her hip. "Then don't."

Branna sighed, bringing their lips together again—tasting and teasing, sucking and biting.

Julia guided Branna over her and Branna kissed her way from Julia's mouth, down her neck to her breasts. She writhed, gasping and clenching against the ache in her core while Branna tormented her nipples with her tongue and teeth, bringing them to hard points. Julia arched, driving their hips together and clutching at Branna's shoulders.

"Tell me if I hurt you," Branna mumbled, her mouth full of Julia's breast, her hips rocking into her rhythmically, in time with the pulsing throb between her legs.

"You will…if you stop," she panted, the pressure of her desire building to nearly unbearable levels.

Branna hummed her approval. Julia shivered and trembled when Branna's tongue and teeth raked and nipped across her belly and she settled between her legs, spreading them to accommodate her as she kissed a path slowly down her body.

Julia's hips jerked at the first touch of Branna's mouth against her swollen center. Branna's tongue danced and darted for several exquisitely agonizing minutes, her strong arms hooking beneath Julia's thighs to hold her in place while she teased.

Julia groaned, her hips rocking up, searching for more while Branna seemed to delight in toying with her, driving her to the brink of madness but holding her back from the release she craved. Her arms pressed into the bulkhead above her, driving her against Branna's waiting mouth. "Bran, please…please…"

Julia's desperate plea for satisfaction was swallowed by her own guttural groan of pleasure when Branna's mouth closed over her fully. Branna devoured her without restraint—sucking and swirling her tongue, pressing into her until Julia bucked wildly, panting and moaning, while a climax without parallel tore her to pieces. Julia arched and cried out with the final burst of sensation and collapsed against the bed, her head lolling to the side with a soft sigh of satisfaction.

She was only vaguely aware of Branna crawling up her body and gathering her into her arms for sleep.

CHAPTER SEVENTEEN

Branna stood out on the main deck in the late morning and stretched slowly, a smile playing across her face, remembering the feel of Julia's hands on her, her warm breath on her skin and the feel of Julia arching and trembling under her hands as she cried out her pleasure.

She held Julia as she slept, long into the night, stroking a hand along her back and marveling in a feeling of completeness she had never known before. Julia, it seemed, had begun the impossible and worked her way into her heart with her fierce spirit, passion, and courage.

Branna squinted into the morning sun and laughed as she saw the bodies of her crew littered along the beach. The ashes from the fires still smoldered and a few of the men were stirring, some of them crawling along the beach, retching into the sand.

They would stay today as well, though the rum rationing would be back in effect. She needed the men well rested but sharp and alert. Food, rest, and recreation were in order. Jack emerged from the tree line, holding his stomach and looking a little green. A sharp two-fingered whistle got his attention. When he looked up, she motioned for him to come and get her.

Branna turned at a thump. Julia was walking gingerly up the two steps to the main deck. "What do you think you're doing?" Branna hurried to meet her.

"I want to come with you," she replied a little breathlessly. Branna led her to the starboard gunwale and leaned her against it. Julia grimaced and held her side, her breathing slightly labored.

"Absolutely not, Julia. You're staying here."

"Is that an order, Captain?"

"Yes. It is."

Julia straightened as best she could, eyes glittering in anger. "I'm crew and I should be allowed—"

"That's right. You're crew and expected to follow my command without comment, question or complaint."

"You're enjoying this aren't you?"

"No, Julia, I'm not," Branna replied, her expression softening as she placed her hands on her shoulders. "Look, this doesn't have anything to do with you and me. You are injured and cannot move around well on your own. I can't worry about you or anyone else who may run into trouble trying to help you. I have a responsibility to keep you and everyone on this ship safe. So, if that means you stay here, then you stay here. Is that understood?"

Julia crossed her arms. "You weren't *worried* about my injuries last night and I moved just fine, thank you."

Julia wasn't wrong and Branna's face flushed. "It's not the same thing and this is not a discussion."

"What trouble could there possibly be—"

"Julia, that's enough. My decision is made."

Her jaw clenched and eyes flashed before she turned away. "Aye, aye, Captain."

Branna ran her hand down the side of her face and turned her back so she could look at her. "If you like I can send someone back to keep you company."

"I would like that."

"Okay, who?"

"Bartholomew, if you don't mind."

"Bartholomew, is it? I think I may mind."

"Don't be absurd. I enjoy his company. He's good-natured, funny, and easy to get along with."

It was not lost on Branna that Julia had just described everything she wasn't and her mood quickly soured. She glanced out to see Jack come alongside the ship with the boat. "One more thing, as long as we're on the subject. While you're on this crew you can't be my…" Her what?

"On the subject of what? You lording your power over me? Don't worry, Captain Kelly. Your reputation of being a miserable, insufferable, brute will remain intact."

Branna snorted. "If there is a power imbalance here, Miss Farrow, it is most certainly not in my favor."

Branna discussed with Mr. Griggs spending the day on the ship with Julia and he was all too happy to comply, which inflamed her ire further while she watched Jack row him out to the ship.

She spent the afternoon in counsel with her senior officers while the crew went in search of fresh water to replace their stores. As suppertime neared another turtle was caught and a spit fire started again. The mood was far more subdued as the men began to turn their attention to the coming battle.

Branna adjourned her meeting with the officers and called all hands, save for Mr. Griggs, to discuss her plans with them. She smoothed over a patch of beach with a branch and then used a stick to map out their various routes, attacks, and defenses. The men crowded around her in a circle. She went over and over their plan and answered as many questions as her men could think to ask.

Branna stood and tossed the stick she had been using down into the sand. "That's it. Is everyone clear on what we're about?"

"Aye, Captain," they replied.

She eyed them each in turn. They looked ready, intent, and focused. Her gaze swept over them again, tensing with the feeling something was wrong. Her head swiveled. She was flanked by Nat and Gus. Jack stood off to her left. She scanned the men a third time, making eye contact with each in turn, unable to place her unease. "Sound off!" she ordered.

Gus stiffened. "Captain?"

"Do it!"

"Hawke," he barked.

"Hooper."

"Massey."

"Ollie."

"Spinks."

"Rathbone."

"Wickersham."

"Linnington."

"Kitts."

"Merton."

"Clifton."

"Ashfield."

"Brewer."

"Caswell."

"Davy."

"Fletcher."

"Gribble."

"Harvey."

"Jenkins."

"Moyle."

"Needham."

"Overton."

"Scott."

"Worsham."

"Where the bloody hell is Hurst?" She looked frantically around and all the men wore similar expressions of ignorance and confusion. Her gaze was drawn out to the ship in time to see Cuddy Hurst hauling himself over the gunwale and onto the deck.

"Hurst!" she screamed and ran to the edge of the water. He wiped water from his face and grinned wickedly before moving off along the deck.

Branna ran to the boat. "Get me out there. Now!"

Hurst was out of his mind, either believing he could get away with whatever he was planning or because he didn't care that he was a dead man. It didn't matter. Branna was filled with rage and worry at what he could do before they got to him. She pushed the boat into the water, jumping in as it floated out from shore, with Gus and Nat splashing through the shallows to catch up.

Julia pushed open the door to Branna's cabin. She didn't think Branna would mind if she borrowed *Robinson Crusoe*. She and Bartholomew had been discussing it earlier and she wanted to read him a passage. She scooped up Morrigan and stroked her head as she gazed around the cabin looking for it.

She tucked the book under her arm and climbed down the steps to the crew quarters, careful not to jar her ribs. Bartholomew had offered to retrieve the book for her but she couldn't very well tell him it was in the captain's quarters. He would be punished severely for going in, and instead she had insisted he wait for her in the galley.

"Found it," she called as she poked her head in the galley but didn't see him. "Bartholomew?"

Perhaps he thought she was heading to her own quarters to get the book and made her way farther down the passageway to the officers' quarters. She turned a bulkhead and stumbled, her foot catching on something on the floor. She crashed down with a shriek of pain and gripped her side. Her pain quickly turned to horror when she realized she was lying atop the unmoving form of Bartholomew Griggs.

"Bartholomew!" she cried and tried to turn him over, her ribs protesting ferociously. He was too heavy and the passage too narrow for her to get any leverage. She ran her hands over his head and neck, her fingers coming away sticky with blood.

He had a gash across his temple that was oozing blood. She could see the slow rise and fall of his back with his even breathing and sighed with relief—until she saw the iron mallet on the floor. She realized he had been struck and that she was most likely alone with whoever had done it.

Julia pushed herself up, looking down the dim passageway to see Cuddy Hurst stepping out the door of her quarters.

"There you are. Looks like it's just me and you now, girlie." He smiled menacingly and charged.

"No!" She scrambled to her feet and ran back the way she had come. If she could get to the deck and call for help or jump… Surely, someone would see her.

He was a big man and couldn't move well belowdecks. If it weren't for her ribs, she would have had the advantage of speed, but with her injury, he caught up to her as she was halfway up the steps.

He gripped her leg and dragged her back down. Her heart hammered in her chest and her breath came in short, painful gasps. She could smell his stink of sweat and filth when he turned her, slamming her back against the steps.

She grunted and fought against him as he pressed against her. "Get off!" she screamed when he grabbed at her clothes, ripping her shirt as he leaned in and ran his tongue across her cheek. She groaned and turned her head. His breath was hot and foul-smelling. She raised her hands and clawed at his face, gouging at his eyes.

Hurst howled in pain and released her, his hands covering his face. She shoved him hard and he staggered back far enough that she could turn and pull herself up the steps.

She burst out of the hatch, landing on her hands and knees on the deck, with a strangled cry. "Help me!" she screamed hoarsely, as she tried to push herself up and away from the hatch.

She reached her feet as Hurst emerged from below, his face purple with rage and bleeding from the eyes. His hand lashed out, gripping her ankle and pulling her feet out from under her, sending her crashing back to the deck.

The pain in her chest left her dizzy and sick as he flipped her on her back. He gripped her by the neck and slammed her head onto the deck. Her vision grayed at the edges and she fought to stay awake.

"Stupid bitch!" he snarled and fumbled with his belt.

Julia reached out blindly for anything to use as a weapon, her fist closing around a gaff hook left near the hatch. She gripped it hard, swinging it up toward him as he descended on her again.

The hook embedded deeply into his shoulder at the base of his neck with a wet crunch and his left arm immediately went limp. Hurst howled, clutching at his neck with his right hand. Julia yanked the hook from his body and blood fountained from the wound, showering them both. She scrambled out from under him.

She stood unsteadily, wincing with every ragged breath while holding her left arm across her chest to support her aching ribs. Her right hand gripped the gaff hook dripping blood onto her feet. Cuddy Hurst staggered around trying to stem the fount of blood, shrieking like an animal. He finally dropped to his knees, gurgled a breath, and fell forward onto the deck.

Branna was frantic. They were close but too much time had passed. She leapt from the boat to the ladder while they were still several feet away when she heard Julia scream for help. Her heart was in her throat, afraid she was too late.

She vaulted the gunwale and froze when she saw Julia standing and staring at the still body of Cuddy Hurst, as a pool of blood grew steadily around him.

"Julia?"

Julia whirled, bringing the gaff hook up to defend herself and Branna sucked in a sharp breath at the sight of her—blood-soaked and ghostly pale. Her eyes were wide and glittering with fear, and she trembled when she finally focused on Branna. "I think I killed him."

"Don't worry about him," Branna said, approaching her cautiously. She was clearly still in survival mode and Branna didn't want that hook through her eye.

Julia lowered the hook but didn't let it go, taking a step back from Branna's outstretched hand. "Is he dead?"

Branna looked at Hurst's still form. She heard Nat and Gus climb over the side but they didn't come closer. She crouched over Hurst's body and held the back of her hand beneath his nose to check for breath. There was none. Julia watched her with wide, fearful eyes. She didn't need the burden of this, too. However righteous her actions, this would make her a killer. Branna pulled a knife, gripping Hurst by the hair to lift his head, and slit his throat. "He is now."

Branna called to Nat and Gus, "Find Griggs. Get the crew back here now and send Jack to me."

Gus motioned to Hurst. "What about the body?"

"Leave it. I want everyone to see."

CHAPTER EIGHTEEN

Branna clamped down on her emotions and moved back toward Julia. She was shockingly pale and so visibly tense she thought she might shatter and Branna didn't want to do anything that might traumatize her further. "Julia, put the hook down. You're safe now."

Julia nodded, staring at her hand as if willing her muscles to release the handle. The gaff hook clattered to the deck at her feet. Her brow furrowed at the blood, congealing and tacky on her hand and she scrubbed it against her shirt, her breath hitching with distress.

Branna reached out a hand to her. "It's okay."

Julia was clawing at the blood on her palm with her nails. "It's not coming off."

"I'll help you. I promise." Branna wrapped an arm around her waist and guided her toward her cabin. She sat her on the bed and Julia frantically began wiping her hands against her pants.

Branna grabbed the bottle of rum and a cup and sat on the edge of the bed next to her. "No one is going to hurt you. Julia, look at me." She tugged gently at her arm to get her to turn. "I need to see if you're all right."

Julia swallowed hard, her breath shuddering in and out, but lifted her head to meet Branna's gaze.

"That's it," Branna soothed and brushed her fingers gently over her face. Blessedly, she had no visible injuries. She poured a cup of rum. "This will help," she said and held it to Julia's lips. She winced but swallowed. "A little more," Branna encouraged and Julia drained it. She rose again and came back with the basin of water, setting it down by the bed. She soaked a cloth in cool water. "I'm going to help you clean up."

Julia nodded and raised her arms, allowing Branna to strip off her blood-soaked shirt. "I'm sor...sorry," she stammered, crossing her arms to cover herself despite them being alone.

"What? What for?" Branna slipped a clean shirt over her head.

"I should...shouldn't be here. I'm only distracting you and the crew."

Branna's guts twisted with rage, but she made every effort to stay calm. She stalled by beginning to wipe gently at the blood on Julia's face and neck, giving her time to get her emotions under control. "You are a member of this crew. Hurst's actions are his own and he can't hurt you anymore."

"This was a mistake," she whispered.

"The mistake was his—and mine for bringing him aboard."

"This was all a terrible mistake. I'm not supposed to be here and I would take it all back if I could."

Branna knew Julia was hurting and scared right now, but she couldn't help being stung by her words. "I don't think so," she said softly, taking Julia's hands one at a time and carefully scrubbing them clean of blood.

"You're lying," Julia challenged, her eyes glittering.

Branna didn't take offense this time. This time Julia was wrong. She dropped the cloth back in the water and cupped

Julia's face gently so she couldn't look away. "I'm not. Julia, ever since I left you and my parents were killed, I've always had something to fight for and a cause to die for, from which I've never wavered. Until you came back into my life I've never had something to live for."

Julia just stared, her mouth moving like she wanted to speak but couldn't find the words.

Branna smiled. "Do you understand what I'm saying?"

Before Julia could answer there was a quick knock at the door and Jack let himself in, his arms laden with supplies. "You, my dear, are good job security."

Julia smiled shakily. "I'm not hurt."

"More rum, Captain," Jack said as he eyed his patient. "Let me make sure."

Branna poured another cup and offered it to him.

"The men are waiting for you on deck," he said, looking pointedly at her as he took the cup. "I'll take care of her."

Branna nodded. She had business to attend to. She gripped Julia's hand briefly before stalking onto the deck.

"Captain on deck!" Nat bellowed when she emerged and the crew snapped to attention.

Branna stood before them, her expression stony. She had lectured Julia on not going ashore because she was injured and it was the captain's job to protect her crew. She had failed. In so many ways she had failed and her anger knew no bounds.

She would make this right. Starting now. Her eyes flicked over her crew, looking anxious and uneasy as they fidgeted where they stood. Bartholomew Griggs leaned against the gunwale, a bloody rag to his head. The body of Cuddy Hurst lay, face down, where she had left him.

"Mr. Hurst's contract with this ship and her crew has been terminated," she began icily. "He assaulted two members of this crew. An offense to me, this ship, and all of you for which I wish there were a punishment more severe than death."

She scanned their faces, some were hard and blank, but most wore similar expressions of rage and betrayal. Hurst's actions were a black mark on them all. "Pick him up," she commanded.

Nat and Gus, with considerable effort, hoisted the body of the big man and propped it between them.

"Take a good look," she said and lifted his head, the wound in his neck gaping open, pouring more blood and flashing innards beneath. "This is what crossing me looks like. I want you all to remember this the next time someone may feel like taking advantage of my good nature. Get this filth off my ship."

Nat and Gus dragged him to the side and hoisted him over the gunwale. A second later his body splashed into the sea— meat for the turtles. "We sail for the *Serpent's Mistress* with the morning's tide." She gestured to the blood on the deck. "Someone clean this mess up. Dismissed."

The men wandered off silently, only Griggs remained. "Captain, a word, please?"

Branna was in no mood. She wanted to blame him for what happened, but he was as much a victim as Julia. She had sent him to keep her company. She had failed to anticipate the danger and she had no one to blame but herself. She hired Hurst and she thought she could handle him and she had been wrong.

"How bad is it?" she asked, nodding to his wound.

He pulled the rag away to reveal a jagged gash over his eye and temple, still oozing blood. "It's fine."

She frowned. "I'll send the quartermaster to find you when he's through with Miss Farrow."

"Julia, um, Miss Farrow? Is she all right?"

"She will be."

"Thank god. Miss Farrow told me you had ordered her out of the conflict with the *Serpent's Mistress*. With your permission, I would like to offer to stand with her on the ship. See that no harm comes to her tomorrow."

Branna narrowed her eyes suspiciously. "For what reason?" She did need someone to stay with Julia. Ollie couldn't do it, though he wouldn't be fighting either. With Griggs injured also he was the obvious choice.

"I owe her."

"You and me both," she muttered before she could stop herself.

"You can't blame yourself for the actions of a deranged man."

"You are aware of what will happen to you if any harm were to befall her?"

"Aye, Captain."

"Very well."

Julia dozed off and on with the help of the rum while Jack kept vigil. She wished she could sleep but her muscles spasmed relentlessly, keeping her awake. She finally heard Branna come in. She was tense, vibrating with pent-up energy, her face a mask of frustration and fury. "Branna, what happened out there?"

Branna sat at the edge of the bed and picked up her hand, lacing her fingers together. "I reiterated a few finer points about the expectations of being a member of this crew. Nothing you need to worry about."

Julia's mouth quirked into the beginnings of a smile. "I bet you said it just like that, too."

"Not in those words, exactly. How are you?"

"Better."

Branna turned to Jack and raised her eyebrows in question. "She'll be all right with rest."

Branna nodded her thanks. "Will you attend to Mr. Griggs, please, Jack?"

"Of course." He collected his things before slipping quietly out of the cabin.

Julia squeezed Branna's hand. "How is Bartholomew?"

"His head is probably pounding and he may be a little less pretty from now on, but otherwise, he's fine."

"You didn't, um, punish him?"

"Why would you think that?"

"I thought, maybe, you held him responsible for what happened."

"No." She looked away, dropping Julia's hand. "I should've been here. I could've stopped him."

"Don't. You couldn't have known."

"Yes, I could have. I did. I saw the way he watched you. Like you were on display for him. Christ, I just served you up to him. I'm sorry, Julia. This is all my fault."

"I'm all right, Branna," Julia said and was immediately seized with a brutal muscle spasm, twisting her face with a grunt of pain.

Branna's eyes went wide. "What the hell was that?"

Julia exhaled slowly and relaxed. "It's been happening all night. It's just tension."

"What can I do?"

"Can you just hold me?"

Branna rose and locked the door before kicking off her boots and stripping off her pants. Julia had moved over to make room for her. Branna settled herself and pulled Julia into her arms, Julia's head resting on her chest.

Another spasm gripped her and Julia gasped, twisting Branna's shirt in her hand until it passed. Branna winced in sympathy and held her as tightly as she dared, running her hand gently over her back.

"Mmm, that's uncomfortable." Julia sighed.

"I'm so sorry this happened."

"Just talk to me and help me take my mind off it, please," Julia mumbled into her chest.

"Okay." Branna settled back more comfortably. "What would you like to know?"

Julia considered for a moment, enjoying the feel of Branna's hand caressing her neck and running through her hair. "What are your plans after this?"

"My plans?"

"You know? For the future?"

"Christ, with the life we lead out here, the work we do, we're lucky to live past..." She paused for a long moment. "That was a stupid thing to say. I didn't mean—"

"It's okay. I'm not blind to this lifestyle. Have you never thought about what your life could be like without the *Serpent's Mistress*?"

"Not until recently."

"And?"

"What if you don't care for me after all this is over? I mean, you've only ever seen me at my most charming. I would hate for you to discover I could be...off-putting."

Julia laughed. "You forget, Captain, you don't scare me. I know you of old."

Branna sighed heavily. "I haven't been the person you knew for many years."

"We shall see."

"Will we?"

"Would you like to find out if I still care for you when this is over, Captain Kelly?"

"I would like that very much, Miss Farrow."

CHAPTER NINETEEN

Julia stayed out of the way and watched Branna move around the cabin in the early dawn light. She dressed slowly and with precision. Black on black as she carefully tucked her shirt tails into her pants and buttoned the waist. She stepped into her boots and buckled her belt of knives around her hips, ensuring the blades were secure. In addition, she pulled on a black leather gauntlet over each forearm, lacing them tightly before sliding another knife in a sheath, hidden on the inside of each forearm.

Julia's anxiety built while Branna dressed for battle. She may not be scared *of* her but she was certainly scared *for* her. She bit her tongue to keep from saying as much. It would only serve to distract her.

She swung her legs over the side of the bed and sat up. Branna's hair was still loose, the breeze through the doors rippling through it. "Come here," Julia said softly.

Branna's brows rose in question, but she did as instructed. Julia pulled her down to the bed, raking her fingers through her hair to untangle it. Without a word, she braided her hair tightly, tying the end with a leather cord.

She sat back when she was finished and turned Branna toward her, studying her face. "How do you feel?"

Branna didn't answer for a long time. "I was thinking, maybe, when we get back to Nassau we could visit that juice vendor again?"

Julia smiled and traced her scar down her face. "I'd like that very much."

Branna cupped Julia's cheek. "How do *you* feel?"

Julia swallowed several times and thought of all the ways in which she could answer and settled on what she hoped was the least troublesome. "I'd like to be on deck with the crew," she said and hurried on as soon as Branna opened her mouth to protest. "At least for a little while. We have a full day's sail and I'd like to help."

"Julia—"

"Please. I want to be a part of this. I know these men, some of them probably better than you. I care what happens to them."

"Stay on the deck. Don't do anything to risk yourself or anyone else—"

"I won't. I won't get in your way."

"And when I say, as soon as I say, you're to return back here and stay here."

Julia nodded. "Aye, Captain."

Branna sighed, her face softening. "I wish you weren't here, right now."

"I don't." Julia wrapped her arms around Branna's neck, pulling her into a fierce embrace. "Please, come back to me this time."

The intensity with which the crew worked was palpable. Gus stood stoically at the helm, Branna next to him while Nat shouted commands to the crew from the main deck. They were at full sail and the *Banshee* crashed her way through the sea to meet the *Serpent's Mistress*.

The men showed no signs of fatigue even as encumbered as they were with weaponry. The blades of short swords, cutlasses, boarding axes, and pikes glinted in the sun. Everyone was dressed for battle and Branna could taste revenge on her lips.

She kept an eye on Julia, working alongside the crew. She moved slowly but was determined to pull her weight, tending the lines and adjusting the sails as needed to stay on course.

The afternoon wore on and Nat called for the crew to reef the fore- and mizzensails. From now on they would move under the mainsail only, slowing the ship as they approached the islands. Branna pulled the spyglass and scanned the horizon. There was no sign of the *Serpent's Mistress* but she knew the ship was close by. She could feel it.

There were two ways into the island cluster: from the open sea or through the thread, a deep, narrow channel between two of the outer islands. It was more protected and far more treacherous. It was the route they would take in. Branna knew Jagger would be expecting her through there and she would be ready for him. She could see the entrance to the thread through her lens. It was time.

Branna replaced the spyglass and nodded to Gus.

"Cannon crew, report below," he called. "Load all guns. Keep the ports closed until you hear from Ollie."

Three men dropped what they were doing and scrambled to get below to the gun deck.

Branna sought out Nat on the deck and waited for him to meet her gaze, giving him a sharp nod. Nat crossed the deck and laid a hand on Julia's shoulder.

Julia straightened and looked at him before turning her gaze to the helm. Branna nodded to her, her mouth grimly set. There was nothing more to discuss and Branna could see the tears burning behind Julia's eyes as she let Nat lead her back to the captain's quarters where Bartholomew Griggs was already standing sentinel.

Nat returned and gave her a nod. Branna exhaled slowly. Julia would be safe, or as safe as she could be. She turned to Gus. "Arm the men."

Gus leapt from the quarterdeck to distribute the long arms and Branna took his place at the wheel. Eight men returned to the deck armed with flintlock pistols and muskatoons usually kept in the armory.

The sun was lowering and the entrance to the thread was in sight. They sailed on and Nat called for the men to take up battle stations. The men scattered to their assigned posts, only a handful remaining on deck to tend the sail.

She was careful to keep her eyes forward while they entered the thread. The ship slowed again as soon as they were protected from the wind, and their crawling pace made it possible to feel the *almost* imperceptible tug on the ship when they crossed the line she anticipated would be there.

The men felt it too, and she could see them gripping their weapons, their eyes shining with violence as they crouched beneath the gunwales, waiting for the first attack.

It was a daring trick and one she suspected Jagger would risk to try and get the early upper hand by wearing down her crew. She had been a part of it herself once, as one of her early positions. It had failed miserably, costing the lives of several men. A line was laid in the water across the thread attached to a small boat on either side, hiding out of sight in the island foliage. When the keel of the passing ship snagged the line and sailed past, it would tighten, pulling the two boats in alongside the ship silently, allowing the men to board fast and unexpectedly.

She was ready, as were her men. Her heart pounded in her chest while she waited for the first sign of the boarding party to throw their hooks and climb up from below.

A shout rang out and pistols fired. Her men along the gunwales leapt to their feet, howling, cursing, firing, and hacking at the boarding party when they attempted to clamber over the side. The ship rocked with the motion of the added weight and Branna watched stonily, as the snarling, filthy faces of the first attackers appeared. Blood sprayed and the sound of battle filled the deck. Her crew cleaved the heads and arms of the invaders as soon as they appeared over the side, sending them screaming and splashing back into the sea. The water darkened with the blood of a dozen bodies.

She tried to keep her focus on the channel to keep from running them aground, but was inevitably drawn back to the fight. Gus fired his pistol into the face of one attacker while severing the hands of another. The man screamed, looking wild eyed at his bloody stumps as he peeled off the side and fell away.

It was over in a matter of minutes and all the invaders were dispatched swiftly and brutally. The men knew better than to celebrate. This was only the beginning. They had killed efficiently but there would be many more where they came from.

The crew moved about, reloading pistols, wiping blades clean and tossing severed body parts back over the side. They had suffered only one injury, the young man, Spinks, received a knife through his hand when he got caught leaning over the side for too long. They had acquitted themselves well and Branna had no complaints.

She pulled the spyglass out again. Still no sign of the *Serpent's Mistress*. It was just as well; it would give them time for their next cover. If she couldn't see them they couldn't see her.

Tattered, blood-smeared sails were raised and flapped uselessly against the foremast. Purposefully frayed lines dragged in the water, all carefully designed to look as if they had sustained damage in the initial assault.

Jagger sent those men to a sure death, but at first glance he may believe the *Banshee*, too, had taken a blow. The armed crew remained out of sight. She wanted Jagger to think their numbers had been thinned.

Branna pulled the spyglass again. There she was. The *Serpent's Mistress*. She was at full sail coming around the point of the large island, heading just to port of them. Branna could see the cannon ports open, ready to fire as soon as the *Banshee* passed alongside of her. She didn't intend to give them the chance.

Gus came to take the wheel from her. "Stay the course," she commanded and hopped down to the main deck. The *Serpent's Mistress* was closing the distance fast and Branna's heart thudded in her chest with the thrill of the oncoming battle. She had waited fifteen long years for this, but she didn't want it drawn out. She wanted to hit them hard and fast, cripple the ship, board and take out the crew.

She motioned to Ollie who was at her side in an instant. "Starboard cannons only. Keep the port side closed. If that's all they can see and he thinks we're not ready or incapable of firing, they'll wait to fire until they're right on top of us. Then take cover."

"Aye, aye, Captain." He scampered away and disappeared below.

Nat crouched at the port bow, his eyes never leaving her, waiting for her signal. Everyone knew what to do and she trusted them to carry out their duties efficiently and effectively. A cloud passed over the sun, darkening the sky as the two ships moved toward their inevitable confrontation.

They were close now and Branna could see the crew working along the deck tending their sails and positioning themselves for the fight. She trained the spyglass on the quarterdeck. Jagger was there, grinning maniacally and screeching orders.

"Hold." She raised her hand to Nat. They needed to be close. "Hold." She no longer needed the spyglass to see the men moving about on the *Serpent's Mistress*. "Hold." The ship was nearly on them and she could hear the shouts of their crew as they prepared to fire.

"Now!"

Nat hit the winch that released the kedge anchor off the port bow and the heavy iron chain rattled and rocked the ship as it slid into the sea. The *Banshee* sailed on while the anchor plummeted to the shallow seafloor along the shoals.

Branna gripped the gunwale to steady herself. "Prepare to fire all starboard guns!" she shouted. She could see Jagger well enough to know he wasn't smiling any longer as the anchor chain pulled taut with a grinding squeal.

The *Banshee* creaked and groaned loudly at the strain and the men were nearly jerked off their feet when the bow snapped around, bringing the starboard side into firing sight of the *Serpent's Mistress* at only fifty yards away.

"Fire all guns!" Branna yelled.

The report of six cannons, loaded with both round and bundle shot, was deafening and five of the six rounds hit their mark. Two of the rounds smashed through the hull and the other three caused maximum damage across the deck—shredding sails, fouling lines and partially splintering the foremast. The screams of men told her there was some human damage as well.

"Reload!" she screamed as the *Serpent's Mistress*, still holding course, let fly with her own barrage.

The deck near where she stood exploded when a round hit home, sending sword-size pieces of the deck raining down on them. Only three of Jagger's cannons fired. The others were either disabled or the men manning them were. The air filled with the acrid smell of gunpowder and smoke.

"Cut loose the kedge!"

Nat released the chain on the anchor, letting it drop into the sea, freeing them to maneuver as the *Serpent's Mistress* sailed past.

"Get after her!"

CHAPTER TWENTY

The men scrambled, dodging around the damaged deck, shouting and pushing each other to bring in the tattered sails and hoist the sound ones. Gus spun the wheel and the ship lurched forward as the sails filled. The *Serpent's Mistress* was smaller and faster, but with damaged sails and hull, she was slowing. Branna eyed them through the spyglass. It looked as if the *Serpent's Mistress* listed to port. With any luck she was taking on water.

The *Banshee* closed in on her port side. "Prepare to fire starboard guns," Branna shouted as they came upon her. It also meant the *Banshee* would be in the *Serpent's Mistress's* firing range as well. She was counting on their guns not being at full force.

Branna waited until the first two fore cannons were in range. "Fire one and two!" she shouted. At close range the blast was devastating as the rounds smashed through the *Serpent's Mistress's* quarterdeck. The *Banshee* surged ahead and came alongside. "Fire all guns!" Three through six unloaded with a deafening explosion along the port side followed immediately by the booming of a return volley.

She was blown off her feet when the deck buckled under her. She hit it hard, her head banging off a cleat. She wiped blood from her eye and shook her head to clear it. Peering through the smoke she saw the torn-up bodies of Moyle and Gribble nearby, eyes staring unseeing to the sky.

Branna pushed herself to her feet, her ears ringing. The two ships sailed within yards of each other and the frantic shouting of both crews could be heard over the crashing waves. The metal on metal grinding from the gun decks told her both crews were fighting to reload. "Throw the boarding hooks!" she roared over the din. "Board! Board!"

Her crew organized along the starboard gunwale and let loose the lines with heavy three-pronged hooks attached. The hooks thunked into the wood of the *Serpent's Mistress*, effectively securing the ships together.

The crew swarmed over the side, screaming and snarling, teeth bared and blades flashing as they engaged the *Serpent's Mistress's* crew. The fighting was fierce, but the *Serpent's Mistress's* crew had already taken heavy casualties from their cannon fire and was weakened. Her gaze darted around the deck, checking on her men.

Nat vaulted the gunwale, slashing the throat of a man struggling to his feet, nearly severing his head. His blade didn't stop there but swung around to split the face of another as he came to engage him. The smell of blood and smoke was overpowering and gore slickened the deck.

Jack held his ground on the foredeck of the *Serpent's Mistress*, swinging a cutlass in each hand, piercing the heart of one man before kicking another from the steps into Gus's waiting axe. The man's head exploded under the blow, showering Gus in blood and tissue.

Branna pulled herself atop the gunwale and looked for Jagger. She saw him, his sword a blur as he defended the helm from two of her best fighters, Kitts and Merton. Jagger went down on his knees under a blow from the hilt of Kitts's sword and her men closed in on him—falling right into his trap.

He swept his blade across their legs, staggering them and leapt to his feet to drive his sword through Merton's throat.

"Jagger!" she roared and leapt from the gunwale onto the ragged deck of the *Serpent's Mistress*.

He looked at her with wicked, hate-filled eyes before slashing across the belly of Kitts, spilling entrails onto the quarterdeck. "Take her down!" he bellowed at the remaining crew between him and Branna. "And bring the Raven to me!"

Three men, bloody and crazed, one of them with an arm hanging grotesquely, turned and charged her.

She dropped to one knee, reaching for her knives, her arms a blur as she threw her blades. One man dropped instantly, a blade through his eye. Another staggered as the blade hit home deep into his gut before dropping to his knees. The third man rushed on and she drew her sword with a shriek of metal.

He was big and inhumanly strong as he struck at her furiously. She blocked each strike but quickly tired, her arms trembling. The next blow came down like a hammer and she ducked under it sending him staggering forward, his sword cracking into the deck. She came up under him, swinging her blade up and severing his arm at the shoulder.

He screamed and frothed, staring stupidly at the ragged bloody stump before she ran him through the middle and kicked his body back off the end of her blade. She turned to face Jagger, her snarl of rage turning to a menacing smile.

The battle among the crews lessened. There were fewer sword clashes and more screaming as the *Serpent's Mistress's* numbers continued to diminish. She blocked out the noise as she stalked slowly toward him. He shifted uneasily, gripping his sword in his blood slicked hand. His earlier cruel bravado faltered as his gaze darted across the deck in search of his crew. There was no one left to help him.

Julia's heart pounded so hard she thought it would burst out of her chest. Her shirt clung damply to her and her breath came raggedly as she listened to the horrors of the fight. Without any way to know what was going on she feared the worst and screamed when the door crashed open and Bartholomew burst into the cabin.

"Julia! You have to come."

"What's happened?"

"It's the captain."

She leapt up and pushed past him, her throat painfully tight. She ran out onto the deck, blinking furiously against the sunshine, and looked around uncertainly.

The ships were locked together, their hulls creaking and crashing together as they sailed out into the open sea. The battle on the *Serpent's Mistress* had waned to a few one-on-one skirmishes which were over quickly with either Jagger's man surrendering or being run though.

She looked toward the quarterdeck to see Branna fighting the man she knew as Captain Jagger. Branna's head was bloody and sweat poured down her face and neck. She was ferocious as she smashed her blade down on him relentlessly, howling in rage.

Jagger's eyes were wild with fright as he tried to parry her blows. He was forced farther and farther back as she rained down her fury, fifteen years in the making. He hit the capstan and stumbled and she drove her sword down onto his, knocking it from his hands.

Julia sucked in a sharp breath. Branna had done it. It was over. Her eyes flicked across the deck to see the *Banshee's* crew standing over the few survivors of the *Serpent's Mistress*, holding them on their knees at sword point.

Bartholomew must have been mistaken and her eyes turned back to Branna just as a strong arm went around her neck and the point of a blade pricked into her side. She gasped and jerked, freezing as the blade pierced her skin and she felt blood flow beneath her shirt.

He breathed into her ear. "Stay still, Julia, and you might yet live through this."

Branna straightened, panting heavily, and smiled, bringing the point of her blade to his throat. "You're dead."

"Stay your sword, Captain!" a voice rang out from the deck of the *Banshee*.

Bartholomew Griggs was on the deck, his arm tight around Julia's throat and a blade pressed to her side. "No," Branna breathed. Her vision narrowed to a pinpoint and the deck seemed to sway beneath her.

Captain Jagger tore his eyes from Branna to follow her gaze. He frowned in confusion for a moment before breaking into a face-splitting grin. He pushed Branna's blade from his neck.

"Why, if it isn't the captivating Miss Farrow." He stood and looked from Branna, trembling with helpless rage in front of him, to Griggs on the deck of her ship. "I must admit, Griggs, I was thinking you'd been discovered and your body was feeding the fishes long before now. I'm pleased to see you are cleverer than I believed."

Julia's voice was shaky with fear and confusion. "Bartholomew? What is this?"

"This, my dear, is my duty," he answered.

Her eyes slid closed, tears tracking down her face. "You're Jagger's man."

"And a far finer man for which I ever gave him credit." Jagger picked up his sword and leveled it at Branna's chest. "Drop your weapon."

Branna couldn't take her eyes off Julia. Her heart pounded and blood roared in her ears. How could she have let this happen? How could she have failed so completely?

Julia met her eyes, shaking her head, her eyes pleading with her not to comply. Branna let her sword drop to the deck with a clatter as Jagger moved close, his hot breath on her face while he slid the remaining blades from the belt at her waist, tossing them to the deck.

Branna's gaze flicked to the rest of her crew. They watched with hatred as the few living *Serpent's Mistress* crew struggled to their feet and armed themselves again. No one else moved beyond that.

"On your knees, Captain—where you belong." Jagger laughed, forcing Branna down with the tip of his sword drawing blood at the hollow of her throat. "Hands on your head."

Branna dropped to the deck, lacing her fingers on top of her head, her chest heaving with fatigue and fury.

"Don't worry, Captain, I didn't see this coming either. Griggs was placed on your ship to...I don't even know. Cause havoc, sabotage, foment unrest, or whatever he could to cause problems, slow you down or exploit a weakness." He laughed as if he'd just told the funniest joke. "Exploit a weakness indeed, Captain. Jesus Christ, I can't believe it. I see my invitation was better received than I had ever intended."

Branna didn't look at him but instead focused on Julia. She stood, unmoving, pinned tightly against Griggs, watching Jagger in horrified defeat. Branna moved her fingers, unlacing them and shifting a hand under each opposite forearm, feeling for the hilt of the blades hidden there. She needed Julia to see her—needed her to understand.

"Were you helping her deal with her grief, Captain Kelly?" Jagger went on nastily. "Because I understand you both have had similar tragedies in your past."

"Fuck you," Branna growled.

Jagger leered at her. "I'll just bet you did, too. Take advantage of her? Tell her you understood her pain so you could get up her skirt? Yes, I've heard the stories and I know all about your... proclivities. You're every bit as ruthless as they say, aren't you, Raven? I'd call you depraved, but really what fault can I assign you for your love of a good woman, hmm? I really was loath to give up Miss Farrow to you, but my sacrifice was rewarded tenfold and here she is, back in my care."

Branna gritted her teeth to keep herself from lunging at him, tearing out his throat with her bare hands and showing him how ruthless she could be. She gazed past him, searching for Gus and met his eyes, imploring him to be ready when she made her move. He stood rigid and expressionless, though his eyes flashed with understanding.

Jagger went on, high on his perceived victory. "Now, I'm going to slaughter your officers and take your crew and your ship. The only question that remains is, do I gut Miss Farrow slowly so you can hear her screams as her blood spills all over your deck? Or do I take her with me and send you to your grave with the vision of her chained in your own hold, savaged by me and my men at a whim?"

Branna's gaze flicked to Julia. Her eyes were glassy and her breathing fast and shallow. Branna tried to let her know it would be all right. She wouldn't let this happen. She would protect her, but Julia was too far gone.

Branna let her eyes drift closed, focusing her mind and slowing her breathing, praying she had the strength to finish this and keep them all alive. When she opened them again, Jagger was looking at her curiously. "Nothing to say, Captain?"

She moved lightning fast, knocking his blade from her throat with her knife and jumping to her feet to send a blade hurtling across the deck to plunge through the throat of Bartholomew Griggs. Julia screamed and fell back with him to the deck, but Branna couldn't yet spare her attention.

Jagger's mouth dropped open in shock and he spun toward her as she lunged, sinking her last blade deep into his chest. He had the oddest look of surprise as he stared at it before staggering back a few steps and falling to the deck on his side.

As soon as Branna moved, Gus and Nat made short work of the rest of the *Serpent's Mistress's* crew. Branna didn't bother checking Jagger but jumped to the gunwale. "Julia!"

CHAPTER TWENTY-ONE

Julia never saw the knife. It all happened so fast. She felt the breeze and heard it whistle past her ear before piercing Griggs's neck. He toppled back, dragging her with him as blood spurted from his neck and his last few breaths came out as wheezing, gurgles, bubbles of blood forming at his lips.

Julia scrambled away from him and pushed herself to her knees as she watched him die. She tore her gaze away when Branna called her name. Even through the day's horrors a small smile came to her lips, seeing Branna standing atop the gunwale—alive, magnificent, and victorious.

The pistol shot startled them all and Branna spun, her legs buckling, before toppling over the side and splashing into the water between the ships.

"Branna!" Julia screamed.

Gus leapt across the deck and skewered Jagger through the eye, the pistol he had taken off one of the bodies falling from his hand.

Julia ran along the gunwale. "I can't see her! Oh, my god, where is she?"

Gus dropped his weapons and kicked out of his boots before grabbing the end of a coiled rope. He tied it around his waist as he ran aft and launched himself from the stern into the sea.

A handful of the crew ran to the side and peered over to watch, all with expressions of varying levels of distress as they played out the rope from the deck to Gus in the water. The rest scrambled to cut down the sails and slow them.

Gus surfaced for a breath some ways behind them now. He peered around through the water, before diving down again, his legs kicking up behind him. Again he came up, this time yelling angrily, "Come on, Branna, come on!" He sucked in a huge breath and dove again.

He was down for a long time. Julia raced back and forth along the gunwale. She didn't remember when she started crying, but she swiped at her eyes with her hands, her vision blurry with tears.

Gus broke the surface, his mouth gulping air loudly, and he wasn't alone. He had Branna, an arm across her chest, her face ashen and slack. He rattled her hard as best as he could from the water and smacked her back while looping the rope around them both to keep them with the ship. After a moment she coughed and gasped with a groan and Julia let out a bark of hysterical laughter.

Gus grinned up at her. "Let down the ladder!"

Julia ran to it and pushed it over the gunwale. The rest of the crew drew in the line and tugged the boarding lines to pull the ships nearer each other so they could get back across. Nat ordered a few men to stay aboard and sweep the *Serpent's Mistress*.

Between Gus, Nat, and Jack they were able to get Branna back on the *Banshee*, sitting her up on the deck. Blood stained the sleeve of her sodden clothes from the pistol round through her upper left arm. Julia dropped to the deck and pulled her into her arms, laying kisses across her face and neck.

"You're okay," she whispered. "Oh, thank god, you're okay."

Branna coughed and returned her embrace weakly. "I'm okay."

Jack left the captain's cabin after cleaning and stitching Branna's wound. He bound her arm tightly across her body. She had resisted getting treatment until the men were attended to. There were some in far worse shape and seven men had been killed—two from cannon fire and five others from the fight on the deck.

The sails of both ships had been reefed, bringing them to a standstill and the bodies of the *Serpent's Mistress's* crew, including Jagger, stacked on the foredeck out of the way. The search and stripping of the *Serpent's Mistress* was ongoing but they were almost through. There were a few other items to attend to before they could get underway back to Nassau.

"Julia, I'm fine," Branna insisted and batted at her hand with her good arm.

Julia continued to dab at the gash on her head with a rum-ooaked oloth. "You're not fine. You have an iron ball in your arm."

Branna took another pull from the rum bottle. "Nah, it went all the way through."

A knock heralded Gus's entrance. He poked his head in the cabin. "We're ready, Captain."

Branna nodded and pushed herself to her feet. "I'll be right there." She turned to Julia and held out her hand. "This is your victory as much as it is mine. Stand with me."

Julia swallowed heavily. "Victory?"

Branna nodded, her lips pressed together, thinly. Part of her struggled with seeing the death of so many as a victory for anyone. "I understand what you're not saying, Julia, but the *Serpent's Mistress* and her crew were a blight on humanity and the absence of them in this world will make it a safer place."

"Captain on deck!" Nat called and the men straightened, those who weren't too seriously injured.

They had mustered on the main deck surrounding the shrouded bodies of their seven dead crew. Branna stood amongst them. "All hands," she called. "Bury the dead."

Gus handed her a battered book of Common Prayer and Branna opened it to the marked passage, the only one she used with any regularity, while Nat called out the names of their fallen crew.

"Cal Moyle, William Gribble, George Kitts, Alden Scott, William Linnington, Robert Rathbone, and Alec Merton."

Branna read in a clear strong voice. "We brought nothing into this world, and it is certain we carry nothing out. The Lord gave, and the Lord hath taken away, blessed be the name of the Lord. We therefore commit these bodies to the deep, looking for the general Resurrection in the last day, and the life of the world to come, through our Lord Jesus Christ."

Silence hung in the air for a moment before the burial detail moved to hoist the first body, throwing it over the side to the sea. Seven times the bodies splashed down and Branna's throat tightened and she saw from the corner of her eye, Julia shudder as each one fell.

The moon was high and the sky clear when Gus cut the lines to the *Serpent's Mistress* and shoved the ship away with a pike. It drifted off their starboard bow as the crew raised the mainsail and set a course for home.

Branna would normally take the shot herself, but wounded, she couldn't shoulder the musket. "Can you see well enough?" she asked Gus as she handed him the weapon.

"Aye," he replied. Several barrels of gunpowder had been brought up from the *Serpent's Mistress's* hold and stacked on the deck. Gus waited a few more moments, letting the ships separate farther, before dropping to brace himself along the gunwale.

He fired once, the report shattering the still night air, and an instant later the gunpowder ignited and the barrels exploded into a mushroom of fire and smoke, rocking the *Banshee* with a blast of heat and noise. The *Serpent's Mistress* caught flame fast and the ship and bodies of the crew burned, the sails flaming and dropping into the sea with a hiss.

Branna watched for a moment, searching herself to try and name her emotions. She was satisfied, but she thought she would feel differently. She expected joy where she only felt loss.

This fight was all she'd known for so long and its end brought a certain amount of emptiness.

The warmth and comfort of Julia's hand slipped into hers and the emptiness of a moment before began to ease. Julia awakened feelings Branna had abandoned long ago and she believed for the first time that she could be whole again. "There's one more matter to attend to," she said softly as she let go of Julia's hand.

All the men stood watching the *Serpent's Mistress* burn so she didn't need to call them together again. Branna backed up a few steps so she could see them all, the flames still burning high behind them as they sailed for Nassau. She nodded to Nat and Gus who hefted a large, battered wooden chest between them and dropped it on the deck.

"It seems the rumors were true. The late Captain Jagger was a cold-blooded savage, a thief, and a murderer," Branna said. She kicked open the lid to reveal gold and silver coins inside. "He was also a very wealthy man."

She looked around the deck. The mens' eyes widened in disbelief at the riches before them. "Upon our return to port, this money will be divided among you—including the families of our lost shipmates—as the terms of the Articles dictate. The total amount distributed will be less an amount I will be setting aside for a fund with Travers Trading to aid those legitimate merchants sailing these waters who have fallen prey to the violence of ships like the *Serpent's Mistress*."

Branna searched the faces of the men and watched for any sign of anger or resentment at her decision. "The *Banshee* will be in port for several months for repairs. If you wish to be relieved of your appointment with this ship, now is the time. You may take your final payment and be on your way with my gratitude and respect at your loyal service to me and this ship."

Branna suddenly felt exhausted and her arm throbbed in time with her pulse. "Mr. Hawke. Take us home."

"Aye, aye, Captain." Gus called the crew to stations and they scattered, talking excitedly amongst themselves.

Branna's shoulders slumped and she breathed out a heavy sigh. She wanted nothing more than to lie down and she looked up to see Julia watching her with pride and pleasure. "Miss Farrow, would you accompany me to my cabin?"

Branna sat at the edge of her bed and let Julia pull off her boots and unbuckle her knife belt. She pushed Branna gently back onto the bed, encouraging her to move to the side so she could slide down next to her. "How do you feel, now?" Julia asked softly and brushed the hair out of her face.

"Tired and...I don't know...content?"

"Content?"

She shrugged, immediately wincing at the pain it caused in her arm. "Maybe that's not the right word. What's the feeling when you have everything you want?"

"There's nothing else you want?"

Branna eyed her with a small smile and reached her good arm around Julia's neck, pulling her down until their lips barely touched. "Maybe one thing."

Their lips met slowly and tenderly for a moment before Julia pulled away to look at her. "I love you, Captain Kelly."

Branna's heart stopped at her words, her throat tightening and eyes burning. She opened her mouth to speak but could not form the words.

"It's okay. You don't have to say anything."

Branna was grateful for Julia's understanding and her face relaxed, eyes shining brightly with need. She worked the buttons on Julia's shirt with one hand, pulling it down, exposing her shoulders and chest and pressing her lips to her bare skin.

Julia frowned, pulling away to still her caresses. "I don't want to hurt you."

Branna grinned, pulling her back close. "Then don't."

Julia's mouth quirked into a smile and she straddled Branna's hips. Her gaze held Branna's while she slowly unbuttoned her shirt and parted the fabric to reveal her small breasts, hard nipples, and taut belly.

Branna sucked in a sharp breath at the exquisite sensations when Julia ran her hands up and down her bare skin, raking her gently with her nails, causing Branna's muscles to quiver beneath her touch.

"Does that hurt?" Julia asked.

Branna shuddered. "Only when you stop."

"Mmm." Julia moaned and lowered herself to take a nipple into her mouth, sucking hard and flicking it with her tongue, sending Branna into a spasm on pleasure. "Nothing to worry about then."

CHAPTER TWENTY-TWO

It took a week to return to Nassau. The *Banshee* had taken considerable damage to the foremast and the spar of the bowsprit had finally given way completely and was lashed to the bow to keep if from dropping into the sea.

Despite the crippled ship and injured crew, spirits were as high as ever as the *Banshee* sailed into their home port. Branna emerged from her cabin, her arm out of the bindings, and stretched carefully, grinning from ear to ear.

There would be a bed waiting for her, for them, and if she could talk Genevieve into setting it up, perhaps a bath large enough for two. She spied Julia on the deck, hair grown long enough to ruffle in the wind as she gazed at the port with her face turned up to the sun. Just the sight of her sent Branna's heart racing and she couldn't stop herself from closing the distance to her quietly and reaching her arms around her waist.

Julia jumped, startled, then leaned back into Branna's embrace. "What about the men?" she asked with a smile.

"I don't care," Branna breathed into her hair. They had been discreet on the trip home, but the ship wasn't that big and they were sure it hadn't gone unnoticed that the purser's quarters were vacant once again. "I've made them all very rich men and if they have a problem with it, they can swim the rest of the way."

"Fair enough." Julia laughed and faced her, lacing her fingers around Branna's neck. "What's the first thing you're going to do after we go ashore?"

"I was thinking a bath followed by a proper meal and a drink and then…" Branna's lips twitched into a smile. "I suppose, I'll see what company I can find."

"Oh? And who do you think is going to be interested in a broken down, sulky, old ship's captain like you?"

"Broken down? I'll take that as a challenge, Miss Farrow."

Julia grinned wickedly. "I meant it as such."

The *Banshee* moored in her usual spot offshore from the port of Nassau but she wouldn't stay long. As soon as the men were paid and ashore and the cargo from the *Serpent's Mistress* offloaded, she would be towed to the repair docks where she would be taken out of the water and the extensive repairs begun.

Branna left Nat aboard to see to the payment of the crew and the unloading of the ship. Jack rowed her, Gus, and Julia to shore. They all sat quietly, their thoughts accompanied by the sound of the rhythmic splashing of the oars as they glided toward the dock.

Branna climbed the ladder and reached her good arm down for Julia. She had healed well but she knew she still ached when she stretched. Julia took her hand, smiling gratefully, as she climbed the ladder and stood with Branna on the dock.

Julia let out a long sigh. "It's good to be home."

"Home?"

"Well, you know what I mean—on land."

"Of course," Branna agreed, fighting a grin. She held out her hand to Julia. "Ready? I'm famished."

Julia laced their fingers together and laid her head on Branna's shoulder as they walked the long dock to shore.

"Hey, there's Genevieve," Jack said from behind them.

From the entrance of Travers, Genevieve was waving to them and Branna waved back with a smile. Genevieve turned to speak with someone behind her and two people emerged from beneath the arch—two women, one their age and one a child—both versions of Julia Farrow. Branna's heart leapt to her throat and her breath caught. She knew who they were immediately—Julia's sisters.

Julia saw them an instant after Branna and stopped on the dock. She blinked, as if uncertain she was seeing correctly. "Oh, my god."

Genevieve chewed her fingers nervously. The Farrow girls were looking as distraught and uncertain as Julia. Branna slipped an arm around Julia's waist. She had paled alarmingly and was still unmoving. "Come on."

Julia began to cry as they neared. She wiped her tearstained face and quickened her pace, breaking into a jog. "Oh, my god! You're here!"

Julia flung herself into Alice's arms and she enveloped her, their tears and cries mingling with each other as they embraced desperately. Young Kelly clung tightly to Julia's waist, sobbing. Branna could only watch, fighting tears of her own and ignoring the slithering dread building in her belly.

"We thought you were dead," Alice sobbed.

"No. No, I'm okay." Julia pulled away to look at her older sister, smiling through her tears.

"What happened to you, Jule? Why didn't you send word?" Kelly cried as she clutched hard to them, both their voices breaking over each other as they all wept and talked at once for several minutes, never letting each other go.

Alice was the first to break from their embrace and straighten, wiping at her eyes. "Branna Kelly? It really is you."

"Yes." Branna cleared her throat. "It's good to see you, Alice."

Kelly Farrow stepped forward, inhaling deeply and squaring her shoulders as she met Branna's eyes and extended her hand in greeting. "I'm Kelly Farrow. Thank you for my sister's life."

Branna swallowed heavily as she shook her namesake's hand. She could only nod in response, her lips pressed together tightly. There was so much she wanted to say but she didn't know how. "It's an honor to meet you, Kelly Farrow."

Alice took a deep breath. "We should go back to the house. We can talk there and Julia can get some rest."

A man strode down toward them, grinning widely. It was Alice's husband, Arnold Ainsworth. "Miss Travers has been very kind and put us up in one of her vacant properties, Julia," he said as he bent to embrace her and kiss her cheek. "There's enough room for you, too, and we won't be here much longer anyway."

Julia wiped at her face and took a deep shuddering breath. "What do you mean?"

Branna felt her heart stop—the dread uncoiling and rising within her. She knew what was coming next. Her gaze flicked to Genevieve whose sympathetic expression told her she was right.

"We came down on the *Starlight*," Arnold said. "It returns to Charlestown the day after tomorrow."

Julia turned and met Branna's gaze in an unnamable expression of disbelief. Branna wondered if Julia could hear her heart breaking and she felt a pain so acute she thought for sure a knife had just been plunged into her chest.

"So soon?" Julia whispered, her eyes never leaving Branna.

Branna clamped down on her grief, unwilling to let Julia see, and forced a smile. "You must be anxious to get home," she said in a voice much steadier than she thought possible.

Genevieve looked between them. "I'll see you back to the house," she said and gestured for Julia's family to head back up the pathway.

Julia had supper with her family at the house, the doors open to let in the warm harbor breeze, fluttering the drapes and bringing in the smell of the sea. Her head had calmed somewhat and she could see her sisters clearly for the first time.

They told her what it had been like when word of the attack on the *Firelight* had reached them. It was awful to hear and all three began to cry again as they spoke of all the people they lost and how hurt and terrified they had been for her.

Julia briefly spoke of what had happened to her, her rescue and her eventual time aboard the *Banshee*. She left out a lot—her stowing away, her part in the battle with the *Serpent's Mistress*, and her relationship with Branna Kelly. She couldn't even speak Branna's name without her throat closing in sadness at the thought of leaving her again.

It didn't matter. None of them were too keen to dwell on the details of the horrors they had all faced. It was over and they were all together again. They were going home. Julia sat, legs curled under her on a bench, and watched the ships coming and going in the harbor. She couldn't see the *Banshee* but she knew she was there and she knew Branna was nearby.

Julia found Genevieve in the morning going through her usual cleanup, emptying ash cans and collecting cups from the night before. As soon as Genevieve saw her, she dropped what she was doing and pulled Julia into a tight embrace.

"Oh, Julia," she said and hugged her fiercely. "I'm so glad you're all right. I was so worried about you."

"I'm okay. I'm happy to be back."

Genevieve pulled away but glared at her sharply. "What the bloody hell did you think you were doing? You could've been killed."

"I know. I'm so sorry, Gen. I never wanted to betray your trust or seem ungrateful for everything you've done for me. I just wanted…I needed to…"

Genevieve's face softened. "It's all right. I was scared for you and I'm so happy to see you safe—both of you."

"Where is she?"

She released Julia's arms and steepled her hands in front of her mouth. "I don't know."

"What do you mean? What did she say?"

"I'm sorry, Julia. She wouldn't talk to me. She didn't say anything and then she left. I don't know where she is and neither does anyone else."

"I don't understand." She looked around as if Branna would somehow mysteriously appear. "She knows I'm leaving tomorrow morning?"

"She knows."

"I see." Julia pushed away her hurt and disappointment. "I should get back to my sisters."

"Julia," Genevieve called to her back. "I'm sorry."

* * *

The wind was high and the sky clear as they stood on the dock ready to be rowed out to the Farrow Company ship that would take them home. Julia turned when she heard booted feet thundering across the wooden dock. Jack, Gus, Genevieve and Merriam were racing toward them.

"You didn't think we'd let you leave without saying goodbye, did you?" Jack said, sweeping Julia up into his arms and hugging her tightly.

Julia laughed and kissed his cheek. "Thank you for coming."

Jack set her down and Gus moved in, hugging her close. "Stay safe," he whispered.

She nodded, her throat clogging with emotion. Merriam's eyes shone brightly with unshed tears as she pulled her into an embrace. "We're gonna miss ya 'round here. 'Cept for Gen, I never had a real friend."

"I'm going to miss you all, too." She struggled not to cry as she released her.

"There's always a place for you here," Genevieve said before wrapping her in her arms.

"Thank you. For everything."

She smiled at each of them in turn. Her next words died in her throat when her gaze was drawn to movement behind them. The dock workers split down the middle to get out of the way of Captain Kelly, striding down the dock toward them.

Her heart lurched. She didn't think Branna was coming and she couldn't take her eyes off her as she walked, straight and proud, stopping a few feet from her. "You're here," she breathed.

"I wanted to give you this." She held out a small leather satchel, heavy and bulging. It clinked slightly when Branna shifted her grip on it. "It's your share of the money from the *Serpent's Mistress*. Enough to cover repairs to your ship and loss of cargo and see that the families of the crew are taken care of."

Julia stared at the satchel and then back at Branna, making no move to take it. "I don't need or want your money."

Arnold Ainsworth stepped over. "Don't be foolish, Julia," he said and took the satchel from Branna. "Thank you, Captain Kelly. Your honor and generosity are very much appreciated. I'll see that this gets distributed to the families of the men that were lost. Is there anything we can do for you, Captain? There must be someone in Charlestown we can contact for you and tell them—"

"No, thank you, Mr. Ainsworth. I would thank you *not* to mention my name at all. If you must speak of me, use the name Raven. There is no one in Charlestown that needs to know or would care to know of my survival."

"As you wish. Thank you again. We have to go now, Julia," he said and stepped down into the boat waiting to take them to the ship, and joined her sisters already seated in the bow.

Julia's brow furrowed. "Is that all you have to say to me?"

Branna pulled a book from behind her, tucked into her waist, and handed her the battered leather-bound copy of *Robinson Crusoe* tied closed with a leather cord. "I have this for you, too. I thought you might like to finish it."

Julia took the book with a trembling hand and clutched it to her chest. "Branna, I love you. Did this mean nothing to you?"

"Fair winds, Miss Farrow," Branna said before turning away.

"Branna!"

She slowed for a moment but didn't turn around.

"Fair winds, Captain Kelly," Julia whispered.

CHAPTER TWENTY-THREE

Branna felt Julia's arm slip around her hip, her fingers fanning out to caress her belly and slide up to cup her breast from behind. Branna shifted in the bed, pressing herself back against her, feeling Julia's curves as they molded against her back, and sighed with the first stirrings of arousal.

She loved waking up to Julia's hands on her, teasing and stroking her desire until she could barely breathe with the wanting. Julia was so beautiful and she bit down on her lip as a soft groan of pleasure escaped her. She turned in Julia's arms, smiling lazily, searching for her lips.

Branna's eyes slid open with a deep shuddering breath and she sat up alone in the bed, choking back a sob. She hugged her knees to her chest to tamp down her deep aching need. Julia was gone. It had been nearly a month, and every day Branna awoke, praying the hole in her heart would close over. The pain of her heartache was so great she thought she would surely die of it, and often wished it to be the case.

Julia would be home by now, safe and with her family. She could return to her life and soon her time in the Caribbean would be a distant memory, a healed-over wound, or an exciting story to tell her friends.

Branna had stayed at Travers while the *Banshee* was being repaired. It would be another month yet. Since Branna had the money, she was having her refitted and upgraded as well. Soon it would be time to round up the crew, see who wanted to sign back on and get back to work.

In the meantime, somehow she thought it would be a good idea to stay in Julia's old room. The linens had been laundered but Branna imagined she could still smell Julia on the pillow. She regretted it now. All it did was bring back the memories, once so deliciously sweet but now excruciatingly painful.

She wouldn't tell Genevieve, though, and instead she'd put on a brave face. When she wasn't patrolling the island with her officers, routing out men still loyal to Jagger, she oversaw the repairs and upgrades to the ship, stayed abreast of what was going on out on the water by conversing with the other captains and making plans for when she would return to her life at sea.

The atmosphere at Travers, the docks, and everywhere in town was noticeably lighter with the knowledge that Captain Jagger and the *Serpent's Mistress* were no longer out there. Before, crowds parted for her out of fear, but now it was out of reverence, gratitude, and respect. She had rid the world of a singular evil, and it seemed even the sun shone brighter. She wished Julia, who had thought the town vibrant before, could see what they had accomplished.

Morrigan leapt up onto the bed and let out a yowl for attention that snapped her out of her reverie. She scratched the cat behind her ear. "You miss her too, don't you?" she said as she purred and nuzzled her hand.

* * *

Julia sat on the veranda of their house overlooking the gardens. They had been home nearly a fortnight. The weather had been good and the winds high. Her ribs had fully healed and she had helped the crew on the journey home. Anything to keep her mind off Branna and everything she had left behind.

Alice had returned to her life in Charlestown society and Kelly to her schooling, both of them excited to share the story of their adventure to Nassau to rescue Julia. Julia saw to it that the families of their lost crew had received the money Branna had offered them. It wasn't enough, could never be enough to cover the loss of their husbands, fathers, sons and brothers, but Branna had been very generous.

Julia's gaze swept across the green grass and gently swaying trees before returning to the table in front of her and resting on the book Branna had given her. She carried it everywhere, never opening it. It was the only thing she had of Branna's besides the memory, still raw and sweet in her heart.

Alice set a cup of tea in front of her. "May I join you?"

"Of course."

"You look a million miles away. Tell me what you're thinking about."

Julia shrugged and let out a long sigh. "It's nothing."

"Julia, the last time you looked like this was right after the *Rebellion* left when we were young. You may think I don't know you or know what happened between you and father, but I do. I know heartache when I see it."

Julia's head snapped up to her sister and her mouth opened wordlessly in surprise. She had wanted to talk to her sister about it so badly but she didn't want her to think she wasn't happy to be home and back with them. "Oh."

Alice smiled. "My marriage to Arnie may not have been born of love but love has grown deeply between us and I cannot imagine life without him now. We have suffered many losses, you and I, but when I feared you were dead, it was the worst pain I've ever felt in my life. But I had Arnie and our children and we were alive. We would go on."

"I'm so happy for you, Alice, I am."

"I want that for you, too, Julia. Arnie and I both do."

"What are you saying?"

Her sister reached across the table and gripped Julia's hands in her own and met her gaze with the love, understanding and encouragement only a sister could provide. "I'm saying, Julia, you need to follow your heart. If there is someone out there for you that can be what Arnold and I are to each other, then you need to hold on to that. I'll make Arnie understand. We won't stand in your way and we won't let society turn their back on you for your…unconventional relationship."

"Oh, god, I love her so much, Alice," she whispered as tears spilled down her face.

"And does she feel the same?"

"I don't know. I thought so, but then she just walked away. I just don't know."

"Just to be clear, we're talking about Branna Kelly, right?"

"Why do you say it like that?"

Her sister shrugged. "I never knew her like you did when we were children, and certainly, I don't know her at all now, but I got the impression she's not particularly demonstrative."

Julia couldn't help a small laugh. She smiled and looked out at the gardens, lost again in thoughts of Branna. "She is with me—sometimes. There's so much more to her, though. She's smart and compassionate. Fiercely protective and loyal. And she has so much courage. She can be so gentle and no one has ever infuriated me as much as she does."

"She strikes me as quite a remarkable woman."

"She is. But I can't just do whatever I want. What about Kelly?"

Alice rose, her fingers tapping on the book, before she slid it in front of her sister. "Kelly and I want nothing but for you to be happy, Julia. Kelly positively worships you, and god help us, wants to be just like you. You know that. She would hate to know you held yourself back for her. Don't you dare let us stand in your way. Do you hear me?"

Julia swallowed around the tightness in her throat and managed a nod before her sister disappeared back into the house.

* * *

Branna had declined to accompany the men on yet another search of the ruins of Fort Nassau when they had received a report that some of Jagger's agents may be hiding out there. For the last several weeks she had tried to ease her pain by inflicting it on others. Deserving of her wrath or not, it failed to make her feel better and holding on to her rage only seemed to make her feel even more distant from the memory of Julia.

She chose instead to walk through the market in the afternoon, in no particular hurry, and with no agenda. She stopped to browse the crafts and tools. She ate grilled chicken on a stick and kicked a ball back to some children whose game got away from them.

She could feel the eyes on her, wary and disbelieving. Perhaps they thought she had lost her mind when she stopped at the juice vendor and asked for a drink. The taste reminded her of Julia and pain squeezed her chest and tightened her throat as she continued through the square.

Now she didn't want to be the Captain Kelly everyone feared. She wanted to be the woman Julia saw in her. She tried to school her expression into one more pleasant and even tried smiling at people as they walked by. Folks still kept their distance. She supposed it would take some time.

She was surprised when she was jostled from behind and she dropped her drink. She spun around, opening her mouth to apologize, when the man's fist shot out, punching her in the stomach. She doubled over with a grunt and clutched her abdomen. She looked curiously at her hands as dark red blood spilled through her fingers.

"Not so tough now, are you, Raven?" Virgil Bunt's words came out on a hiss of fetid breath.

Branna blinked stupidly as he walked away, before blinding pain sent her to her knees in the middle of the square. She tried to call out for help but made only a strangled sound as her body failed and dropped her onto her back. She could feel blood pumping out around her with every frantic beat of her heart as she stared up at the clear blue sky.

People screamed and booted feet thundered along the stone ground. Hands pressed against her middle and distant voices called her name. She couldn't feel any more pain. "Julia..." she whispered before her eyes slid closed.

An inhuman scream rang in her ears and Julia bolted up in her bed, her hands clawing frantically at her stomach. She was overwhelmed with panic and a flash of pain knifed through her.

"Bloody hell," she gasped when she realized she was in her room at home. She hadn't intended to fall asleep. Branna's book lay open next to her on the bed where it must have fallen when she sat up, the cord coming loose. She picked it up carefully, realizing the pages were carved out in the middle in a small square from which tumbled a piece of gold.

Her breath caught. It was Branna's ring, the one she had given her all those years ago as a promise of her love, and the one she thought she had lost. She slipped it on the first finger of her left hand and clutched her hand tightly to her breast, her heart filled with love—and fear.

She paced her room, spinning the ring around on her finger, throwing open the windows to let in the fresh air and dispel her unease. Something was wrong. Racing down the stairs, she found her family at the table having supper.

"Julia?" Alice said, seeing her panic. "You were sleeping so soundly we didn't want to wake you. Is everything all right?"

"I don't know. I must have been dreaming." Her sisters appeared fine but a bit confused and concerned for her. "You're both okay?"

Kelly and Alice shared a worried glance. "We're fine, Jule," Kelly answered.

"Come and sit down, Julia," Arnold said. "There's something I want to talk to you about."

Julia took a steadying breath and tried to ignore her anxiety as she pulled up a chair at the table. "What is it?"

"I managed Farrow Company while you were away, and with the *Starlight's* most recent successful voyage, we're going to be sending her back to honor the trade agreements you set up with the Swansboroughs in Port Royal." His eyes flicked to Alice and she gave him a small nod of encouragement. "The *Starlight* is leaving again for the Caribbean at the end of the week."

Julia stared at him, unable to wrap her head around whatever he was trying to say.

Kelly sighed loudly, frowning at her sister's silence. "Jule, do you want to go back? It's okay if you do."

Julia's head whipped to her little sister, her eyes going wide. Go back? That was absurd. She just got here. Fear tightened around her heart again and she struggled to focus on her sisters. "I don't...I can't think..." she mumbled, unsure if she was even speaking aloud. She wiped at the sweat beading across her forehead.

"Julia?" Alice asked, concerned. "What's wrong? Are you ill?"

"No. I don't know. I just have this overwhelming feeling something terrible has happened."

CHAPTER TWENTY-FOUR

Despite her unease, Julia stood steady on the deck of the *Starlight* as Nassau came into view. She could see land and her heart thudded in her chest at how close she was. The journey had been fast, only a week. After the attacks on the Farrow Company ships they decided the best defense was speed.

The ship was efficient and light, at least without cargo, and the winds had been in their favor the entire way. Julia had enjoyed working alongside the crew, as much as she could enjoy anything. It was the only thing she could do to keep fear from overwhelming her. She was terrified of what she was going to find, but she knew she had to come back as fast as she could.

"Tacking!" the first mate bellowed, snapping her out of her head.

She jumped to tend to her lines. She would be there soon. She would find Branna and ease her troubled heart.

She changed quickly in her quarters from the pants and shirt she crewed in to a simple skirt and blouse, sliding Branna's ring onto her finger. She slung her satchel across her chest and hurried back out to the deck to get a spot on the first boat to shore. She had brought little with her. Only some clothes, money, and a few personal items. She didn't need much.

The ship would be staying in port for only a few days before heading on to Port Royal and from there making the journey back to Charlestown. She didn't intend to be on it but she was still confused with the way Branna had treated her when she left nearly two months ago. She supposed Branna and the *Banshee* may not even be here.

She chewed her lip and spun the ring around her finger as the boat made its way to shore, the men talking excitedly around her. The boat had barely pulled alongside the dock when she scrambled up the ladder and hurried her way to Travers Trading.

Julia stepped beneath the archway and slowed, uncertain of what she was seeing. It was midday and the courtyard was full of sailors and ladies alike, but instead of the raucous lively energy, there was a heavy pall hanging in the air. The low rumble of conversation sounded like thunder before a storm about to break, and in fact, there appeared to be more than one brawl simmering.

Julia saw no one she knew, though more than a few heads turned her way. She didn't see Genevieve or Merri anywhere and she made her way to the stairs and ascended swiftly to the second floor. A familiar flash of orange and white stalked over. A much-grown Morrigan stopped her hunt as Julia came up the steps.

"Hello, sweetheart," she murmured, for a second believing everything was fine as she stroked the cat for a moment before she streaked off again about her business.

The heaviness in her heart grew anew with every step she took toward the open door of the room she'd used during what felt like a lifetime ago. She recognized the voices coming from within.

"If I have to listen to that fool say one more time how lucky she is that the blade was so dull it didn't shred her guts, I'm going to punch him in the throat," Gus growled.

"He's the best there is," Genevieve replied, sounding exhausted.

"Well, he's bloody well cracked if he thinks putting those things in her is a treatment. Bloody disgusting little worms."

"It's the only way, Gus. They eat the infected tissue, keep the wound clean and keep the infection from getting into her blood."

"It's mad!"

"She'll die, otherwise!"

"Maybe… Oh, god help me, maybe that's for the best."

"What did you say?"

"She wouldn't want this, Gen. Look at her."

"I have! I do! Every goddamn day and night!"

"You know I'm right. You know she would hate this. Being so sick and weak, and the pain…"

"We're managing it."

"Yeah. By having your girl breathe that fucking poison into her."

"Opium is the only thing that works. Goddamn it, Gus, I'm doing the best I can. I love her, too."

"I know. I'm sorry, Gen. I just wish there was something more we could do."

Julia trembled. She'd heard enough. She knew now what she was going to find in that room, but her heart refused to believe. "Hello?"

Gus and Genevieve whirled around with similar expressions of shock at the sight of her.

"Julia!" Genevieve rushed to her, pulling her into her arms. "What are you doing here? How did you get here?"

Julia looked frantically from Genevieve to Gus. "What's happened?" she asked, as she took in the hazy air and her mind registered the smell of infection and sweet, pungent smoke. Julia could see the outline of someone in the bed through the filmy netting and moved toward it.

"Julia." Genevieve gripped her arm to stop her. "You can't go in there right now. Wait for the smoke to clear."

"Branna?" She pulled out of Genevieve's grip.

Her hands shook and her heart beat madly in her chest as she pulled the netting aside. Branna lay unmoving, her head turned toward the open doors to the sea, her heavy-lidded eyes unseeing and dull. "Oh, god, Branna," she breathed and dropped to her knees at the side of the bed.

Genevieve came to stand behind her. "Julia, we're doing everything we can."

Tears sprang to her eyes, flowing steadily down her face as she took in the sight of Branna. She was thin, her skin clammy and flushed. Her hair was lank and her face slack, showing no hint of recognition that anyone was there. Julia looked down the length of her. She wore only a thin shirt, buttoned across her chest. Her middle was exposed but wrapped heavily in bandages stained with pink and yellow fluid seeping from an unseen wound in her belly, the rest of her covered with a sheet.

She picked up Branna's limp hand. "How did this happen?"

"We have to go, Julia," Genevieve insisted and pulled Julia away. "Let's talk outside and we'll explain everything. We'll come back later."

Julia sobbed a breath and let Genevieve pull her from the room. Gus closed the door and the three of them headed back to the courtyard.

Julia dropped her head into her hands. The source of all her fear was obvious. Branna was near death and somehow she'd felt it.

She gratefully accepted the glass of rum from Gus when the three of them settled at a table in the courtyard. "What happened?"

Gus shrugged. "Branna was attacked in the square and stabbed once. It happened fast from what I understand, though there were plenty of witnesses. We know it was Virgil Bunt. Nat and Jack are running him to ground. The filthy coward is proving surprisingly elusive. He has help on the island—Jagger's men, for sure. We've been clearing them out as fast as we can, but…"

"I don't understand. She was just stabbed?" Julia looked between them, incredulously. "Branna would never let that happen. I mean she was so vigilant. Was she armed?"

Genevieve and Gus shared a look.

"No," Genevieve said.

Julia frowned, shaking her head. This wasn't the Captain Kelly she knew—wary, cautious, and prepared for anything. "I don't understand."

"She was just out for a walk, Julia. She'd been doing that a lot since you left."

"A walk?"

"To get to know the town better, she told me," Gus added.

Julia stared at them, understanding. She steepled her hands in front of her face to cover her pained expression. She didn't know whether to laugh or cry. "Oh, Branna."

Genevieve poured herself more rum and topped up Julia's glass. "Julia, we're thrilled to see you, but what are you doing here? Did you even get home?"

"Yes. We got home safely. My family is all fine and settled back in their lives."

"Do they know you're here?" Gus asked.

She couldn't help a small laugh. It was an obvious question given her track record. "Yes. It was almost their idea."

"Christ, I'm so bloody glad you're here," Gen blurted and tossed back her drink.

"When did this happen? How long has she been like this?"

Gus answered, "About two weeks ago."

Julia covered her mouth with her hand and looked away, tears springing to her eyes. It was true. She had felt it, perhaps in the moment it happened.

"Are you all right?" Genevieve asked.

"Yes." She didn't want to try and explain. It didn't matter anyway. She was here now. "Tell me what I can do."

Gus offered a hard stare. "Give her something to live for."

Julia carried the basin of cool water and cloths to Branna's room. She entered quietly, not wanting to disturb Branna, though Gus and Genevieve had insisted Branna wasn't aware of anything. She set the water on the floor and pulled back the netting. Branna lay as she had before, her eyes closed to slits, her body still and breathing shallow.

Julia sat gently on the edge of the bed and placed a hand across her forehead. Her skin was damp and she burned with the fight raging inside her body. She unbuttoned her shirt, exposing her chest, and ran the cool cloth across her face, neck and chest, wiping away the sick sweat. She had offered to change Branna's dressings but Genevieve had said no. The doctor was taking care of that and would be there in the morning. She told her about the gruesome treatment to keep blood poisoning at bay and Julia had not pushed too hard. She knew Genevieve was right and she didn't want to see that. Just the knowledge that the wound was infested with maggots, however helpful they were being, was enough to set her hand to shaking.

She soaked the cloth again, running it along Branna's arms. She laced their fingers together and took a shuddering breath as Branna's hand lay limply in her own. "Branna," she whispered. "I'm here." She waited for any sign of recognition but got nothing.

It didn't matter and Julia was determined to stay by her side, to either help her get well or see her through to the end. She knew Branna might not recover from this. She would be here for her, regardless of the outcome.

Genevieve came in with bedding and set it down on the divan. "Are you sure you wouldn't rather have your own room? I can put you—"

"No. Thank you. I need to be here."

Genevieve nodded and made no secret she was grateful for the help. She had been caring for Branna since the attack and Julia could see she was worn out and her business was suffering.

The sound of breaking glass and angry voices from the courtyard brought Julia to her feet.

Genevieve sighed, her eyes drifting closed. "Nearly every night, now."

"Who is it? Surely Jagger's men wouldn't dare come here."

"It's…unclear," Gen admitted. "There are still some followers of Jagger's ways on the island. Some trouble comes from men just looking to be the next worst thing, and with Branna…" She gestured vaguely. "Well, tensions are running high."

"Are we safe?"

Gen smiled wanly. "As safe here as you would be anywhere in Nassau. I have some things to take care of but I'll never be far. You know where to find me. Nat is staying on the hunt for the scum who did this, but Gus is around and Jack will be with Merriam when he returns. You know where her room is, right?"

Julia nodded. "Thank you."

CHAPTER TWENTY-FIVE

Morning came quickly and Julia sat up, rubbing grainy eyes. She levered herself off the divan, which she had pushed to the side of the bed.

Branna's eyes were partially open again and staring toward the sea. Julia couldn't help believing that deep down some part of Branna was completely aware and drawn to the view of the clear sky and rolling waves. She knew it would be soothing for her.

Her breathing was slow and even and her skin looked a little less flushed and felt a little less hot this morning. It could only be a good thing. There was a soft knock before Genevieve opened the door and entered followed by a slightly built, good-looking man maybe a few years older than her.

"Julia, this is Benjamin Tuttle," Genevieve said. "He's been treating Branna and he's here to change her dressing and check the wound." She gestured to Julia. "This is Julia Farrow. She's a close friend of Captain Kelly."

"Pleased to meet you, Miss Farrow," Benjamin said as he came around to the side of the bed, arms laden with supplies.

Julia moved out of the way to let him sit next to Branna. He placed his hand across her head, lifted her lids to peer into her eyes, and placed his ear to her chest to listen to her heartbeat.

"She seems to be doing well today," he said. "How was her night?"

"Quiet, I guess." She didn't know what other information he wanted to hear.

He pulled gently at the soiled bandages. "Let's see what we have here."

Julia bit down on her lip, grimacing as he peeled away wet bandages to reveal the open wound, roiling with wriggling, white larva—spilling out onto Branna's belly.

"Oh, god," she choked, her hand covering her mouth.

"Hmm," Benjamin mused as he began to clear out the maggots with tweezers and place them in a cup. "This looks good. Well done, fellas." He inspected the edges of the wound, prodding gently and nodding to himself. He turned to them finally with a small smile. "I think she has a real chance."

"What happens now?" Genevieve asked.

Benjamin bobbed his head back and forth as if undecided. "I'm going to close this wound and god willing, it will start to heal and we won't have to open it again." He began to unpack his instruments next to Branna on the bed.

"Do you need anything from us right now?" Genevieve asked.

"No, thank you," he chirped, humming to himself as he threaded suture through a sharp, hooked needle. "I'll come find you when I'm through."

Genevieve slipped an arm around Julia's waist. "She's in good hands. Let's get some coffee."

Julia let Genevieve guide her out of the room. She wanted to stay but there was nothing she could do, and she would be the first to admit she could use some fresh air.

Gus and Merriam were at a table in the courtyard when they came down. Gus stood when he saw them, pulling out chairs for them. Merriam jumped to her feet and pulled Julia into a fierce embrace.

"When Gus told me ya was here I didn't believe him." She shrieked and squeezed Julia tightly. "How did ya know to come back?"

Julia barked a laugh at the question, wondering if Merriam would believe she had a feeling she was needed and that something had been gravely wrong. "Um, I didn't. I just—"

"It don't matter. We're so glad ya did, though. We've missed ya and Branna had been wanderin' 'round like a little lost pup, pining away since ya left. And I mean, if this hadn't happened, she probably woulda died of a broken heart."

"Merriam." Genevieve and Gus cut her off simultaneously.

Julia stared at her. "I don't know what to say. When I left she didn't say anything. I didn't know what to think."

Whatever they were going to say next was interrupted when Benjamin Tuttle came down the stairs. They all stood, looking at him expectantly.

"The wound closed nicely, all things considered," he said. "Her fever should break now that the infection is under control."

The four breathed a collective sigh of relief. "Thank you, Benjamin," Genevieve said.

"Closing the wound was hard on her. She's experiencing a considerable amount of discomfort. Whatever you've been doing to ease her pain..." He cleared his throat. "You may want to proceed."

"I'll get Selina," Merriam said and moved off across the courtyard to interrupt a woman at work with a table of sailors.

Julia remembered her as the woman Branna was with the first night she spent at Travers after her rescue. She was uncertain of Selina's role in this and headed upstairs behind Gus and Genevieve.

Branna was agitated, her eyes rolling erratically and she tried to pluck at the bandages across her middle with a low groan of pain. Beads of sweat dotted her brow and her breathing was labored.

Julia sucked in a breath. She couldn't stand to see her like this and stroked a hand down her face. "Shhh. Just breathe, Branna."

Branna couldn't hear her and was wracked with pain, her mouth open in wordless agony.

Tears sprang to Julia's eyes. "What can we do?"

"Selina's coming," Genevieve offered by way of explanation. "She can help."

Julia frowned as the woman swept into the room and gestured for Julia to move.

"Let me," Selina said and took Julia's place at the edge of the bed. She smoothed her hand across Branna's brow much as Julia had done moments before. "Rest easy, love, you'll feel better soon."

Genevieve pulled Julia away to the doorway with them. Selina lit a pipe, drawing deeply on it to suck the smoke into her lungs. She placed her hands on either side of Branna's head to still her and covered her mouth with her own, exhaling into her.

Branna stilled as the smoke filled her for a moment before trickling up out of her nose and mouth as she exhaled raggedly.

Selina repeated the procedure several times. The room filled again with the sickly sweet stench and Julia could see when Branna's body relaxed and her eyes glazed with the stupor of drugs.

Selina's eyes drifted closed for a few moments before she collected her things and rose from the bed. She moved slowly toward the door, her eyes glassy and a languid smile on her face. "She'll be okay now for a while."

"Thank you, Selina," Genevieve said tightly.

Genevieve pulled Julia from the room again and jerked her head to Gus and Merriam to follow as she headed back downstairs to the courtyard. "You can return later."

* * *

"'And which I take notice of here, to put those discontented people in mind of it, who cannot enjoy comfortably what God has given them, because they see and covet something that he has not given them. All our discontents about what we want appeared to me to spring from the want of thankfulness for what we have.'" Julia read to Branna from a new copy of *Robinson Crusoe*, her left hand turning the pages of the book resting in her lap, the fingers of her right laced with Branna's. Morrigan had taken time out of her busy day to wind around Julia's feet and she was grateful for the company.

She turned the page, her head snapping up when she felt a twitch in her hand so slight she wondered if it had been real. Branna's eyes were closed and a single tear slid down her face. She moved the book from her lap and leaned closer to her, lifting Branna's hand and pressing it to her lips. "Branna? Can you hear me?"

There it was again. A twitch of Branna's finger and this time Julia felt it against her lips. She was in there and she knew she was here, or she knew someone was. Julia sucked in a breath. "Branna, I love you. Please, come back to me."

Julia refused to leave Branna again, lest she miss some sign of her waking. It had been two days since her wound had been closed and her fever had broken. She had beaten the infection that raged in her. Julia spent the long days reading to her and spooning water and broth into her.

She remained unconscious but seemingly comfortable and Selina had not returned, a blessing for which Julia was tremendously grateful. Genevieve had warned her to look for signs of withdrawal from the drugs but Julia had seen none thus far.

A change in Branna's breathing had Julia sitting up from the divan with a start. She pushed her growing mop of hair out of her face to see Branna staring at her, her brow furrowed and her mouth moving soundlessly around Julia's name.

"Branna," Julia breathed and clutched her hand desperately. "Oh, my god, Branna. Can you hear me?"

Branna swallowed, her eyes drifting closed until she could drag them back open. "Julia," she whispered before she slipped away again.

Julia laughed through her tears and brought Branna's hand to her lips, kissing her palm. "Yes, I'm here. I'm here."

Julia was washing up when she heard a weak cry from Branna. She whirled at the sound and crossed the room, jerking the netting from the bed. Branna's eyes were open, her face tight with pain, her hands clenched into the bedding by her sides as she struggled to breathe.

"Easy. Easy," Julia soothed as she sank down on the edge of the bed and smoothed a hand across Branna's brow. Her eyes were bright and wild, her breathing ragged, and Julia wondered if she should get help. "Branna, breathe." She placed a hand gently over her chest and could feel her heart racing against her palm. She fixed Branna with her eyes and took a slow deep breath. "Breathe. Come on, breathe with me."

Branna blinked, confused and disoriented, before she focused on Julia's face. She let out a slow shuddering breath along with Julia.

"That's it," Julia murmured as Branna's breathing evened out and her face began to relax.

"You're okay. Just breathe." She continued to chant, her hand on Branna's chest feeling her heartbeat slow.

Branna's eyes drifted closed and she swallowed with difficulty before dragging them open again. "Julia," she said with effort.

Julia reached for the water on the table and moved her hand around the back of Branna's head to lift her gently. "Small sips."

Branna rolled the water around in her mouth before swallowing. Her hand trembled and jerked as she attempted to raise it.

Julia saw and gripped it tightly between her two. "I'm here." She smiled and brushed a kiss across the back of Branna's hand. "You're going to be okay."

"What...are you...doing..."

"I left something here I had to come back for."

"What?"

"My heart," she breathed and the tears finally fell when she saw Branna's lips twitch in the beginnings of a smile before she sighed deeply, her body claimed by sleep once again.

CHAPTER TWENTY-SIX

Julia ran the cool damp cloth across Branna's chest once more before dropping it back into the bowl. Branna hadn't awakened again but her breathing was deep and even and her face free of pain. She picked up the brush and ran it gently through Branna's hair as best she could without moving her.

Branna came awake slowly and she turned into the hands on her head and struggled to open her eyes.

"Hi," Julia said softly.

"What happened?" she rasped.

Julia was quick with the water glass again and encouraged Branna to drink. "You were attacked in the market. Do you remember?"

Branna's head sank back into the pillow, her eyes sliding closed as she gave a small shake of her head. "I don't...I don't know. Who?"

"I'm not sure. I heard Gus say it was a man you refused work to right before the *Banshee* sailed last—Virgil something." Julia studied Branna's reaction and could see she was getting agitated with the inability to remember. She laid a hand on her shoulder.

"Bunt," she said and shifted in the bed to try and sit up. "He stabbed me—I remember."

"Don't," Julia warned too late and Branna groaned, squeezed her eyes shut, and brought her arm across her middle as she gasped for breath.

Branna grasped Julia's hand as she worked through the pain. After a moment she opened her eyes and looked down at their joined hands. "You're wearing my ring."

"I am. Thank you for giving it back to me."

"When did this happen? The attack?"

Julia had to think for a minute. "The better part of a month ago."

Whatever Branna was going to say next was stopped by a soft thump as Genevieve pushed the door open with her foot, her arms laden with a tray of food. She saw Branna was awake and she hurriedly set the tray on the table and moved to the bed.

Genevieve looked hard at her friend, her expression alternating between elated relief, concern, and anger. "Goddamn you, Branna." Her voice was thick with emotion as she picked up Branna's hand.

Branna breathed a small laugh followed immediately by a grimace. "Damn."

"Well, that's what you get when you let some bottom-feeder skewer you in the marketplace."

Branna smiled more carefully this time. "I appreciate your sympathy, Gen."

Genevieve eyed her carefully. "How do you feel?"

"How do I look?"

"Like pig shit. But a hell of a lot better than a few days ago."

"I have you to thank for that?"

"It was a group effort." It was clear she didn't want Branna to know how hard she had fought for her. It would embarrass them both.

Branna's expression said she knew how much Genevieve wasn't saying but let it drop. They weren't the sentimental kind. "Thank you."

Genevieve grunted. "You owe me."

Branna's eyes drifted toward the tray Genevieve had brought in. "Food?"

"Don't get too excited. It's just marrow broth. I'll let Julia deal with your pathetic inability to feed yourself and go let the others know how you're doing."

Branna nodded, swallowing hard and fighting tears.

"They'll want to see you," Genevieve added. "Are you up for it?"

Branna nodded. "In a little while."

"Later, then." She smiled and headed for the door.

Julia turned away quickly when she saw Genevieve's shoulders begin to shake with silent tears. Her hands covered her face as she swept out the door. She hadn't wanted them to see and Julia didn't want to intrude.

She propped pillows behind her and fed Branna carefully, making every effort not to spill on her or do anything to draw attention to how weak she still was. Julia knew Branna must be horrified at needing this kind of help when her whole life had been built around her strength, determination, and resolve. She needed Branna to hang on to all that in order to get well and not feel defeated.

Branna only managed to get half the bowl of broth down before what little strength she had left failed her. Some color had returned with the food but she still looked frightfully pale. "Do you want to lie back down?"

"No. I've been lying down enough."

Julia could feel Branna's eyes on her while she replaced the bowl on the tray, and for the moment, set it on the floor by the divan.

"How long have you been here?" Branna asked.

"Not yet a fortnight."

"Why did you come back?"

There were a thousand ways she could answer that question. She wondered if she should guard herself and hedge her answer or just put herself out there. In the short seconds she allowed herself to consider, she knew there was only one right answer. "Because I love you beyond measure and I want to be with you."

"Oh."

"But you knew that already." Branna was silent for so long Julia began to doubt herself and everything she felt. Had she been wrong about what they shared? She knew she hadn't but maybe something had changed since she'd been away. "Do you want me to go?"

"Never."

Julia's eyes flew open at the soft thump onto the balcony. Her eyes rolled to Branna who was heavily asleep. Julia had been a light sleeper since becoming the primary caregiver for her little sister and her worry for Branna for the last two weeks kept her on high alert for any sound lest Branna need help overnight. She heard movement again, and the whisper of voices.

She remained still, sensing immediately that there was danger. She controlled her breathing with effort lest her panic give her away. She thought frantically about what she had to defend them. The only thing within reach was the tray with the bowl and spoon, still on the floor where she set it.

Her heart pounded so loud she feared they could hear her. She could see them now—their silhouettes in the moonlight cast through the open balcony doors. One man stood in the doorway. "Make sure she's dead this time, ya stupid bastard," he hissed to the man creeping into the room.

Julia sighed softly—a sound she desperately hoped made it clear she was still asleep—and rolled over, letting her arm drape over the side of the divan. She could see them better now through eyes barely open to slits. He froze at the end of the bed—his beady, glittering eyes staring her way. She focused on breathing deep and slow.

He moved again, quicker now, propelled to act either out of confidence or fear. Her nostrils flared at the stench of him as he moved between the divan and the bed—smoke, cheap rum, and ocean rot. Her fingers tickled the handle of the spoon and the metal tinged softly against the bowl.

Leather creaked and there was a rush of air over her before a filthy hand clamped hard over her mouth. Foul breath wafted in her face through the stained scarf he had wrapped around his head to hide his features and his voice was a low growl. "I ain't here for you."

Her eyes bulged when he pulled a wicked looking knife and her mind went blank, her world filling with rage and terror. Her left hand moved of its own accord, swinging up and plunging the spoon into his right eye with a sickening pop.

His knife clattered to the floor and he released her, covering his face and howling in pain while staggering backward toward the balcony.

Julia leapt up, the spoon still clutched in her hand, and stood protectively beside Branna who was struggling up in bed. "Get out!" Julia screamed.

"Fuckin' run, ya fool!" The man by the balcony grabbed his partner by the shoulder and dragged him from the room in a mad shuffle of bodies. The injured man's shrieks grew distant as they disappeared however they arrived.

Julia spun with a startled cry when the door burst open and Gus charged in, sword drawn, with Gen right behind him.

"Julia, Branna?" Gus shouted.

"I'm okay," Julia gasped, a hand going to her heart. "Bran?"

Branna blinked furiously. "Aye. Julia, what happened?"

"There were two men here to kill you. He had a knife." She gestured to the balcony. "They came over the side."

Gus hurried across the room and disappeared out onto the balcony while Genevieve lit a lantern, filling the room with soft light.

"Are you two sure you're all right?" Gen looked them over, her eyes narrowing at the spoon Julia held. Her gaze flicked to the knife on the floor.

"I stabbed him," Julia blurted.

"With a spoon?" Branna gaped.

"In the eye."

"Well, that's horrible," Gen said dryly. She picked up the tray and held it for Julia to replace the spoon.

"There's a boat hook and rope over the railing. Probably took a dory beyond the harbor and then came through the bush on this side. I should have seen this coming." Gus dropped the hook and coiled rope onto the floor with a growl of disgust.

"The bastards were in my bloody room. Julia could have been..." Branna swallowed heavily. Her gaze flicked to her with worry before hardening at Gus. "We need to talk about this."

Gus nodded sharply. "We will."

"Now."

Julia opened her mouth to protest but held her tongue. Branna's expression was as furious as she'd ever seen it, her eyes glittering with anger. Her strength wouldn't last long, but for the moment Captain Kelly was back—fueled by her rage and another attempt on her life that put them *both* at risk.

"I'll get the others." Gus stalked from the room.

Genevieve sighed dramatically. "I'll get the rum."

Julia sat at the edge of the divan resisting the urge to reach for Branna's hand. Branna was radiating tension and she suspected her touch would not be welcomed as long as Captain Kelly was the one leading the charge.

"Why now?" Nat rumbled from where he leaned against the wall. He had only just returned that morning from his latest search of the very man that brought about their dead of night meeting.

Jack nodded. "They must have known Julia was here and if they didn't intend to hurt her, they left her able to sound the alarm. Seems poorly planned."

Gus grunted. "They've already proven they're not the most capable of Jagger's lot."

"Capable enough to evade you lot," Branna said dangerously and everyone's mouth slammed shut at her angry rebuke.

The silence was broken by the burble of liquid as Merriam refilled her glass. "They were 'spectin' Branna to give up the ghost by now," she said cheerily and raised her glass.

"Merri!" Jack hissed.

"What? She's been knockin' on death's door for weeks. How many of us really thought she was gonna live?"

Everyone found something interesting to look at as far away from Branna's gaze as possible.

"Sorry to disappoint," Branna snarled.

"Bran," Julia said, laying a hand on her arm. "I know you're upset, but you're taking your anger out on the wrong people. If not for everyone in this room, you most certainly *would* have died. I can't even bear to think about that. Not only did they save your life, but by extension, mine as well."

At Julia's gentle admonishment Branna's furious expression settled and she relaxed against the bed. Her gaze swept the room. As her anger dissipated so did her strength. "Forgive me," she said wearily, her face paling dramatically without the flush of anger.

Gus straightened. "There's nothing to forgive, Captain. We should've rid this island of Jagger's poison by now, but they remain well hidden."

"Except when they come out." Jack gestured to Branna.

Gen sneered. "My ire at the thought they're watching my place closely enough that they know she's on the mend, knows no bounds."

Nat said, "I'll assign additional men outside the door and have a patrol around the building."

Branna shook her head slowly, her eyes heavy with fatigue and her face pinched with discomfort. "No...let them come... use me to draw them out."

Gus grunted his displeasure. "You can't defend yourself."

Branna's eyes drifted closed. "It's an order..."

Julia laced their fingers together and could feel when Branna drifted away again in sleep. "I don't know if I get a vote here..."

"You do," Gen said, daring anyone to contradict her.

"Don't worry, Julia. We won't put her in danger again," Gus said. "We'll think of something else."

"I 'ave an idea." Merri sipped her drink and grinned slyly. "Branna'll hate it."

CHAPTER TWENTY-SEVEN

Julia sighed deeply and stood, stretching her back and rolling her shoulders. She was bored, exhausted, and afraid. It had been three days since the attack on Branna and they had all—with the exception of Branna—agreed to put Merri's plan into action. Fortunately, Branna was in no condition to put up much of a fight and the rest were prepared to defy whatever orders she gave no matter how viciously she swore and screamed at them. Her constant protestations were tedious and Julia feared it would slow her recovery.

Nat had been positioned outside their door and Gus and Jack had organized a new search of the island in an effort to rout out Jagger's agents. Still, Julia was tense all the time. She slept poorly and ate little and prayed for this to end.

"I'll be back in a few minutes," she said to the grumpy body under the bedclothes and received a mere grunt of acknowledgement. She wasn't the only one at the end of their rope.

The balcony doors stood open, the curtains barely moving in the still, night air. The heady smell of the sea hung heavy in the air and a shiver crawled up her spine. Before she had the opportunity to consider the source of her unease there was a loud crack of splintering wood and shattering glass from the courtyard and gruff voices raised in anger. Nat's rage-filled bellow could be heard as if there wasn't a wall between them and his footsteps thundered down the stairs so heavily the vibrations could be felt through the floor.

Julia flew out of their room and stood at the railing, worriedly watching the fracas in the courtyard below. Tables and chairs were upended, tankards of ale crushed and bottles of rum smashed as bodies were tossed about the space. She leapt out of the way when Genevieve burst out of her room next door and flew past her, not even sparing a glance.

Her heart beat frantically and she pressed her hand to her chest in a futile attempt to quell her rising anxiety. She looked right and left down the walkway as men continued to pour out of rooms and join the fray while scantily clad women jeered the drunken combatants from above.

She gasped and covered her eyes when one man climbed the second-floor railing and hurled himself into the surging mob down below. She ducked back into the room before discovering what became of him.

She leaned her back against the closed door and took several deep breaths. A sharp knock at the door had her heart leaping into her throat again. "Who's out there?"

"Miss Farrow!" a gruff voice barked. "There's a fight in the courtyard. Miss Travers asked me to check on you. Open the door...please."

Julia stepped back uncertainly. "How do I know it's safe?"

"It's not safe, miss. That's why I'm here. Miss Travers will skin me if I don't make sure you and yours are unharmed."

"We're fine."

"Please, miss."

Julia swallowed hard, with every instinct telling her not to open the door. She turned the handle and cracked the door, peering out. Before she could do anything else a meaty hand shot through the space and gripped her around the throat.

She gasped and scrabbled desperately at the thick, greasy fingers crushing her airway as Virgil Bunt shouldered his way into the room followed by another man who moved quickly, not even bothering to close the door.

Julia's vision swam and she pounded against his wrist and clawed at his hairy arm in an effort to draw a full breath. His scraggly, filthy face loomed in front of her wavering vision. A grimy rag, crusty with blood, was tied about his head covering his right eye.

"I owe you, slag," he snarled in her face.

"I'll take care of Kelly," the other man growled and headed toward the bed.

Julia rolled her eyes toward the bed, but before he even pulled his blade, the mound of linens sat bolt up and a pistol report echoed through the room. The man dropped, screaming, when his leg folded backward with an iron ball through his knee.

Gus shook the sheet from his head and raised his other hand, pistol cocked and at the ready toward Virgil Bunt. "Let her go, Bunt."

His grip never loosened, but Julia was jerked around when he pulled her in tight to his body in an effort to shield himself. "Bugger off, Hawke. I'll snap her neck."

The curtains in front of them rustled and Jack stepped out from behind, training his own pistol on the man. "There's nowhere for you to go and we only need one of you alive."

Bunt snarled in fear and anger, his grip tightening. Julia wheezed, her vision graying at the edges and her legs threatening to collapse. She sagged in Bunt's grip and couldn't stop the tears that rolled down her face.

"I only regret I won't get to see the life leave your eyes," Branna growled from behind them.

There was a rush of movement, a thick spray of warmth down the back of Julia's neck and a gurgling sound before the crushing pressure left her throat and Julia dropped to the floor. She coughed and dragged ragged breaths, her head pounding viciously in time with her heartbeat. Hands pulled her across the floor and onto the bed. Despite knowing every aspect of the plan, the lack of air had her struggling now to understand what was going on in the room.

Jack knelt on the man shot through the leg, binding his arms and his wound so he wouldn't bleed to death. Gus dragged Virgil Bunt's body out of the room, leaving a trail of blood from the gaping ear-to-ear slash in his throat. Nat had appeared and was scooping a nearly unconscious Branna up from where she had collapsed against the railing outside the door, covered only in a blood-splattered shirt, the knife still clutched in her hand. She had *not* been part of the plan. Julia remembered that much. She was supposed to be safely tucked away in Genevieve's bed next door.

Nat carried her in and lay her next to Julia on the bed. "Stay here," he rumbled and disappeared again.

Whatever else was going on in the room faded to the background and Julia pushed herself over to Branna. Her eyes were barely open and her breathing came in short sharp pants. She ran her hands over Branna's sweaty face. "Bran, talk to me."

Branna's mouth twitched into a smile. "Did we get 'em?"

"We did."

Branna frowned, her hand raising shakily to brush her fingertips along Julia's bruised throat. "You're hurt."

"I'm fine. You on the other hand…" She began to unbutton Branna's shirt. Several small spots of blood were blooming through bandages swathed around her middle. "Oh, Bran."

"S'nothing."

"What in god's name were you thinking? We agreed."

"*You* agreed."

Julia rolled her eyes but before the conversation could escalate, Genevieve swept in, holding a cloth to the side of her face. "Are you two all right?" she asked while surveying the condition of the room.

"Yes…" Julia winced and cleared her throat.

"Hmm." Gen frowned at them. "I'll send for Tuttle to look at you."

"What happened to you?" Branna asked.

"Oh." Gen moved the cloth from her face to show them the dusky bruise across her cheek. "That ratty lot took their assignment of causing the distraction to heart."

"It worked, though." Branna sighed, relaxing back against the bed.

"Like a charm. Merriam is annoyingly pleased with herself," Gen said. "Figured those two fools wouldn't be able to pass up a chance to sneak in here when it looked like everyone was involved in a brawl in the courtyard."

"It was a good plan," Branna agreed.

"I'll be sure to tell Merri you said—"

"Don't you dare."

"Are there others we need to worry about?" Julia asked.

Genevieve smiled grimly. "Gus and Nat will be questioning the one still living. If there are, he'll tell us pretty quick and then it can be handled."

"Mmm." Julia couldn't help the sympathetic groan. She pressed her lips together tightly and looked away. She felt Branna's hand reaching for hers.

"Don't think about it," Branna said, gripping her hand hard. "We're safe now. That's what matters."

CHAPTER TWENTY-EIGHT

"I'm not so sure this is a good idea, Bran. A week ago you could barely get from the bed to the chair." Julia stood, hand on her hips, as Branna struggled into her pants and stood on shaky legs.

"That was a week ago. But your opposition is noted," Branna said, not without humor as she fumbled with the buttons at her waist.

They didn't have to worry about the waistband aggravating the wound because she had lost so much weight her pants dipped low on her hips. "Will you bring me my boots, please?"

Gus had announced the *Banshee* had been put back in the water yesterday and Branna was determined to go check out her ship.

She had tried to convince Branna she wasn't ready but Branna was having none of it and Julia could think of no other argument. She had been eating solid food for weeks. Her wound, at least superficially, had healed and for the past several days she had been moving around on her own quite well. She had even been making trips up and down to the courtyard a few times a day though Julia knew, from the tension in her face, she still had a lot of pain and tired quickly.

She had attempted to enlist Gus and Genevieve's help in convincing Branna not to go but Gus had been no help, even encouraging her by saying she needed to get out and Gen was simply resigned to the inevitable—Branna wouldn't stay put. Julia sighed and brought Branna's boots to her.

She swayed unsteadily as she bent to pull them on and Julia shot a hand out to steady her. "Sit down," she said gently and pushed her back to the bed, crouching in front of her. "I'll do it."

"Thank you."

The door crashed open and Gus stood there excitedly bouncing up and down on his toes. "Ready, Captain?"

"Aye." Branna stood and set her mouth determinedly.

It wasn't far—a ten-minute walk at most if she had been healthy—but Branna was still weak. She concentrated on the ground in front of her, slightly hunched with an arm across her middle. Gus and Julia walked closely on either side ready to help and Genevieve followed along behind. Morrigan graced them with her presence again and weaved in and out of their legs along the way.

The day was typical for Nassau—bright and breezy with the sun high and hot in the afternoon. Swarms of people filed along the docks and the laneway, and as usual, parted for Captain Branna Kelly.

Julia noted immediately, instead of the usual tense stares or averting of eyes as Branna walked by people smiled, called her name and shouted greetings to the Raven. Children approached delightedly, tugging gently at her free hand and shirt and smiling at her with bright faces.

Branna's eyes widened at the smiling faces of the people that stopped to watch their slow procession to the repair dock. She offered a smile and small wave in return, seemingly stunned at their reaction to seeing her out.

Julia shook her head, bewildered at the change in attitude toward Branna, though she knew it was a result of having rid the world of Captain Jagger and the *Serpent's Mistress*.

She kept a wary eye on Branna as they made their way along the path. Sweat glistened on her skin and her shirt clung damply to her back. She was struggling and Julia could clearly hear her labored breathing. She moved in closer and slipped her hand around Branna's waist, uncertain how she would react.

Branna gave her a grateful smile and Julia tightened her grip at her waist and took some of her weight. "Almost there," she encouraged.

Julia focused on the dock and sucked in a breath as it came into view. The *Banshee* bobbed majestically against the dock, the water dredged deep enough here that the ship could rest in the water this close to land.

Branna heard Julia's breath hitch and raised her head. Nat and Jack stood at the end of the dock and lined up behind them was Branna's crew. Though they were mostly all the familiar faces, they were nearly unrecognizable. They were clean, trimmed, and turned out in well-fitting leather, shined boots and gleaming blades.

Branna's mouth dropped as she moved closer and took them all in. She had made the offer for them to be released from their contracts after defeating the *Serpent's Mistress* and she expected, at least some of them, now rich men, would have taken her up on it. They were all here, every one of them along with some faces she didn't recognize.

She moved away from Julia's supporting arm as she approached her men. She had to go the rest of the way on her own. She hadn't seen her friends since the night they had set the trap for Jagger's men in her room.

"Mr. Hooper. Mr. Massey." She extended her hand and they each shook it firmly, their faces breaking out into enormous grins. "It's really nice to see you."

Nat enveloped her hand in both of his giant ones, eyes bright with emotion. "Happy to have you back, Captain."

Branna turned her gaze to the line of crew and tried to keep her voice even. "What's all this then?"

Nat grinned. "The men are ready to sail, Captain."

Branna took a deep breath, overcome with emotion at the sight of her crew waiting to greet her. She moved down the dock slowly, mindful of every step, and stood in front of them. "I'm pleased to see you all," she began and let her eyes scan the line of men. They looked back at her, some with anticipation, some with concern, some with awe, but all with pride. She had missed her crew, her ship, and the sea. That all of them chose to remain with her, despite her injury, spoke volumes of the trust and belief they had in her and her command. Perhaps potential mutiny was no longer one of her concerns.

"Thank you. I'm sure you are all anxious to get back to sea. I am, too. More than I can say. We have been through much together and I believe..." Her voice cracked with emotion, forcing her to look away in frustration. She hadn't expected them to see her like this and she was angry that she hadn't the energy for one of her rousing speeches. She took a step and swayed dangerously.

She was a breath from going down when Ollie, the ship's boy, stepped forward and gripped her arm to steady her. He extended his other hand smoothly as if he was only wanting to shake her hand.

"It's awfully good to have you back, Captain Kelly," he said, his voice finally having broken into a smooth, deep timbre.

Branna's eyes went wide as she took his hand, grateful for his support. She looked him over. He must have shot up two inches and gained a full stone since she saw him last. "Thank you, Ollie."

"It's Oliver now, Captain," he corrected with a lopsided grin.

Branna blinked at him before laughing, wincing and throwing her arm up against her wound. "Oliver, it is."

Their good-natured exchange broke the awkwardness and more of the men stepped forward to shake her hand and offer words of greeting to her.

Branna moved down the line, greeting each man by name, asking after them, hearing their stories of how they'd spent the last two months and their money and thanking them for their well wishes for her recovery.

As she moved to the end, Nat, Gus, and Jack stepped alongside her and introduced her to the seven young, fresh and eager faces hired to replace the men they had lost against the *Serpent's Mistress*. Branna spent some time with them, learning their names and hearing the backgrounds as the other crew mingled along the dock speaking excitedly with each other about getting back to sea and the repairs to the ship.

Branna felt her mind clouding as the young men continued to chatter at her. She was done in and needed to get back to her room before she collapsed in front of them. She stopped the man speaking with a raise of her hand and turned to the rest of the men, gathering what little strength she had left. "All hands," she called.

The men turned and snapped to attention.

"The *Banshee* will sail again in a fortnight!"

A cheer went up among the men that sent a shiver of excitement and pride down her spine. She nodded to Gus for him to follow and turned to head back down to the dock.

"Branna, are you sure? You know the crew will wait as long as you need."

"I'm sure. I'll be ready." She eyed him from the side and saw him press his lips together unconvinced, and changed the subject. "Is the crew complete?"

"We still don't have a purser." His eyes flicked to the head of the dock where Julia and Genevieve waited for them. "I thought, perhaps, you'd have someone in mind and like to make the offer yourself."

"I may be able to come up with someone," she said without expression. She stopped suddenly on the dock and Gus had to come back to meet her. "Is there time for a few more upgrades to the ship before we sail?"

"What did you have in mind?"

By the time they made it back to the courtyard her officers were already there. Branna was leaning heavily on Julia and breathing hard. She wasn't sure she was going to make it up the stairs to their room at all. Her abdomen burned and throbbed, her legs felt like rubber and she wasn't at all sure she wouldn't vomit any second.

"How'd it go?" Merriam bounced out from behind the bar and skipped over to them.

Branna was uncharacteristically grateful for Merriam's interruption as it gave her a moment to rest before taking on the stairs.

"It was great," Julia said. "The ship looks beautiful."

Jack joined them and slipped an arm around Merriam. "The captain has said we'll be sailing again in two weeks."

Merriam cocked an eyebrow at Jack and then Branna, taking in how ragged she looked in a quick glance. "Has she now? Is that before or after she falls over and hurls all over our feet?"

Branna stiffened, her eyes going hard and she pushed off from the railing toward Merriam.

"Merri!" Jack snapped.

Merriam's eyes flashed a challenge at Branna. "What are ya gonna to do, Kelly? You gonna lead yer crew from yer knees? Maybe get Ollie to carry yer sword for ya?"

"Fuck you, Beeson!" Branna growled, anger and frustration welling up inside her. She balled her hands and took a step before a bolt of pain across her middle sent her staggering to her knees with a gasp, her hands clutching her side.

"Branna!" Julia dropped to the ground next to her and wrapped a protective arm around her before glaring up at Merriam.

"Merriam, that's enough!" Jack shouted.

Merri blanched, realizing she had gone too far. "I'm sorry. Jack, I'm sorry."

Jack ignored her and reached for Branna to help her stand.

"I'm fine!" Branna smacked his hand away.

Merriam was right. She was in no condition to take responsibility of the ship and the crew and the knowledge cut her more deeply than any blade in the gut. She wasn't going to go back on her word. They would leave in two weeks and she would make sure she was ready. She pushed herself to her feet and eyed Merriam hard.

"Branna, I'm sorry," Merriam blurted. "I didn't mean ta—"

"Yes, you did." Branna took a step toward Merri, her arm outstretched.

Merri flinched but held her ground as Branna gripped the back of her neck and brought her mouth to Merriam's ear. Merriam listened as Branna whispered. Her eyes went wide, then narrowed. A laugh erupted from her lips as she nodded.

Branna pulled away from her. "Are we in accord?"

"We are, Captain." Merriam grinned as Julia and Jack looked on confused.

Branna turned to Julia and smiled weakly. "Help me to bed?"

Julia slipped her arm around Branna again and together they ascended the stairs.

Julia lay awake in bed for a long time listening to Branna's slow, even breathing. She had wanted to talk to Branna about what had happened. Though Merriam's words had been harsh and out of line, she understood the sentiment behind them. Branna wasn't ready and Julia was worried she would push herself too hard and do something to endanger herself and her crew. She had expected to speak with Branna about it when they returned to their room but Branna was exhausted and dropped into bed without so much as removing her boots. Julia had helped her undress before pulling the sheet over her. She let her sleep undisturbed for hours before waking her to eat something.

She had wanted again to bring up her concerns as they sat at the table, but the set of Branna's jaw and the fire in her eyes as she spoke of what still needed to be arranged before they set sail let Julia know her worry would be, at best, unwelcomed.

Julia comforted herself with the thought that there was still time. The *Banshee* didn't sail for two weeks. Branna would be stronger and there would be plenty of other opportunities to address her concerns between now and then.

In the meantime, Julia began to worry about her position in Branna's life when she returned to sea. Though she hadn't yet said the words, she knew Branna loved her deeply but she feared she could never compete with the siren song of the sea. Would she be welcome on the *Banshee* or would she be keeping counsel with Genevieve and Merriam as she stayed back at Travers and waited for the ship to return to port?

She turned over again with a sigh and pressed herself into Branna's back, breathing in the scent of her and feeling her warmth as she willed her body to relax and made to banish the worry from her mind.

CHAPTER TWENTY-NINE

Julia awoke with a warm breeze blowing through the balcony doors and sun streaming into the room. She stretched and reached a hand to Branna. She came up empty and pushed herself up, her grainy eyes scanning the room. The room was clearly empty and Julia's heart thudded in her chest with the memory of the last time she woke to find Branna gone from their bed.

She knew that hadn't happened this time, but she tensed just the same and quickly dressed to go look for her. As she neared the door she heard Merriam's mocking laugh and voice drifting through the door.

"That all ya've got, Kelly?" Merriam shouted.

Julia flung the door open and stepped out onto the walkway to be greeted by a steaming cup of coffee thrust in her face.

"Was wondering when you were going to make an appearance," Genevieve said dryly.

Julia took the mug from her gratefully and looked around. "What's going on?" she asked when she saw Merriam sitting at the top of the stairs staring down to the bottom with a grin. Julia followed her gaze to see Branna, red-faced and sweating, as she stepped off the last stair and turned to start her way back up.

"Branna asked Merri to help her regain her strength," Genevieve answered, a half-smile playing at her lips.

"Really? Merri? Why in heaven's name would she do that?"

"Come on, Kelly!" Merri barked and flicked her eyes to the two of them. "Julia's watchin'. How'd ya reckon yer weak, sickly arse is gonna keep a luscious woman like 'er satisfied?"

Julia's mouth dropped open in horror and Genevieve choked on her coffee.

"You're...such a...bitch...Beeson," Branna panted as she crested the top of the stairs. She bent, her hands resting on her knees, and gasped for air. Her eyes widened and she swallowed heavily several times.

"No way, Kelly!" Merri jumped up and spun Branna away from her. "I don't want yer filth near me."

Branna lunged for the railing and vomited over the side. Julia and Genevieve cringed when they heard the contents of her stomach splatter onto the stones below.

Genevieve sighed and headed down the stairs. "For the love of Christ, you two. I have to find someone to clean that up."

"Branna, please, stop." Julia gathered the loose strands of Branna's hair and pulled them off her face as she hung over the rail, spitting to clear her mouth and trying to catch her breath.

"I've got three more to do and then I'm done for the morning."

Julia frowned. She knew what Branna was doing and why it was important and she understood why she'd asked Merriam to help her. "And then what?"

"Massage?"

Julia shook her head in disbelief but couldn't help the small smile that tugged at the corner of her mouth. Branna's strength of will and her resolve were so much of what made her the person she was. Julia would never stand in the way of that.

"Come on, Captain," Merri snapped. "I 'aven't got all day."

Branna glared at her. "When I asked you to help me, I thought you'd be doing this with me."

"What for? I can get up and down the stairs without puking my guts out. Now move!"

Branna sucked in a deep breath and headed back down the stairs on shaky legs.

Julia frowned in worry as Branna staggered and caught herself on the railing halfway down.

"Don't worry," Merriam said. "I won't let anything happen to 'er."

Julia chewed her lip. "Thanks."

"I think she was serious about the massage," Merri said with a grin as Julia turned to head back to the room.

Julia flashed her a look over her shoulder. "Only if you get her cleaned up first."

* * *

As Captain Kelly's strength and spirit returned, so too did the liveliness of Travers Trading, but Julia barely noticed when the courtyard began filling up with revelers. She sat, elbows on the table, and rolled her empty glass around in her hand. Nat and Branna's swords clashed as they dodged around the tables of sailors and evening ladies in a slow spar to further prepare Branna for sailing again.

Genevieve dropped into a chair across from her and filled Julia's empty glass. "She looks good," she said, watching Nat and Branna as they thrust and parried at one another.

Julia's head rose and she stared at her now-full glass in confusion. "Hmm?"

"Branna. She's come a hell of a long way in the last week."

"Yes."

"You don't sound excited."

"What? Of course, I am."

Genevieve nodded, unconvinced. "What about you?"

"What about me?"

"You came a hell of a long way. You gave up a great deal to be here. You've supported Branna unfailingly. Are you having regrets?"

"No. Why would you even ask me that?"

"I know a woman who is not getting what she needs when I see one."

She opened her mouth to argue and then snapped it shut and looked away. Genevieve's intuition was unparalleled and she knew it was no use denying the truth of what she said. She stalled by taking another sip of rum and letting her eyes close as the liquid burned her throat and warmed her chest. "I know Branna needs this. It's who she is. I'm so proud of her and I want her to be well and strong and happy.

"But?" Genevieve encouraged.

"I don't know where I fit in her life now." She turned and watched as Branna rolled across a table with a bark of laughter to dodge a swing of Nat's sword. She landed on her feet, their swords striking again. Julia smiled at the fire in Branna's eyes and the determination on her face. She was amazing and Julia never tired of watching her.

"Have you talked to her about it?" Genevieve asked.

"No. She's been so busy and I don't want to distract her with my silly—"

"Stop." Genevieve held up her hand. "Nothing about what's happened here is silly, Julia. Branna nearly died, and I for one believe if not for you, she would have."

"That's ridiculous."

"Trust me. It's not. You're the reason she's where she is now and Branna knows it. You know how single-minded she can be. She's caught up in preparing to sail again and maybe has lost sight of what got her here. She loves you, Julia, more than anything. Talk to her, or better yet, show her."

"Show her what?"

Genevieve flashed a wicked grin. "What she's been missing."

"You're as bad as Merri," Julia accused, though she couldn't stop herself from smiling.

Julia headed to their room shortly after their conversation, Genevieve's words ringing in her head. She was right. She needed to talk to Branna. Tonight though, she didn't want to talk. Tonight, she wanted Branna to see her. Tonight, she wanted Branna to want her.

Branna dropped into the chair across from Genevieve and ran her hands through sweat-damp hair and reached for an ale Genevieve had poured for her. "Where's Julia?"

"She turned in already," Genevieve answered evenly.

"Oh. I thought we would get something to eat together. She must have been tired."

"Must have been."

Branna frowned at Genevieve's odd expression. "Do you mind if I get cleaned up in your room? I don't want to wake Julia."

"Pretty sure she's not sleeping. But, no, I don't mind, help yourself to whatever."

"What's with you?"

"Get going. You're needed elsewhere."

"Aye, aye."

Branna pushed the door open as quietly as she could, setting her sword and sweaty clothes inside the door. She was dressed in only a shirt of Genevieve's as she only had to get from her room next door. She looked up and her breath caught.

Julia wasn't sleeping. She stood across the dark room in the open door to the balcony looking out over the sea. The moonlight filtered in around her, highlighting the long, sheer, curve-hugging shift she wore.

Branna felt an immediate rush of heat and a tightening in her belly at the sight of her bare shoulders, the line of her neck, the curve of her hip and the way the sea air floated through her hair.

Julia turned toward her and Branna's lips parted at the sight of the light skimming across her smooth skin, the hollow of her throat, the swell of her breasts. Julia's eyes glittered with humor at Branna's obvious reaction. She snapped her mouth closed with a click of her teeth and swallowed heavily. Why, all of the sudden, did she feel so nervous?

Julia crossed the room in smooth quiet steps and stopped a breath from Branna. She ran a slow finger down Branna's neck and between her breasts. "I've missed you," Julia said, her voice husky with intent.

Branna sucked in a breath at Julia's teasing caress and felt liquid heat pool between her legs. Her heart hammered in her chest and she raised her trembling hands to lightly brush up and down Julia's arms. "You're so beautiful, *machree*."

"I was hoping you would notice."

Branna was quickly losing control. If Julia set out to light her on fire she had succeeded. She gripped the back of Julia's head, winding her fingers through her hair and drew Julia to her in a crushingly deep kiss.

Julia moaned into Branna's mouth, wrapping her arms around her neck and holding them close as Branna's mouth devoured her. Julia's head dropped back with a gasp and Branna moved along behind her ear and down her neck raking her teeth across her collarbone. She slid her free hand to the small of Julia's back for support as she pressed her toward the bed, never removing her lips from her skin. She settled her weight on her, their breasts pressed together through the thin material of their clothes.

Branna didn't wait for discussion or direction but slipped the straps of the shift down Julia's shoulders with one hand and slid the other hand beneath the thin material to get at the silky skin of her leg, all the while raining kisses and nips of her teeth along Julia's neck and chest.

Julia arched under her as Branna trailed her fingers along the inside of her thighs, teasing between her legs. Julia moaned deeply and Branna nearly came apart when Julia's body tensed beneath her. "I don't know if I can be gentle," Branna growled as she slid Julia's shift up around her hips and over her head.

Julia ripped open Branna's shirt in response and licked her lips as her gaze raked over Branna's bare chest. "Please, don't try," she rasped and roughly kneaded Branna's breasts.

Branna was mindless with need for Julia and removed her hands only long enough to rip the rest of their clothes away and fling them from the bed. She descended on Julia, gripping her hands and pressing them into the bed over her head as she bruised her mouth with her desire, sliding down to suck a hard nipple, alternating the attention she lavished upon each breast with her tongue and teeth.

Julia moaned her name and writhed beneath Branna's weight as their skin slickened and the smell of their arousal mingled together in the room. Branna shifted and pressed her thigh between Julia's legs, feeling how ready she was.

"Please, Bran," Julia groaned. "Don't wait."

She didn't need to be told twice and Branna slid her right hand down between her legs, parting her, and plunged inside. She sucked in a breath at her wet heat and enjoyed the quivering of Julia's insides.

"Oh, god!" Julia cried and her hips bucked against Branna's hand and her walls clenched around her, signaling her need for more.

Branna slid an arm around Julia's waist, tilting her hips as she thrust in and out of her in a smooth, determined rhythm. Her thumb alternately circled and pressed against Julia's swollen center, sending her into a frenzy of spasms, one hand clutching at the sheets and the other covering her face as her mouth dropped open in a silent scream of ecstasy.

"Look at me, Julia," Branna demanded as she continued stroking her. Julia was almost over the edge and Branna wanted to see her face when she came.

Julia groaned, her breath ragged as she let her arm drop to the bed and dragged her eyes open. "Oh, my god, Bran," she gasped. "Don't stop. Don't ever stop."

Julia's eyes were glazed over and Branna doubted if she could actually see her. She doubted she could see anything as Branna increased her pace and her pressure and sent her spiraling out of control.

Branna's heart pounded frantically and pulsed between her legs. She gentled her thrusts through Julia's climax but didn't stop. Julia quickly responded to the continued stimulation, tightening and fluttering against her fingers. "Again, *machree*," she whispered.

Julia was beyond words, her eyes unseeing while her hands clutched blindly at Branna's shoulders and her hips rocked powerfully with every stroke.

Branna could feel her climax building in ripples of contractions around her hand and pumped and curled her fingers inside her, bringing her ever closer to release. Julia clamped down hard on Branna's hand and arched off the bed with a cry when her climax erupted from deep within her a second time.

Julia shuddered when Branna slid out of her and dropped into a sweaty heap next to her, her arm flung carelessly across Julia's chest. "Bloody hell, Julia," she breathed into her neck.

Julia's laugh came out a raspy breath. "Just, give me a minute."

Branna laughed, pleased with herself. "Take your time."

For a long time the room was filled only with the sound of satisfied, uneven breathing and the pungent smell of sex. Finally, Julia rolled, somewhat ungracefully, on top of Branna and rested her chin on Branna's chest, holding her gaze.

"What?" Branna asked suspiciously.

"Your turn," Julia purred and kissed her way down Branna's body.

"Oh, hell." Branna groaned and grabbed for the headboard.

CHAPTER THIRTY

Julia woke hours before dawn, her body aching deliciously but her mind still troubled. For a few hours she had felt so connected with Branna and she thought everything was going to be all right. Now, in the stillness of the night with only the sound of Branna's deep, even breathing, her unease returned.

She slid her arm from beneath Branna and put some space between them to try and clear her head. Branna woke and turned with her.

"Hey," Branna murmured and ran her fingertips over Julia's hip lightly. "Why aren't you asleep?"

Julia didn't mean to give herself away but she must have waited too long to answer or sighed or tensed. Branna pushed herself up on her elbow and turned Julia's face toward her. "Julia?"

Julia cupped Branna's cheek. "I love you," she whispered. She meant for it to be calming, but even to her own ears, it sounded sad.

"What's wrong?"

Julia let her eyes slide closed and swallowed heavily. "I don't know what I'm supposed to do now."

"I don't understand."

"The *Banshee* sails in less than a week."

"And? I thought you were excited for that."

Julia laughed humorlessly and pushed herself up to sit against the headboard. "We haven't talked about what that means for me, Branna. Should I be looking for work or do I just drift around aimlessly and check the harbor once a day to see when you've returned?"

Branna sat straight up and blinked stupidly at her. "What?"

Julia sighed and raked her hands through her hair. "I'm not really the wringing my hands waiting for my sailor to return from sea kind of woman, Branna. I need more than that."

"Julia, I have no idea—"

"I don't either. I'm at a loss here, Bran, and I don't know what to do."

Branna gripped Julia's hands to still them. "I have no idea what you're talking about."

It was Julia's turn to stare blankly. Before she could speak again Branna jumped off the bed and began scrabbling around the floor for their clothes. "Get dressed," she said in her commanding voice.

"Branna, what?"

"There's something you need to see."

Julia struggled into her clothes in the dark and then Branna gripped her by the hand and led her from the room.

Branna moved quickly, pulling Julia behind. The courtyard was silent as she slipped a dim lantern off a hook by the archway and continued down the path toward the repair docks.

Julia was tired and confused but she let Branna lead her on. "Where are we going?"

"To the ship."

"You're angry."

"Yes."

Julia stopped and jerked her hand from Branna's grasp. She'd had enough and if they were going to have it out, here was as good a place as any. "Stop."

Branna turned and looked at Julia and must have realized her mistake. "No, Julia." She closed the distance between them and smoothed the lines of worry across her brow. "Not with you. I'm angry with myself. Please, just come with me and I'll explain everything."

Julia looked hard at her for another moment before she relaxed slightly and let Branna take her hand again.

Branna kicked at the legs of the chair of the man sleeping at the head of the dock. He grunted awake and lurched blearily to his feet when he saw who it was. "Captain Kelly. What—"

"I'm taking the boat out to the *Banshee*," she said sternly. Earlier in the week the ship had been towed a little way into the harbor to make room for another in need of repair.

"Do you want me to row you out, Captain?" he asked in an attempt to make up for sleeping at his post.

"No. I'll do it. See to it we aren't disturbed."

"Aye, Captain."

Branna stepped off the dock into a small rowboat and reached out a hand to help Julia.

Julia settled into the bow and Branna gathered the oars. One powerful stroke sent the boat shooting away from the dock and Branna doubled over, hissing in pain.

"Branna." Julia moved carefully to sit beside her and took the oars from her. "Are you all right?"

"Yes," Branna said, her voice tight as she sat hunched and breathing hard. "We don't have far to go."

"I'll do it," Julia said sharply and pinned Branna with a look that brooked no argument.

They switched places and Julia guided the boat alongside the *Banshee* and Branna tied it off.

Julia watched Branna eying the rope ladder, aware of the concern. "Branna, we can go back."

"No. This is important. I'll be fine." To prove her point, she swung herself onto the ladder and started the climb.

Julia carried the lantern and handed it up to Branna who extended her hand to help her over the gunwale. It was difficult to see much in the dark but Julia could tell that the deck was new. She could feel the smooth wood under her feet and smell the fresh cut boards and new pitch. She looked forward and could just make out the replaced bowsprit.

"This way." Branna reached for her hand again but waited for Julia to take it on her own. She did and they moved across the deck to the captain's quarters.

Branna's cabin was very dark and their weak lantern did little to illuminate the space. Branna found her way to her navigation table and lit the larger lantern the workers had been using.

Julia blinked as the room became clear. It, too, smelled of sawdust, new wood and tar. She looked around, and at first didn't see much change. Branna's desk, chair, table, and built-in shelves were all as they should be.

She looked to the bed and frowned. It hadn't changed but something wasn't right. She looked from the bed to the navigation table. Was the room smaller? Julia walked around, judging the distance and glanced to Branna who was watching her and chewing on her fingernails. Branna met her eyes and shrugged, a smile tugging at her mouth.

She turned back to the bulkhead the bed was against and studied it again. Branna's cabin was definitely smaller. By nearly a third. She felt along the new bulkhead and noticed the narrow, sliding door at the foot of the bed. There wasn't a door handle but a cutout where she could slide in her hand. She glanced back at Branna.

"Open it."

Julia slid the door open and stepped into the room. Tools and wood scraps still littered the floor. It was obviously still being worked on but the design of it was clear. There was a desk at one end with a chair. There were built-in shelves much like the captain's cabin, a small built-in closet and chest of drawers, and a single bunk along one wall with more storage underneath.

Julia walked toward the stern. Much like Branna's cabin there were two, waist-high aft windows that could be opened to the sea air. She turned to see Branna standing in the doorway looking around herself.

"It turned out well, I think," Branna said.

"What is this?"

"The new purser's office."

"I didn't know you'd hired a purser."

"I haven't made the offer yet."

"To whom?"

"To you, Julia. I did this for you—for us."

Julia looked around again as if seeing it for the first time. "I don't understand."

Branna closed the distance between them and grasped Julia's hands. "I want you to sail with me. Work with me. Be my partner in all ways. I hope we spend most of our time together in my cabin but I knew you would need your own space and a place to work." Her excited words spilled out of her mouth in a rush. "And I'll need privacy sometimes, too. I wish it could be bigger but this was the only way it worked. I tried to think of everything you may need but there's still time and if there's something else you want just tell me and I'll have them—"

"Branna, stop." Julia put a hand on her lips to quiet her.

"You don't like it?"

"No, it's not that. Why didn't you tell me?"

"Oh. I wanted it to be a surprise." She looked at Julia, sheepishly. "Surprise."

Julia scrubbed her face. "Oh, god, I feel so foolish. I thought you were leaving me behind."

"God, no. I'm so sorry you thought that. I had no idea that's what you were afraid of. I should have been paying attention but I was too caught up in everything else."

"It's not your fault."

"It is my fault. You've given up so much for me. You've saved my life, Julia. I haven't been there for you and I'm sorry."

Julia smiled gently. In her heart all was forgiven. Her anxiety eased and in its place excitement began to build. "I love you."

"And I love you. Beyond reason. I let you go once. I'm never letting you go again," Branna vowed and pulled her into her arms, burying her face in Julia's neck. "Do you believe me?"

Julia swallowed around the thick knot of emotion in her throat as she wrapped her hands around Branna's back and clung to her tightly. "Yes."

"If I ever lose sight of you again, of what's important, just kick me. No wait." She thought a moment and smiled wickedly. "Do what you did last night to me."

"Agreed."

"So, what do you say, Miss Farrow? Would you like to sail with me?" she asked, grinning lopsidedly.

"Yes, I would."

Before the last word was past her lips, she crushed her mouth to Branna's, pouring all her love into that one kiss. Her enthusiasm forced Branna back against the bulkhead as Julia worked her hands under Branna's shirt and her mouth around her lips and neck.

"In the other room," Branna mumbled around Julia's lips and worked them both back through the narrow door, their hands ripping at each other's clothes. They stumbled their way to the bed and Julia pushed Branna down and stripped off her blouse in one smooth motion, laughing at the shocked look on Branna's face while she climbed in after her and straddled her hips.

Branna's hands came up to cup Julia's breasts, her thumbs rolling across her nipples reverently.

"Wait," Julia blurted.

Branna froze, a breast filling each hand. "What's wrong?"

Julia placed her hands on Branna's chest and leaned forward. "What about the crew?"

"What about them?"

"Aren't you worried they'll find out about us?"

"Are you serious? Julia, how can you possibly think that they all don't already know?

"We've been together on this ship and you're not exactly as quiet as you think."

"Oh, really? And you, Captain Kelly, are the picture of decency and restraint, I presume?"

"All I'm saying is, it may not be discussed during mealtime, but a ship is close quarters. Besides, who do you think they're rubbing up against when we're at sea for months?"

"Who?"

Branna rolled her eyes. "Each other."

"Oh."

"They are all well aware as to the nature of our relationship, and you saw them. They can't wait to go back to sea with me. With us."

"Hmph." Julia frowned harder and considered Branna beneath her for a long moment, her mouth turning up into a mischievous grin. "I think the crew should hear from you as to the nature of our relationship." She reached down to lace her fingers with Branna's and move her hands above her head, pinning them to the bed, before descending on her mouth with teasing kisses.

"I doubt anyone is going to hear us from here."

"Challenge accepted, Captain Kelly."

Bella Books, Inc.

Women. Books. Even Better Together.

P.O. Box 10543
Tallahassee, FL 32302

Phone: 800-729-4992
www.bellabooks.com